The Nephilim:
A Monster Among Us

Dane Cramer

The Nephilim: A Monster Among Us

Published by Feathered Press Publications

All rights reserved.

Copyright © 2014 by Dane Cramer.

ISBN: 978-0-9904474-0-5

Cover Art Designed by SimCloud

Author Web Site: www.danecramer.com or www.featheredprop.com

Scripture quotes are from King James Version, 1611.

First Printing, July 2014

10 9 8 7 6 5 4 3

Also available from Dane Cramer:

Romancing the Trail: Six Days Atop Laurel Ridge

Romancing the Trail takes the reader on an enchanting journey along the Laurel Highlands Hiking Trail, located in Western Pennsylvania. Discover some of its lesser-known mysteries, and learn about the history of this scenic footpath. Along the way, meet others who, for their own sacred reasons, are wandering the trail.

As the beauty of the Laurel Highlands vividly comes to life in this enjoyable account, the reader will be caught up in the great splendor that is Western Pennsylvania.

To Reese, Ivy, and Alexander.
May your imaginations always run wild.

Chapter One

"Did you hear that?"

The sound of her voice was familiar to him. Yet, it seemed distant.

"Cliff? Did you hear that?" Carly whispered again.

His eyes fluttered open. They searched the heavy dark, trying to find a reference point, but he was only half awake.

Bits of information returned to him: a long hike, a lonely campsite, a warming campfire deep in the timberland of Lycona National Forest.

"Hear what?" Cliff found his voice.

"There's something out there!" Carly whispered, her words stretched thin with tension.

Cliff lifted his head slightly and stared into the dark. He listened for the sound that had apparently startled his wife.

"What? I don't hear anything," he sighed, as he rolled over and vainly tried to find a comfortable position on his thin sleeping pad.

"There is something out there! It woke me up," she insisted.

There was something in his wife's voice that stirred Cliff to try listening again. By nature, Carly was calm. That's what made her an excellent 911 operator. Nothing shook her. If surprised, she seemed indifferent. If confronted, she stood her ground. If frightened, she didn't let it show. This was different. There was an alarm in her voice that he had not heard before. An alarm that now fully awakened him.

Cliff rolled over and strained his ears to listen. But all that he perceived was perfect quiet. And that's when he became concerned. The spring night seemed completely still, too still. The usual sounds of the nocturnal forest were deafeningly absent. The only sound Cliff could hear was his wife's shallow and rapid breathing.

"There! That's it!" Carly whispered again.

This time Cliff heard it. Something heavy had moved at what seemed to be just yards from their tent. It sounded like a single footstep, but Cliff needed to hear it again to get a better sense of what it was and what it was doing. He lifted his head again. His eyes began adjusting to the dark. His ears searched the night air. The sound, however, was followed only by an unnerving silence.

"A deer might have wandered into camp," Cliff suggested, hoping to alleviate his wife's fears. He knew, however, that the noise had sounded like a heavy footfall, one much too unwieldy for a deer.

"It's not a deer." Carly was too level-headed to be swayed by his weak attempt. "Whatever it is, it's moved in a circle around us. It started down here," she whispered pointing toward their feet, "and I've listened to it move slowly around us." Carly made a sweeping motion to show that the source of the sound had moved about halfway around the camp.

"It could be a bear," Cliff whispered, trying to conceal his growing concern. He had suspected this from the first, but he didn't want to alarm his wife. It was now too late for that.

Cliff knew that the black bear population was on the rise in mountainous Lycona County. As their numbers increased and territory diminished, it was not uncommon to have them occasionally wander into a camp site, especially when the smell of food hung in the air. But Cliff had always been careful with food scraps near the campsite. Before they had crawled into their tent, he had suspended their food bag about twenty feet above the ground on a nylon rope. Yet, even with the proper precautions he knew that bears may still visit a campsite. He and Carly had encountered a number of them throughout their years of outdoor activities, always without incident.

"It might be a bear," Carly answered as she tightly grabbed Cliff's arm, "but ..."

Her sentence was interrupted by more movement; four very heavy steps in quick succession.

"...something is different about the way it sounds," she finished her sentence.

Cliff was surprised by how tightly Carly was clinging to his arm. He now felt the fear that he had heard in her voice. He had grown up on a local farm and had hunted these woods all of his life. He was familiar with the herbivores that roamed the woods and the predators that pursued them. During his childhood, he'd spent many summer nights camping in the woods with his brothers. The only time he recalled being frightened in the forest was when his brothers would sit around the fire and tell ghost stories. But the forest itself never frightened him. And that's what bothered him most now; his own fright. It felt so uncharacteristic. And it felt different. It was more than just an emotion; it was more than the pounding of his heart, and the sweat forming on his palms; more than something he heard in his wife's voice. It was as though fear itself had crawled into their tent.

These strange new emotions made Cliff feel paralyzed. It seemed he could do nothing but listen to the unknown intruder as it continued to move at irregular intervals. The steps were slow, and the sounds seemed to indicate that its source was trying to move with stealth. And to Cliff, stealth translated into intelligence; and purpose.

There was something else about the sound that unnerved Cliff. The sounds were not being made by an animal on four legs. Whatever was creating the sounds was walking *upright* on *two legs*.

"What should we do?" Carly whispered anxiously. "Should we try to scare it off?"

"I don't know," Cliff replied. He now wished that they had chosen to sleep on the open ground near the fire rather than in the tent. Not being able to see beyond the confines of the nylon walls made him feel terribly vulnerable. But the forecast had suggested the possibility of showers, and he hadn't wanted to be caught unprotected if a storm struck during the night. So, they had pitched their tent and let the fire go out.

As they lay listening in their sleeping bags, the footsteps continued. Carly was right; the sound they were hearing suggested that it was circling their camp. The rustling of leaves and the occasional breaking of twigs revealed that it had almost made a full circle from where Carly had first heard it. Although Cliff suspected a very large bear, he could not understand why it didn't drop down on all fours. Bears are capable of walking on their two hind legs, but they don't generally move about for so long in that manner.

"Ugh, what is that smell?" Carly whispered.

As if a fan had been turned in their direction, a nauseating odor suddenly filled the tent. Cliff smelled it at the same time and felt sick.

"It smells like something died," Cliff said in reaction. Instantly, he regretted using the words that he had just chosen.

"What should we do?" Carly breathed. The panic was rising in her voice.

"Let me take a look," Cliff whispered as he slowly rose to a seated position. "Maybe I can frighten it away."

Instinctively he reached down for his sidearm. As a deputy, he was rarely without it. But on a short weekend trip like this, and in the confines of very familiar forest, he had decided to leave it behind. He now breathed a silent curse over that decision.

His sleeping bag fell down around him as he moved to his haunches. The tent had a zippered door near their feet. Cautiously, he raised the zipper until a small flap could be peeled back. He took the flap in his right hand and moved it out of the way, allowing him to peer into the night.

Cliff stared in the direction from where the sound was last heard. Though a near-full moon hung in the sky, its light was impeded by darkened rain clouds.

His eyes soon adapted to the available light. Cliff studied the surrounding landscape. He could make out the shape of trees and some smaller bushes at the camp's perimeter. The smoke of their smoldering campfire was rising lazily upward. It all seemed like a peaceful camp under a lovely, night sky.

Then, as the clouds moved past the moon and light was suddenly showered upon the campsite, Cliff saw something. It was partially obscured by a large black oak. The object was dark, making it difficult to see. And it was tall; it was very tall. Cliff saw movement. As his eyes continued to focus, he realized that the movement was the animal's breathing. A long, deep breath in. A long breath out. A light whistling sound suggested to Cliff this was a massive animal. But there was nothing about the animal that suggested that it was a bear. It was unlike anything he had ever encountered.

Cliff thought about calling out to it. A lump had formed in his throat, and he was not sure his voice would even work. His mind rapidly played with available options, but he had never faced a situation like this. He could not develop a workable game plan.

Meanwhile, the strain of the moment overpowered Carly's will to remain calm. She grabbed tightly onto Cliff's arm as she pulled herself up to a seated position. "What is it?" she begged, her voice much too loud.

Not being able to balance himself in a crouched position with her pulling on him, Cliff flailed, trying to keep from falling backward. He lunged to counter the momentum, and then lurched forward to his knees, grunting loudly.

Their noise and sudden movement changed the situation. Suddenly, Cliff saw the figure step completely away from the tree and into full view. Cliff felt the blood drain from his face. His mouth went dry. His arms and legs felt like jelly. He had never seen anything like this before. He had never felt so terrified in all of his life.

Chapter Two

Sandy Kelly turned his rusting Honda Civic into his driveway and eased the car to a stop. Turning off the engine, he closed his eyes and leaned his head back. After a few moments, it dawned on him that both hands were still tightly gripping the steering wheel. Slowly, he loosened his intense grip and relaxed his arms. He unbuttoned his collar and undid his dark tie. As if he had been holding it for days, he let out a long breath.

It had been the most difficult funeral he had officiated since coming to pastor at Lycona Community Church just over a year ago. Funerals were always hard, but today he'd felt particularly exhausted. It was Sunday, and after leading regular morning services at the church, Sandy had conducted the funeral of Ardelle Bingham. The funeral home had been filled to overflowing, and at times the grief had hung like thick sap. Sandy had felt it physically pressing against him. Now his neck and shoulders were aching from the strain of the invisible yoke that intense grief had laid upon him.

Ardelle had been a much-loved member of the church and community. She had also been very close to Sandy, and had been one of his biggest supporters. She had always been active at Lycona Community Church, but when her husband died six years ago she had begun to turn her attention to community affairs. The daycare center had been her first notable achievement. Small, hard-working families, who had been forced to commute out of town for employment, now had a safe place for their children. A number of those families had even begun attending church.

Ardelle's sharp mind and proactive stance had then earned her a seat on the City Council. This had allowed her to extend her influence even further.

Her untimely death now stunned the town. She had been visiting a friend for an extended weekend trip and was returning home late on the rounding, steep hills of forested Lycona. A passing motorist had happened to see headlights off the side of the road and had stopped to investigate. It was Ardelle's Buick. The Sheriff had concluded that she'd fallen asleep at the wheel, or lost control of her vehicle while rounding the sharp curve. Unfortunately, the guardrails had been removed from a previous accident. She had been breathing when they'd pulled her from the wreckage, but two hours and five pints of blood later she'd lost her fight in the operating room. She had never regained consciousness.

Sandy looked out of his Honda's windshield to the greening mountain landscape and sighed heavily. In spite of the difficulty of the day, Lycona was an idyllic appointment. The quiet town was sandwiched between two rugged mountain tops and was completely surrounded by lush Lycona National Forest. Washback River splashed playfully through the town, dividing the uptown business district on the east side from the rows of restored Victorian homes neatly arranged on perpendicular streets and avenues on the west. Washback then tumbled off a fifteen-foot waterfall in Falls Park, the town's centerpiece, before it danced its merry way out of town.

Long ago, the river had enabled the timber industry to export its produce to mill towns that were built farther downstream. The railroad eventually had replaced the river as the transportation of choice. Next had come the tractor-trailers, which still traced the dangerously steep roads in and out of the valley. Timbering remained the most significant source of income for the town. However, when much of the surrounding land had been preserved by the National Parks Department, the hunters, fishermen, and vacationers had migrated to the picturesque town to enjoy the tranquil scenery.

Tourism was now the second highest contributor to the town's economy. But even that was changing. Construction of a modern resort was nearing completion on one of the highest peaks in the valley. Slated to open by fall, the resort was already ushering financial relief into the community through badly needed jobs. By conservative estimates, the complex would eventually pump millions of dollars into the local economy every year through taxes and other revenues. Ardelle had been a strong supporter of the resort. This had changed, however, when the resort owners had approached the zoning board for approval of a casino to be added to the existing resort plans. Ardelle, in favor of the resort, had been opposed to the problems that would be introduced into the area with gambling.

In spite of these ongoing conflicts, Sandy immediately had fallen in love with the area. He felt at home in the town, and had no regrets. However, there was lots of work to do. The congregation had been without solid pastoral leadership, and they seemed to be remarkably immature believers. He'd found many in the church who lacked a basic understanding of their faith. Some families didn't even own a Bible.

As Sandy was about to open his car door, he heard the crunch of gravel from beneath hard rubber behind him. He glanced into his rearview mirror and saw a blue Jeep. The driver was a young woman he had seen at the funeral. After the service, she'd shaken his hand and introduced herself as Ardelle's niece, Ellie Lawson. Ardelle had two nieces: Caroline and Ellie. They both lived with Ardelle; though only Caroline came to church. At sixteen, Caroline was an active girl in school and in church. Sandy had met her at camp last summer and saw her often when he visited Ardelle. But he had never met her sister. She didn't come to church, and Ardelle didn't talk much about her.

Sandy opened the car door and stepped out onto the driveway. The smell of fresh-cut grass and the fragrance of blooming lilacs greeted him. He sucked the perfumed air into his lungs and savored its sweetness. The winter winds were still a fresh memory, but spring was certainly doing her work in the fertile valley.

"I don't know if you remember me or not, Pastor, but I'm Ardelle's niece, Ellie," she said as she crawled out of the Jeep and made her way to Sandy. "You shook my hand at the funeral and said that if there was anything else you could do to just give you a call. Well...," and then she paused. For a moment, Sandy didn't believe that she was going to finish her thought. But then she continued, "If you have just a minute, I sure could use someone to talk to."

"Yes, of course I remember you," Sandy responded with a smile. At the moment, he was not eager for company, and he would have preferred to collapse on the couch for a much-needed nap. But one look at Ellie's swollen eyes reminded him of why he had become a pastor. "Why don't you come inside and I'll put on some coffee?"

Sandy led the way to the front door of the church parsonage. He unlocked it and swung it open for Ellie, who slipped in behind him. He was hoping that he had left the living room in order, and he breathed a quiet prayer of relief when he saw that it was relatively straightened. As an unmarried pastor, one of the hardest challenges for him was making the change from communal dorm life to that of a professional figure, who often entertained visitors unannounced. After a few embarrassing episodes, he'd made housekeeping a priority.

"Have a seat, Ellie," Sandy said, motioning toward the second, or maybe third-hand sofa. "I'll get the coffee started."

"Don't make any for me, please," Ellie replied, "I'm really not in the mood for anything."

"Okay," Sandy said. He motioned for Ellie to have a seat on the sofa. He then angled a worn, wooden rocker in her direction and sat down, covering the gaping hole in the fabric with his thigh. Pastoring was good work. It just didn't pay well.

Sandy looked at Ellie and waited for her to say something. Instead, she kept her puffy eyes focused on the floor. Others may have been made uncomfortable with the silence, but Sandy had never felt it burdensome. He was becoming increasingly aware of his own ability to remain at ease with those in pain. It was not that he was indifferent; far from it. As of late, he felt a kinship of sorts with the hurting.

"How are you doing?" As soon as he asked the question, he felt like a heel. Feeling at ease was one thing; conversing with ease was another. It was intensely obvious that the young woman across from him was not well. Her long, red hair was tousled and her makeup had been smeared.

"I'm okay. I guess I'm still in shock over this whole thing." She spoke as if she was not offended by his blundering question. She even lifted her eyes from the floor to meet his for a moment.

"I'm not even sure why I stopped in," she continued as she returned her gaze to the floor. "I guess I just feel kinda lost right now."

"That's pretty easy to understand," Sandy reassured her. He hadn't been asked any direct questions yet, so he assumed this was a time for listening.

"Aunt Dell means—meant—so much to me," Ellie said. "She was more of a mother to me than my own mother. Yet, I didn't treat her nicely at times, and now she's gone. I don't know how to go back and change things with her!"

Sandy sensed that there was much more hurt than what was hinted at by those words. His mind quickly scanned through past conversations with Ardelle, searching for nuggets that might lend insight. He couldn't recall anything of significance. When Ardelle had spoken of Ellie, she'd always appeared troubled. But no specific details were ever given, and Sandy had never pressed her.

Sandy got up, retrieved a box of tissues from the end table, and handed it to her. She took a tissue from the box and wiped her nose. She sat quietly with eyes fixed to the floor again.

"Tell me a little about yourself and your Aunt Dell," Sandy prompted. "She talked about you from time to time, but I don't believe you and I met before today."

"Well, my story is not a pretty one," Ellie said with a forced laugh. She again wiped her nose and looked up, but she seemed to avoid Sandy's eyes. "My parents divorced right after Caroline was born. I was ten. Dad moved out of Lycona and I only saw him during the summer months when I went to visit him. It's been years now since I've seen him, and I don't even know where he is these days. Mom was so busy working two jobs and trying to make ends meet that we never spent any good time together. She died of cancer when I was fourteen. That's when her sister, Aunt Dell, took us in. I loved her dearly, but we never got along. I ran away from home a few times, and whatever she wanted me to do; well, I'd just do the opposite. I guess I was just angry. I was angry at Dad for leaving, and at Mom for dying."

Ellie lifted her gaze and looked briefly at Sandy. For a moment, Sandy tried to make a connection with her; to relay the concern he felt. But she wouldn't keep the contact long enough. Her eyes once again fell to the floor. Sandy sensed a wall rise between them. And it seemed Ellie was purposely keeping that wall in place.

"When I was young, Aunt Dell and I fought about everything," Ellie continued. "I know that I gave her so much grief. And I don't know why, because she loved me so much. And I loved her!" She paused and appeared to be struggling to maintain her composure.

Sandy pulled another tissue from the box and extended it toward Ellie. She saw the gesture but didn't take it. After an awkward moment, Sandy pulled his arm back and balled the tissue in his hand.

After a few seconds, Ellie suddenly composed herself. She wiped her nose, cleared her throat, and looked at Sandy. Her green eyes were sad for a moment. But as she appeared to study him, Sandy saw them flash with a new emotion.

"What's the point believing in a God who lets good people die in ugly car wrecks?" Ellie asked, almost as if she were accusing Sandy of something. Her green eyes had become smoking pistols. "What's the point believing in a God who leaves you when you need him most? Aunt Dell was lying in the woods, and God was nowhere to be found!"

Sandy was going to speak, but Ellie continued, "And where was God in my life all these years? He let my parents' divorce, he let my mom be tortured by cancer and then die, and then he allowed ..."

Ellie didn't finish her last thought. Instead, she rolled her eyes and shook her head as if it was pointless to even give it voice. She looked at Sandy again. There were no tears now. There was no hurt. There was only deep frustration. With a slow, determined voice, she said, "I just want to know why!"

Sandy blew out a sigh. He was finally being asked a question; though not one he felt comfortable answering Too much was going on in his own world right now. Too many of the same questions were being asked by him. His stomach churned.

"I don't know why God allows things like this to happen," he said, choosing his words carefully. "Sometimes it seems impossible to make sense of what happens around us. But a believer does not believe because life makes sense. A believer believes because..." Sandy paused, corrected himself and continued. "A believer believes when he determines that God can be trusted."

With that, Ellie rose quickly to her feet. Her eyes now burned with a fire that matched her red hair. A wave of determination washed quickly across her face.

"Well, then I can't be a believer anymore; because God can't be trusted!"

Ellie made her way to the door as Sandy stood up. As she turned the door knob, she looked back to him. The fire may have waned only a fraction. "Thanks for your time."

Ellie stepped outside and closed the door behind her. Sandy stood motionless, wondering what to do. Before he could process his next move, he heard Ellie's Jeep roar to life. He moved to the large picture window and watched her back quickly into the street. She then pulled away. She never glanced back.

The ache in his stomach grew sharper. He set the balled up tissue down on a coffee table. He pulled the tie from around his neck and made his way from the living room window. In the kitchen he grabbed a wooden kitchen chair and carried it with him as he kept walking. *Why does God allow things like this to happen? Where is God when we need him most?* These questions were not just Ellie's; they were Sandy's. They represented *his* doubts; *his* fears.

Sandy walked back the hall to a tiny bedroom that had been converted into an office. He swung the kitchen chair behind his desk, where it would now serve as an office chair. He collapsed into it. The ancient desk was bare, except for a white envelope setting in the middle. It was like a wine stain on a pristine wedding dress.

The contents of the simple, white envelope had forever changed him. Yet, he was unable to discard it. He was unable to do anything with it. And each time he saw it he felt like crying. It was the reason for the knots in his stomach. It was the reason for the doubts that harbored inside of him.

Sandy picked up the envelope and pulled out the now-worn letter from inside. He had received it just a few months ago, not long after Christmas. It had arrived days after a phone call from his sobbing sister. She had explained that their father, a minister of thirty years, had suddenly walked out on their mother and run off with a woman from the church that he had been serving. At that time, Sandy had made a quick trip back home to visit his mother, who was so completely in shock that she seemed thoroughly composed. Later, she'd begun to unravel. Sandy called her often, but had not yet spoken with his father.

Sandy unfolded the letter. He had read it so many times that he nearly had it memorized. It was handwritten by his father from a post office box in another part of the state. He read the letter again, as if to find a hidden clue that he had missed before. But it was a brief correspondence with no frills. No hidden messages. Nothing between the lines. His father simply confirmed the truth and asked his son for understanding. He gave no explanation for his actions. He admitted no guilt. He asked Sandy to write or call. Sandy did neither.

Sandy remembered his father as a stern man who ruled the house with unchallenged authority. He was not a bad father, but because of the distance he'd kept from his family it had been hard to get to know him. It had been hard to get to know him, that is, unless you were in his

16

parish. For it was there that Sandy had seen another side of his father. There, he'd smiled all of the time and warmly greeted the parishioners with handshakes or hugs. It was there that his father had talked with everyone. It was there that he had bent down and warmly laid his hands on the children's shoulders. Sandy still sometimes wished that he belonged to another family so he could feel his father's happy touch. He hated the fact that he felt jealousy whenever he went to church. But he had. He had been very jealous.

Everyone had loved Sandy's father. They'd heard him preach fervently and teach brilliantly. He was always a real master of the Bible and could quote long sections verbatim. He had also taught theology courses at a local college, earning quite a reputation for his intellect. Everyone had loved Sandy's father. Sandy loved him too.

At an early age, Sandy had made up his mind that he wanted to be just like him. After high school Sandy had completed college and entered a Masters of Divinity program. Originally, he'd had designs on teaching the New Testament or Church History at a seminary level. But during his masters, he was required to serve as a student pastor at a very small parish near the college. It was there that he had fallen in love with pastoring and had felt that God was changing his direction. When he'd told his father that he felt he was being called into the pastorate, Sandy recalled seeing one of his father's rare around-the-house smiles. That smile had fueled Sandy's studies more than his father could ever hope to know. It had been his inspiration.

Now the inspiration was dying. What hurt the most was the feeling of betrayal. With a smile, his father had encouraged him into pastoral work, and he had patterned his style of ministry after his father's. Whenever Sandy stood behind the pulpit and preached, he could hear his father's voice in his own. Whenever he spoke about matters of faith, he tried to imitate the confidence that he used to hear in his father's voice. Now, it seemed that all of that was taken away. Sandy felt robbed of his past. Deceived. Betrayed.

If his father could serve the church for thirty years and in a moment leave it all behind, Sandy began to wonder if faith really meant anything at all. How could a person profess to be a certain way all of his life and then overnight decide to live differently? Perhaps his father's life of faith was really just a lie? Perhaps faith was a lie? Maybe God was a lie? At his best moments, he could silence the questions. At his worst, they reverberated in his mind at a deafening volume.

When the questions came, Sandy was no longer certain about life. And the longer he felt uncertain, the more difficult it was to be the man extinguishing doubts in others, like in Ellie

For the most part, he was able to maintain a healthy front. He attended meetings, visited the sick and shut-ins, kept after the church newsletter, and saw that the church ran like a well-oiled machine. On the outside, he looked fine. On the inside, he was coming apart. On the outside, he looked like his father. On the inside, he felt like a failure. That thought terrified Sandy. For hadn't his father looked fine on the outside, but was only a hypocrite on the inside? Was he becoming his father?

He dropped the letter and buried his head in his hands. He tried to pray, but the words would not come. Nothing came easily to him in these moments of doubt. Inspiration fled. Study time was meaningless. Even the quiet sanctuary of the church frightened him. But worst of all, he felt like a hypocrite. Whenever he took to the pulpit in these moments of doubt, he felt like a whitewashed sepulcher; clean on the outside, but inside he was full of dead men's bones. He also felt alienated because he didn't know how to tell the church that there were times when their leader struggled with his own faith. Oh, that would surely make the roll books swell with new members! That would bring them in!

Sandy couldn't take the questions any longer. He got up from his desk, changed his clothes, and spent the evening trying to be distracted by the television. It didn't work.

Chapter Three

The sunshine sprinkled brightly over Lycona. In the flats beyond the mountains, the temperature would soar well into the nineties during the summer months. But in the basin beneath the shading of the two mountain tops, where the tiny town stood, more pleasant temperatures always prevailed.

Uptown Lycona was beginning its Monday bustle. School buses were making their regular stops around town. The students' moods were much lighter now that winter was over and the summer vacation was in sight.

Cheery shop owners were unlocking their doors and setting their wares out onto the sidewalk in an effort to lure passing customers inside. The town's only barber switched on his rotating barber pole, while the hardware store owner next door set out several lawn chairs. Though the lawn chairs were for sale, they would soon be filled by the retired loggers who made their way uptown. After breakfast at the Timber Creek Cafe, they wandered to the chairs where they would sit "logging timber" the rest of the morning.

It was a typical Lycona morning. But the cheerfulness of the beautiful day was lost to Deputy Cliff Janowski. He was returning from a week's vacation that had begun rather oddly and still left him utterly perplexed. He pulled into the City Office Building parking lot, where the Sheriff's Department was located. He parked next to Sheriff Frank Bragg's patrol SUV. He was glad to be working the daylight shift, because it kept him busier. Today would be a twelve-hour shift; the first of three in a row. They would be long, busy days. And he needed to stay busy, because his mind was still reeling from the strange encounter that he and his wife had experienced while camping earlier in the week. The person—or animal or whatever he'd seen—had stepped out from behind the tree when startled by the noise and commotion in their tent. It had then turned very suddenly and disappeared into the woods. Cliff had told Carly that it was a bear, the largest he had ever seen, and that it had left camp. But that hadn't been the truth. It had *not* been a bear. What it really had been, Cliff was not sure. What he *did* know was that he had become completely paralyzed with fear when he saw it. He had never felt such raw, heart-pounding fear; fear that had left him completely unable to move or think.

Eventually, Carly had been able to get back to sleep that night. But Cliff had remained awake until morning, jumping at every sound that he'd heard. The night had passed without further incident, and as the sun had risen, he'd felt better. After breakfast, he had ventured beyond the treeline to look for tracks. He hadn't found any discernible footprints, but its path had been obvious. The Creature had circled the camp site and then retreated into the forest. Cliff had felt no desire to follow its path.

Carly had sensed Cliff becoming edgy, so she'd suggested that they return home early. He hadn't argued, so they had packed their belongings, hiked back out of the woods, and returned home. The remainder of the vacation had been spent working around the house. They hadn't talked about it anymore, yet the memory of what had happened remained fresh in his mind.

It felt good to be getting back to work. Cliff enjoyed doing police work, and he was good at it. He loved the sensation of adrenaline pumping through his system when things became intense. Adventure was something that he always craved, and though his job didn't promise a continual stream of it, it was the only occupation in the area that even came close.

As Cliff crawled out of his car, Deputy Craig Logan pulled in beside him. Logan was a young, part-time officer who, at 6'3", was a giant of man. Cliff suspected he pounded not only the weights at the gym, but also the steroids. The Sheriff had approved Logan's side security jobs so that he could exploit his size and make extra money. Cliff didn't like Logan's cocky attitude, impulsivity, or his love for "bling," as he called it. But when it came time for muscle on the job, Logan was the man you wanted at your side.

Cliff glanced at his reflection in the car window to make sure he was proper. His uniform was spotless and sharply pressed. Though he never really thought so, he was a handsome man. He had striking gray eyes and sharply cut facial features that made looking like a deputy seem natural. His hairline had begun receding while in his twenties, and now that he was in his mid-thirties, his hair was almost gone. Yet, he was the type of man who actually looked better that way.

"Cliff, I need you to check out a call we got," Sheriff Bragg said as Cliff and Logan walked into the office. "Hank Deal off of Willow Road phoned in a report this morning of someone snooping around his barn last night. He apparently frightened him off before anything was taken, but he wants us to go out and take a look. I told him that there isn't much we can do if the perp is gone, but he was pretty insistent about it. I want you to stop by and see him."

Cliff nodded in agreement and took the note extended from Sheriff Bragg's outstretched hand. Bragg was a long-time peace officer who had done his share of grunt work. He had seen active duty as a U.S. Marine, and he'd returned with some horrific stories. He was in his mid-sixties, and his age was really beginning to show. His once coal-black hair was mostly gray now. He was overweight from too much inactivity, and the constant cigar smoking and coffee drinking had stained his teeth yellow. Even as he extended the note, there was a tremor in his hand that Cliff had recently begun to notice. Above all, he looked tired; more weary than Cliff ever recalled seeing him. Though he talked of retirement and enjoying the good life, Cliff seriously doubted that Bragg had enough savings set by to live comfortably.

"I'll take a ride out there, Sheriff," Cliff replied. He paused, and for a moment he considered sharing his strange sighting. Cliff was still trying to sort it out himself, though, and he didn't know how to even talk about it. Besides that, Bragg had a mean streak that needed little provoking to arouse. A story like this one would only set him up for endless ridicule.

Cliff finished his morning cup of coffee and a short morning debrief. He had a summons that he had been trying to serve not far from Willow Road, where Deal's farm was located. Since it was a non-emergency call, he decided to serve the summons first and then stop by

Hank Deal's place before beginning his regular patrol. Within half an hour he was out of the office and on the road.

Cliff served the summons before heading to Deal's farm. Hank Deal operated a small beef farm just outside the city limits. Like most of the local farmers, he was a hardworking man who took advantage of the fields that had been cleared years ago by the loggers. Cliff had grown up on a farm not far from the area. He knew firsthand the hard work and trials of this difficult life. At times, he still missed it. The love he continued to feel for the land fostered a kinship with men like Hank Deal.

Deal had done well enough to buy some decent equipment. Crime in the area was not a huge problem, but Cliff figured Deal's good fortune had probably caught the attention of someone looking for an easy way to make some cash.

A lifetime ago, Hank used to drink heavily. However, after the loss of his only daughter to a drunk driver, he'd never gone back to the bottle. He now lived quietly with his wife, Marge, focusing his entire attention on his livestock and farm. Cliff had met Hank two years ago when he asked to hunt on some of his property. Friendly and polite, Hank was a man who now took life very seriously.

As he drove down the lane, he studied the landscape. The farm was laid out in a fairly open area. It was surrounded on three sides by open fields, but was hemmed in on the rear by some rough-cut bluffs that eventually gave way to a small grove of trees. Cliff speculated that a prowler would not have risked coming in from the roadway since traffic was relatively moderate and the perpetrator would've risked being seen. The bluffs, however, would have allowed a more stealthy approach.

As he brought the patrol car to a halt in front of the house, Hank's German Shepherd came out to greet Cliff with a chorus of enthusiasm. It was a fierce-looking dog, but Cliff knew that Sadie just wanted some attention. He got out of the car and scratched her behind the ears as her wagging tail beat a friendly rhythm on the fender of the patrol car.

"Hey, Cliff," Hank called as he walked up from below his house. He carried a spool of wire and a pair of metal cutters in his hand.

"Hey, Hank," Cliff returned. "Doing some fence mending?"

"Not mending a fence," Hank replied, "But I'm puttin' up one around the spring house where I keep my potatoes."

"Afraid someone is going to steal your potatoes, Hank?" Cliff teased.

"Kind of," Hank said as he put down the tools on a weathered stump in the yard. The tree that had once stood there used to hold a swing for his daughter. He hadn't been able to stand looking at it any longer, so he had cut it down.

"I appreciate you stopping by, Cliff. And I'm glad that it's you, not Sheriff Bragg."

"Why's that?" Cliff wondered out loud.

Hank didn't answer, but motioned for Cliff to follow him. They walked down the slope, past the farmhouse, and toward the barn that stood about fifty feet away. Near the dilapidated outhouse, Hank paused and a very serious look swept over his face. Cliff got the sense that Hank was trying to lead him away from the farm house.

"Ain't nothing like this ever happened to me before, Cliff," Hank said. "And I want you to know that I haven't touched the bottle in years. I'm just an honest man trying to make an honest living. I don't want no trouble from no one, and I ain't interested in makin' any trouble for anyone else."

"What's going on, Hank?" Cliff asked. He knew Deal as a straightforward man, and he could tell he was really struggling to talk.

"Well, that's just it–I don't know what's going on."

"You're confusing me, Hank. I got the word that a prowler was out here. What's happened?"

Hank reached into his pocket and withdrew his pipe. Inside his shirt pocket, he found a pack of tobacco. Cliff watched as he silently filled the pipe and then tried to light it. His hands were shaking. Not until he took a couple of deep puffs from the pipe did he seem to calm down. He looked at Cliff through narrowing eyes.

"I seen something."

"What?"

"I don't know *what*. It was something that I never seen before. And something I hope to God that I never see again."

Hank drew again on his pipe. As he exhaled, Cliff watched the sweet-smelling tobacco swirl around the farmer. Cliff didn't interrupt, but let him talk.

"Last night, sometime after ten-thirty, me and the missus were in the living room watching TV. We were waiting for the news to come on. All of a sudden Sadie, who was at my feet, starting growling. I didn't think nothin' of it at first. I told her to hush, but she just kept on growling real quiet like and looking toward the back door. Finally, I had enough of it so I yelled at her to quiet down. As soon as I yelled, me and the missus both heard something from out back. It sounded like it came from the spring house."

"What kind of sound was it?"

"Kind of like a bang. I thought at first that the spring house door might not have been shut and that the wind knocked it open. But there wasn't much of a breeze blowing last night, and because Sadie was acting up, I figured someone might be snooping around.

I got up and walked to the back door. Sadie followed me. I opened the back door and turned on the yard lights at the same time. I didn't see anything moving, and I could see the spring house door was closed.

Just to be sure, I yelled out that I had a gun and whoever was out there was gonna be in a heap of trouble if I caught them. Thinking back, there's something kind of strange that I hadn't noticed earlier."

"What's that?" Cliff asked.

"Normally, Sadie would have torn out that door the moment I opened it. But she wasn't moving. She just stood there and growled.

I left the light on and walked back to the living room. Marge asked me what the fuss was about. I told her I didn't see nobody and that it was probably nothing. But Sadie was acting real weird. Instead of growling, she started whimpering."

"What happened next?" Cliff asked. He scribbled some notes on a small pad that he carried in his breast pocket.

"Well, I heard the noise again. I jumped up and fetched my twelve-gauge. I loaded her up and walked out into the back yard. I meant business this time. Mind you, I wasn't gonna shoot no one, just scare 'em a bit. Sadie followed me, but she was crying like a baby.

I walked down to the spring house and checked the door. I don't keep it locked; never had a reason to. It was shut, but it looked like someone had been playing with the latch. As I was standing there at the spring house door, it hit me: the worst smell you could imagine. It just drifted over my way. It smelled like something died in a vat of sulfur. Honestly, Cliff, I don't know how to describe it to you. It was just awful."

Hank's account was starting to remind Cliff so much of his own encounter that he could hardly write his notes. He kept his eyes locked on the notepad.

"Go on. What happened next?" Cliff asked without looking up.

"Well, when I smelled that rancid smell I stepped away from the spring house to face the way the wind was blowing. And that's when I saw *it*."

"It?" Cliff asked, looking up.

"It, he? Heck, I don't know. Maybe an animal? Maybe it was a guy? I'm not sure. But if it was a guy, it was the biggest guy I've ever seen!"

"What did you see?" Cliff asked. He stopped his writing.

"Well, like I said, I looked over near the barn, and there he stood. It was the biggest guy I ever seen. He must have stood nine feet tall and had to weigh over four hundred pounds! He was standing near the barn, but he wasn't moving a muscle. He was looking at me and I was looking at him."

"What was he wearing, Hank?" Cliff asked, trying to sound professional.

"I don't know. He was covered in black from head to toe."

"He was dressed in black? Or, was he a black person?"

Hank shook his head and started walking toward the barn. Cliff could tell he was very upset, and it looked like he needed a moment to gather himself. Cliff followed Hank as he walked, studying him very closely. The man carried his pipe in his left hand. The shaking had returned. Cliff had seen accident victims and witnesses react like this while retelling their stories. A person might lie about what they saw, but he knew the difficulty in faking this kind of physical reaction.

Hank stopped as he neared the lower portion of the barn and looked back at the spring house.

"This is where he was standing. The top of his head was just under that beam." Hank gestured upward to a one-by-ten inch plank extending from the barn, holding the sliding door track.

"That plank is nearly ten feet off of the ground, Hank" Cliff said. "Are you sure he was right under it?"

"As sure as I'm standing here!"

"What happened next?"

"Well, when I saw him I got so scared I couldn't do anything but curse. I cursed real loud. I think it startled him, because all of a sudden he turned around and walked off. And Cliff, there ain't *no one* who can move like that. It took him three steps to reach the pasture fence, and then he stepped over without even breaking his stride. That fence is forty inches high, and he stepped over without so much as making an effort. He looked back at me once more, and in a few steps he was gone; disappeared down over the bluff.

I was so scared I turned around and ran back to the house. Marge took one look at me and asked if I had seen a ghost. I didn't know what to say, so I didn't say nothing. That's when I realized that I had brought a loaded and cocked gun into the house. I had been so scared I totally forgot that I was holding it! So I un-cocked the gun and ejected the shells. I was shaking so bad I didn't know what to do.

Marge asked me what happened to Sadie. I looked around and saw her under the coffee table. Marge said that just before I came into the house the dog tore through the living room and hid herself. She asked what was out there. I didn't know what to say, so I told her I had seen a bear. She asked about the foul odor, and I said that I didn't know what it was. Told her I'd check it out in the morning."

"What happened next?"

"Nothing. Marge went to bed after the news. I followed a little bit later. Sadie stayed by our bed all night and never made a sound.

This morning I got up and looked all around. I couldn't find anything that would have caused that smell—but this." Hank punctuated his sentence by pointing straight down between his feet.

Cliff followed the direction of Hank's pointing finger. He didn't see anything in the grass, so he walked to where Hank was standing. Cliff crouched down and found a deep impression in the soft soil. Although it had decayed considerably, he could still make out the form of a very large footprint.

"It's seventeen inches long and about five inches wide. I measured it," Hank said, knowing Cliff was thinking the same thing.

"Find any others?" Cliff asked.

"Nope. This area right here is soft from always being shaded. But in the yard between the spring house and barn the ground is pretty hard. I couldn't find a print anywhere else."

Cliff studied the impression, but too much time had passed to make any firm conclusions about it.

"What do you think it is?" Hank asked. "And don't tell me it's a bear. There ain't no black bear in these parts that stands that tall or walks that fast on two legs. Besides, you and I both know that ain't a bear print."

"No, it's not a bear print. But I don't know what it is, Hank." Cliff didn't know what to say. Normally he would not have felt such alarm. However, memories of his own encounter came flooding back, causing him to feel quite shaken.

"Did anything else happen last night? Did you hear any more noises?" Cliff asked.

"Not a thing. It just took off and was gone."

"Did you find anything missing or out of the ordinary this morning?"

"Nope, nothing was stolen. I think, and this is my theory, I think that the thing smelled my potatoes in the spring house and was trying to get in when I scared it away. And believe me, I'm glad I found it in the yard rather than in the spring house. I wouldn't have wanted to corner that thing."

Cliff made some final notes and closed his notepad.

"I'll write a report and keep it on file, Hank. If it shows up again give us a call. We'll get out here as soon as we can. And if you don't mind, I'd like to talk privately with your wife, just to get her side."

"No problem at all, Cliff. She's inside the house right now." Thanks for stopping by," Hank said. He was relieved that Cliff seemed to accept his story.

Cliff interviewed Mrs. Deal. Her story matched Hank's in every detail but one. She said that when Hank had come back in from seeing the animal, she'd notice that he had wet himself. Understandably, it was a fact that Hank had failed to mention.

Chapter Four

"You've got a call on line one," bellowed Beatrice Maxwell, the Lycona Community Church Secretary.

Beatrice's voice never needed an intercom. Despite years of chain smoking, it remained as strong and loud as ever. She was overweight, had high blood pressure, and was on the verge of diabetes. But instead of heeding her doctor's warnings, Beatrice had decided to stop doctoring. It was easier. She didn't like taking pills anyway. "If the good Lord wanted me to take medicine," she was fond of saying, "He'd figure out a way to put it in a cigarette." That line always ended in one of Beatrice's rare laughs, which then evolved into a full-blown smoker's cough.

"Who is it?" Sandy called from his office. He had been crafting an email when her raspy voice had shattered his concentration.

"I don't know," came the gruff reply. "She didn't say."

This kind of exchange was common in the church office. It had become a constant source of irritation to Sandy. Initially, Sandy had responded to her obnoxious behavior with anger. Unfortunately, that had only led to heated quarrels over office protocol, for which she had little concern. Eventually, he'd realized that Beatrice was only trying to rattle him. She had a fondness for provoking people, and had set out to master the art. It served as an enjoyable hobby for Beatrice. Consequently, Sandy had become a little more selective over which battles to fight.

"This may seem like a novel approach, but could you *ask?*" Sandy replied. He struggled to keep the annoyance out of his voice.

"Rather than both of us getting involved in something like that, why don't you just find out and then come and tell me?"

Sandy sighed. Beatrice *knew* who was on the phone. She always knew. In fact, there wasn't much that Beatrice didn't know around the church or town. As a secretary, her skills were fair; but as a source of information, she was a fountainhead. She thrived on hearing and sharing gossip. She spent only three mornings each week at the church office. That's all that the church budget allowed. If the truth were known, however, Beatrice would have worked for free. A church office is a great place to learn what is going on in a sleepy mountain town.

Sandy moved his laptop aside before picking up the receiver.

"Hello, this is Pastor Sandy."

"Pastor," the caller paused, "this is Ellie Lawson."

"Oh... hello, Ellie," Sandy replied. Awkward silence. "How are you doing?"

"Uhm ... I'm fine, thank you," came the reply. Ellie's voice didn't seem to have the same edge that it had the last time they'd spoken. "I, ah, just wanted to call and tell you that I'm sorry for snapping at you like I did yesterday."

"Oh, don't worry about it, Ellie. I didn't take anything you said personally," Sandy said. He meant it. "Besides, you've got a lot going on right now."

There was a long pause, broken by Ellie clearing her throat. "Thanks." There was measurable relief in her voice. "You're right, I do."

Again, there was a pause. Sandy had a sense that Ellie wanted to talk, but was having trouble starting things.

"How are things going for you?" he asked, trying to keep the conversation moving.

"Okay, I guess," she sighed.

"How is Caroline doing?"

"She's struggling, but doing better than I thought she would. Aunt Dell was the only mother she ever knew. Maybe you could stop by to see her sometime?"

"I'd be happy to," Sandy replied. "I think Jocelyn Rush, our youth leader, has taken a special interest in her."

"Yeah, she has, and I appreciate that," Ellie replied. "She calls her every day, and they talk a lot."

The conversation quieted down again.

"Do you have a job? Are you working?" Sandy pushed the conversation in a different direction. It seemed that Ellie wanted to talk. She just needed some help.

"This past winter I had a job at the resort over in Winston. Then they cut me at the end of the ski season. They said they may call me back if things get busy again, but I haven't heard from them."

"So, what are your plans? Where do you go from here?"

Sandy suddenly noticed that Beatrice's adjoining office had grown quiet. He came around from behind his desk and, reaching as far as the phone cord would extend, pushed his office door closed with his foot. The scowl that he knew would now be on Beatrice's face brought a grin to his own. He sometimes enjoyed a few games, too.

"Well, that's the other reason I called," Ellie continued.

Sandy tried recalling the first reason. Then he remembered the apology. *Nice.*

"I just got a call from Attorney John Williams. I guess Aunt Dell had a will; he wants to give it to Caroline and me. He asked us to come by on Wednesday at five. Uhm ... I was wondering if there's any chance that you could go with us to his office. After the way I treated you the other day, I know that I have no right to ask. But I don't like attorneys, and I really could use having someone along. To be perfectly honest, I don't have anyone else to ask."

Sandy not only heard the sadness in her voice, he felt it.

"Wednesday? Day after tomorrow?" Sandy asked rhetorically. He clicked on his mobile phone calendar and began scrolling. "Yes, I think I can make it at five. Williams' office is just a short walk from here. Why don't you stop in a bit early, and then we'll just walk up together?"

"Oh, thank you so much, Pastor!" Again, there was relief in her voice.

Seeing an opportunity, Sandy assumed a teasing tone, "So, if you're going to call me 'Pastor,' does that mean I'll be seeing you in church?"

"Do you remember the things I said yesterday about God?"

Sandy thought she was avoiding his question.

"Yes."

"Well, this may come as a surprise to you, but I really *do* believe in God." Ellie's voice was pleading for understanding.

"I never thought that you didn't."

Ellie let out another sigh. "I just feel so lost without Aunt Dell. I guess I was just angry. I took that anger out on you and on God. I'm sorry for doing both of those things."

"It's okay, really," Sandy encouraged. "God is big enough to handle our outbursts, even if it's directed toward him. He created us to be emotional people. That's what you were doing, being emotional. If anyone understands, it's God."

Ellie paused. She seemed to be considering what Sandy had just said.

"You know," she continued. "You may not believe me, but I pray to God all the time, and I even read my Bible a little."

"Ellie, why would I not believe you?"

"Well, I assumed that Aunt Dell told you all about me and my past and how *bad* a person I was."

Something was clinging to the word *bad*. Sandy couldn't tell if it was just sarcasm, or if there was something deeper to it.

"Actually," Sandy said, "she never really told me much about you other than to tell me that you stayed with her."

"Hmmm ...." Ellie seemed surprised.

"So, since you believe in God, read your Bible, and pray, the next logical step would be to come to church, right?"

"I don't know. Maybe." She seemed to be reaching for an answer. "The typical church setting never did it for me."

Sandy glanced at his laptop; at the email he had been proofreading when Ellie had called. An idea struck.

"Ellie, if you're not into the 'typical church setting,' then let me suggest something else. This summer, just after school lets out, we're taking a group of kids to camp for a week. We already have about ninety registered to go, and that number is going to climb. I was about to send an email out to the congregation asking for more help. Maybe this is something you'd be interested in doing? You're between jobs right now. It would keep you busy—your mind occupied—and it would help out the church a lot."

"You're kidding me, right?"

"Absolutely not," Sandy replied confidently. "I really could use your help."

"Pastor," Ellie seemed to be looking for the right words. "There's no way I would even come close to being qualified as some kind of camp counselor. I'm not exactly a nun, you know. I mean, I'm not the best person, and I've done some things in the past that I'm not very proud of."

Sandy couldn't help but wonder about the inferences in her last remark. Still, it did not deter him.

"First of all, you wouldn't be a counselor. You would be what we call a Camp Aide. Secondly, we aren't interested in nuns; their habits only get caught in the trees. And thirdly, you just need to pass a state background check. There isn't any special training or qualification needed. You just come along and help!"

"I don't know," Ellie said, her tone skeptical. "I've never done anything like that before."

"I think it would do you some good, Ellie. Besides, your Aunt Ardelle was a huge supporter of the camping program." Sandy was saving his best argument for last. "I think it would have meant so much to her to know you were helping."

Sandy couldn't see Ellie's expression, but the silence that followed told him that his argument had landed a heavy punch.

"Caroline is already registered. It might be fun to go along with her," he added.

"Well, let me think about it," she replied.

"You've got a few more weeks to make a decision, but the sooner the better. Anyway, we can talk about it some more on Wednesday when you stop in."

After the phone call ended, Sandy heard Beatrice moving about her office again.

////

In spite of its massive size, the Creature's passage through the forest was marked by astonishing silence. Its movements were executed with remarkable speed, yet each one was deliberate, as if it had been calculated long in advance. Occasionally, as it moved across the forest floor, it came to an abrupt stop. Then it would raise and cock its head in stiff positions, as if fine-tuning a sensitive antenna. When it retrained itself to the sound, the rapid forward motion resumed. In response to its presence, the forest became deathly silent as it passed by.

A well-worn deer trail provided easy movement for a short distance. As the trail turned over a sharp knoll toward an inviting forest stream, the Creature abandoned the path and once more began moving through the thicket.   Soon, the voices ahead became more easily discernable. The need to stop and reorient itself diminished. Its pace began to slow. Ahead, in the otherwise dense forest, an unnatural clearing began to materialize. The Creature lowered its massive frame closer to the ground. It began to creep with the stealth of a trained sniper. Movement soon became measured in inches as it silently and deliberately drew near the slightly elevated opening.

Four figures slowly came into view. One was sitting atop a large rock. The other three were beyond the first. Finding a position beside a rotund maple where the entire clearing could be seen, the Creature crouched low and became completely still. Unblinking, bloodshot eyes surveilled the scene.

////

Benjamin Walker sat cross-legged on the large boulder.   His eyes were closed, as if asleep. His long black hair was tied in a ponytail, and the fringes of his buckskin shirt waved in the cool morning breeze. His faint Native American ancestry became quite apparent whenever he dressed like this.

Behind Benjamin, three men were unloading tools from the back of a rusted, white Suburban. Two of them were scrawny figures, barely out of their teen years. The first wore a ball cap turned backward; the second donned a red bandana on his head. They were agitated with their surroundings and were constantly casting glances into the forest surrounding them. The third man was at least ten years older than the other two, about the same age as Benjamin. He was heavy, with strong arms and deeply calloused hands. He too was agitated, but not with the surroundings. The source of his disturbance sat cross-legged on the rock.

Suddenly, Benjamin opened his eyes as if he had been jolted from sleep. He instantly scanned the treeline in front of him. He moved his squinted eyes from left to right, as if he was searching for something in the woods. His gaze stopped as he focused just twenty yards from the forest's edge. After a few moments, the muscles around his eyes relaxed as though they were simply reading a familiar book. His lids closed softly again.

"So, you gonna sit there praying all morning, or are you gonna help us get some work done?" the large man with the calloused hands barked angrily.

"Let him alone, Skip!" It was the boy with the ball cap who intervened. "He's not hurting anyone."

"He's a bum. And he's just trying to get out of work!"

"I *am* working," Benjamin said in a steeled voice, eyes remaining closed.

"If you ask me, the work crews have become a bunch of frightened old women!" Skip countered. He pulled a posthole digger from the back of the Suburban and carried it to a growing pile of tools. "We don't need a witch doctor protecting us from some evil spirit. What we need is some people who aren't afraid of doing a little work!" He threw down the heavy digger and returned to the Suburban.

"Shut up, Skip," the young man with the bandana spoke up. "You don't know anything about what happened up here last fall. There's *something* in these woods. And whatever Benjamin has been doing is working 'cause we haven't had any trouble since he started."

"Screw you," Skip spat. "I know a fraud when I see one. And our boy Benny here is as fake as a television preacher. All he needs is a polyester suit and some shiny, white shoes. All religious nuts are the same; they take advantage of a situation to either make themselves rich or famous, or both. Benny here's got everyone thinkin' that there's some ghost running around the woods and he's our Savior."

"But he ain't gettin' rich or famous doing it, you idiot," growled the ball-capped boy, trying to make himself sound tougher than he was.

"Screw you," Skip snarled again as he shot him a warning glance and drew in a breath to puff up. He then looked at Benjamin's back as he still sat on the rock. "The next thing anyone knows, he'll be thinking he's Jesus Christ!"

Benjamin lost his focus, and without concealing the irritation in his voice turned slowly around. "Tell me, Skip," he said, "what do you know about Jesus anyway?"

"A heck of a lot more than you do! While your ancestors were smoking the peace pipe and dancin' naked around a fire, mine were going to a church somewhere learning what it takes to be a sensible human being." Skipped laughed at the image he'd just painted for everyone.

"And what did *they* learn about Jesus?"

"They learnt whatever the good book taught them, that's what they learnt!" The defensiveness in his voice couldn't mask the hint of uncertainty.

"Well, that's the problem, my friend," Benjamin responded coolly. "While your ancestors taught you to believe whatever you read, mine taught me to think for myself."

"Screw you, Benny!" The sledgehammer that he deposited roughly on the tool pile served as an exclamation mark.

But Benjamin's last statement was a warning to Skip that the argument might take a turn out of his intellectual comfort zone. Instead of continuing, he chose to end it. Skip walked to the front of the Suburban and retrieved his thermos. He poured a cup of steaming coffee and shot an angry look at Benjamin, who had turned back to the woods. Cradling the cup of coffee in both hands, Skip walked to the unfinished cabin porch while two bloodshot eyes followed his every move.

The young man with the ball cap saw the impromptu break. Taking advantage of it, he strolled to the rock where Benjamin was sitting, crawled on top, and sat beside him.

"You're a pretty religious person, aren't you?" he asked in earnest.

"Depends what you mean by 'religious,' Mitch," Benjamin replied. He turned to look at the young man. "Everyone is a spiritual being. And we live in a spiritual place. Most people, however, don't know how to connect with their spiritual side or the spiritual world around them. The people who consider themselves religious are mostly following a system that's been handed down to them. They accept it without even thinking about it."

"What do you mean?" Mitch asked, adjusting his ball cap to sit more evenly over his matted blond hair.

"Well, take the Bible, for instance. Most Christians get their beliefs about Jesus from it. They read the first four books of the New Testament–the gospels–and believe that they accurately describe who He is. They don't understand how the Bible has been altered over the years until it barely resembles the real life story of Jesus. To find Him, you have to look beyond what you read. You have to 'read between the lines' a little and figure out what has been added in and what was taken out."

"So, you're saying the Bible isn't true?" the young man asked with eyebrows raised. By this time, the boy-man with the bandana had joined the small session.

"Like everything else in the world, there's truth *in* it. You just have to separate the truth from the non-truth."

"I'm not a real religious person myself," Mitch continued, "but I was raised believing the stories in the Bible. You're telling me those stories aren't true?"

"Some are. Some aren't. Let me explain it this way: the first account of Jesus wasn't written down for many years after He died. In those years, his life was already becoming a legend. People were telling and retelling his story. And you know what happens when people retell stories?"

Benjamin looked at the two young men who were listening. They just stared blankly back at him.

44

"It's kind of like the old 'Telephone Game,'" he answered his own question. "The first person whispers something in the ear of the person beside him, and that person tells the next, and so on. Then the last person repeats out loud what he's just heard. And usually, it has nothing to do with what was first said!"

As a light of understanding clicked on behind their eyes, the two nodded in agreement.

"The gospels are just like that. They were retold so many times, that by the time they were written down they barely contained the story of Jesus. Sure, there's *some* truth to them, but you have to do a little digging to find it."

"You know," Mitch said, while scratching his head, "that really makes some sense to me. I never thought of it that way."

Benjamin flashed a grin. "That's what I meant when I said that no one ever thinks for themselves. They just repeat what they've been taught. And what they've been taught isn't as accurate as they think it is."

Skip had been listening from a distance, and he now walked closer to the rock where the lecture was taking place.

"Well, what about the *thing* in the woods?" the man with the bandana interrupted.

"Chiye-tanka is our older brother," Benjamin glanced at the woods and then back to his small congregation on the rock. "He's not fully human, but he's not fully a spirit, either. He doesn't mean any harm to anyone. In fact, the only time that he appears is when he has a message for us. My people have known him for centuries. Just like we have learned to live in harmony with this world, we've also learned to live in harmony with him. We've learned to listen."

"Is he out there right now?" one of the young men said eyeing the forest that circled them.

Benjamin turned to look again at the treeline. "Yes, he's out there."

"Gives me the creeps!" Mitch exclaimed.

"I don't like working out here, either!" the other man added.

"I don't think any of you like working at all!" Skip interrupted. He slung the last few drops from his coffee cup with a strong arm. "Come on, you bums, let's get some work done before the boogie man goes on the warpath!"

"Shut up, Skip," one of the young men said as he got up from the rock. Benjamin and the other man rose up as well and made their way to the Suburban.

"Screw you," Skip said, watching them walk past. He then opened a can of snuff and put in a pinch of the bitter tobacco behind his lip. As he brushed his fingers against his pants and put the cap back on, he looked into the woods and growled, "and screw *you*."

Chapter Five

Ellie navigated her Jeep through the plaid-laid avenues of Lycona. She was familiar with the town. She had lived here most of her life. However, she could not escape feeling like a foreigner on its streets.

There was a time when she had felt like she fit in. That was long ago. Too much had happened since then; too many things had changed for her. Lycona was still the same; Ellie was not.

She glanced at her sister riding beside her. Caroline had their mother's light blond hair, hazel eyes, and thin lips. She also had their mother's tenacious, free spirit. In spite of all that she had been through, Caroline remained strong. She bounced back with each new obstacle thrown in her path. Caroline had an infectious smile and could always make people laugh. Ellie often felt envious. There had been a time when she'd been like that. She had laughed more often. But there had been too many losses. Too many disappointments. Life had become hard, and Ellie had trained herself to be more serious. Yet, she prayed that someday things might change for her.

Ellie pulled into the church parking lot about half an hour before their scheduled meeting with Attorney Williams. She and Caroline spent the time reminiscing about Aunt Dell. True to her nature, Caroline soon had Ellie laughing. She couldn't remember the last time she had laughed out loud. It felt good.

When they finally entered the church, they were greeted—well, they were *received* by the church secretary. She was a short, crusty woman who spoke with a smoker's hack. Her outdated eyeglasses and outdated hair style matched her detached hospitality. She seemed to eye them both suspiciously as she waved them to a couple of folding chairs against the wall. The office guardian then rapped a gnarled knuckle against an adjoining door and announced that Ardelle's nieces were waiting. Responding to a reply from inside, she pushed the door open. With a jerk of her head, she motioned for them to enter. It seemed to Ellie as though she was an impatient traffic guard at a busy intersection.

As Ellie stepped inside Sandy's office, he was already moving around his desk to greet them. Besides Caroline's, his was the second smile anyone had directed toward her all week. It also happened that his had been the first. Strangely, she found that his smile made her feel safe. She hadn't felt that in a long time.

Ellie sat down and watched Sandy move back to his desk. He was about her age; maybe a few years older. He wasn't "drop-dead gorgeous" as her old girlfriends would say, but he wasn't bad looking either. He was dressed neatly in khakis and a blue, button-down shirt. He was tall and looked as though he had once been athletic. His light blond hair seemed to be on good terms with a comb. He didn't appear to be the typical minister; but she hadn't met enough ministers to know what one was supposed to look like.

Ellie considered herself a good judge of character. She had encountered more than her share of unsavory people, and after some notable failures, had learned to quickly assess a person. Since meeting Sandy at the funeral home; she'd liked him. He had an unassuming air. He had been kind, and soft-spoken. But most importantly, he'd seemed to be genuine. A rare trait.

////

Clay Decker had been praying. Hard. He couldn't recall the last time he'd felt this kind of burden, this kind of darkness. He prayed for over an hour. He prayed for his church, his pastor, and his family. He prayed for his community and he prayed for himself. Eventually, the unseen hands that had fitted the burden to his shoulders lifted it. He felt good again.

The kitchen table had been Clay's prayer closet. He would have preferred to be on his knees. But for the past ten years, that had not been an option. After losing his right leg in a logging accident, it was too difficult to get up and down by himself.

Clay cleared the table of lunch dishes. His wife, Anne, had already been home for lunch and then returned to her job at the bank. The burden to pray had fallen on Clay just after she had left.

After cleaning the kitchen, Clay hobbled to the small barn behind his house. He hated the prosthetic leg, reserving it for trips to town or church. A set of crutches, or sometimes just one, served his purpose most of the time. He leaned his crutch against the barn and slid the faded-red, wooden door open. Anne had taken his truck to work, leaving her Chrysler for Clay to repair. His disability slowed him down, but it never stopped him.

The unblinking stare of the Chrysler's muted headlamps greeted him as he stepped inside of the barn. Clay eased himself onto the mechanic's creeper and slid beneath the car that was held by a hydraulic jack. For about an hour, he worked on attaching the new front exhaust pipe to the engine manifold. At times, the same burden that he had felt in the kitchen surged over him again. When it happened, he paused and prayed. As the sensation passed, he continued working.

With both hands reaching up into the twisting confines of the engine compartment, Clay suddenly thought that he had heard a noise. He paused and listened. Silence. But he felt a presence. It was as if someone or something had entered the barn. At the same time, Clay felt a different presence. A spiritual one. It wasn't another call to pray. Just an unmistakable, benevolent presence.

Before he could process these thoughts, however, things began to happen rapidly. He felt movement. The Chrysler suddenly and without warning began to sink! Clay attempted to free his arms and slide out from beneath the car. But the movement was too fast, and Clay's unbalanced body was far too slow. The great weight of the car quickly pinned him. It happened so rapidly that the cry for help became lodged in his throat.

Clay felt incredible pressure on his stomach and lower chest. It took his breath away, and the weight made it impossible to suck the air back in. He felt a fleeting moment of panic. Then he felt sorrow. For Anne. He was sorry that she would find him like this. He felt sorrow that she would have to face life alone and that he did not have the opportunity to say goodbye.

The sorrow was then quickly replaced by another emotion—peace. It was an overwhelming peace. Glorious, light-filled peace swept over his body and soul. Clay was no longer disabled. He was now more whole than he had ever been.

////

Sandy hardly recognized Ellie. On the day of the funeral, she had been a wreck. Now, her long red hair was neatly pulled back into a ponytail. Her once-swollen eyes were clear and kindly complemented by lightly-applied mascara. Ellie was a tall, slender woman with easy, natural beauty. Sandy was surprised that he hadn't noticed that during their first meeting. He offered them a seat. He and Caroline chatted lightly. Sandy had always found it easy to fall into a conversation with her. Ellie, however, remained silent. Sandy glanced at her a few times as he and Caroline talked. He found Ellie's looks to be a distraction. It was difficult not to stare.

Their visit was brief before they left for John Williams' office. It was a short walk. There they met with the attorney, who presented Ellie and Caroline with Ardelle's will. She and her late husband had had no children. Ellie and Caroline stood as the sole-recipients of their estate. By the shocked looks on their faces, it was apparent that this was something they had not anticipated.

"What are your plans now, Ellie?" Sandy asked as they left the attorney's office. Caroline had wandered a few paces in front of them and had grown quiet.

"My plans?" She asked.

"About your future. What are you going to do?"

"I don't know," she replied. "I haven't given it a lot of thought. Though most of my life has been spent in Lycona, Caroline is my only tie to this town."

Sandy felt a tug of disappointment. He didn't know Ellie well, but something inside of him hoped that she would stay for a while.

They continued walking in silence. Ellie kept her head lowered, appearing to be in thought. Sandy listened to the soft clicking of her heels against the sidewalk.

"Then again," Ellie continued. "I guess I own a home now. So, for now I have no need to go anywhere else."

Sandy felt pleased with her decision. He glanced at his watch. "Say, would you two like to get something to eat? It's my treat!"

They settled into a booth at the Timber Creek Cafe. As Ellie studied the menu, Sandy had an opportunity to steal glances. She was even prettier than he first had noticed in his office. But he was a pastor, a spiritual guide and mentor, not someone who should be bent on his own interests. Isn't that what had gotten his father in trouble? He fought to keep his focus. Yet, he realized how much he was enjoying his time with her.

The clang of dishes and silverware provided the right kind of white noise for conversation. Caroline had become chatty again. As Sandy talked with her, Ellie remained quiet. She seemed to enjoy listening to her sister.

"Tell me, Caroline, what is one of your favorite memories of your Aunt Dell?" Sandy urged.

"Oh, there are so many!" she replied with a smile, her hazel eyes drifting upward in thought.

Suddenly, Caroline laughed. "She loved western movies! Sometimes we would have movie marathons on the weekends. We would watch one after the other, staying up half the night. They were so corny, but she just loved them!"

"I didn't know Aunt Dell liked westerns," Ellie said.

Sandy saw a twinge of sadness in Ellie's eyes.

"They were her favorite," Caroline exclaimed. "I didn't care much for them at first. But after a few thousand, I kind of got hooked!"

Caroline laughed again and leaned back in the booth. Ellie looked at her sister and smiled, though Sandy thought she seemed somewhat troubled.

Their conversation was interrupted as the busy waitress stopped by their table. Ellie and Caroline ordered pasta; Sandy requested a sandwich. As the waitress walked away, Ellie suddenly eyed Sandy with a look of determination. Sandy felt the direction of the conversation was about to change.

"Why would God allow Aunt Dell to be killed like that?" She asked as silence struck the table.

Her question startled Sandy. It jolted him from the pleasure of an enjoyable dinner conversation. "I really don't know," he stammered. The mental gears inside of his head ground together from the sudden change in direction.

The same fire that Sandy had seen in Ellie's eyes during their first meeting was present again. But it wasn't a fire of frustration or anger. Instead, it seemed to be burning with a desire to know; to really know.

"Aunt Dell was a godly woman, a real saint. I mean, I knew she would die someday, but not like that! Not out in the woods, where it was dark and she was alone. Why would God allow that to happen?"

Sandy placed his hands flat on the table. Caroline was looking intently at him. He was a pastor again.

"I'm afraid that I can't answer that question for you, Ellie," he said. "God often doesn't tell us why he does things." His stomach did a twisting flop. He thought of his father. He recalled grieving over the very same question: *why would God allow this to happen?*

"It just doesn't make sense to me," Ellie continued. Her eyes glistened with the earliest hint of tears. "Aunt Dell was a good person. She was also a very good driver! I just don't understand how the accident could even have happened!"

"The Sheriff said she fell asleep at the wheel," Sandy offered. "That kind of stuff happens even to very good drivers."

"I know, I know," Ellie replied with a relenting sigh. "But Aunt Dell was a night owl who drank coffee like water. It just doesn't make sense to me."

Ellie blew out a breath and sank back into the padded booth. She looked at Sandy for a moment, as if searching for something from him. Caroline gave Ellie a caring look, but she didn't say anything.

"Thank you," Ellie said. The corners of her mouth turned up into a slight smile. "Thank you for listening and not preaching to me. You don't know how I appreciate that."

Sandy nodded silently. He felt that he hadn't really contributed, but was glad she felt that he had.

A moment of awkward silence was broken by the waitress bringing two small salads.

"May I offer a word of prayer?" Sandy asked.

Ellie nodded as she and Caroline bowed their heads. Sandy prayed over their food and was pleased to hear Ellie say 'Amen' when he was finished.

The rest of the meal was shared over quiet conversation. In response to his questions, Ellie shared more about her childhood years and her relationship with Ardelle. Much to Sandy's surprise, she then began asking questions about his interests and background. As a pastor, he was used to getting people to open up to him. Most seemed to expect it. After all, they were the sheep, and he was the shepherd. He was there to care for them. It was never the other way around. To have someone turn the tables and take an interest in him was unusual. And for that person to be an attractive woman was an intriguing thought.

After the meal, they made their way back outside and continued walking toward the church. Sandy felt himself slowing the pace. He knew that when they reached the church their evening together would be over. He was enjoying it too much for that to happen.

"Have you given any more thought to coming to camp?" Sandy asked as they walked along together.

Ellie was walking beside Sandy with one hand holding a manila envelope. The other hand was tucked casually in her front jeans pocket. Maybe it was his imagination, but Sandy felt that she had slowed her pace, too.

"I don't know yet, Pastor," she replied. "It's not something that I've ever done before, and I don't know how much I could really help."

Sandy was glad to note that Ellie had not refused the invitation.

"What do you think your aunt would want you to do?"

"I *know* what she would want," Ellie replied with a hint of a smile.

"So, what do you think?" Sandy asked hopefully.

"I just don't know yet."

Just then, Sandy's cell phone vibrated in his pocket. He glanced at the caller ID and excused himself from their conversation. He would always take a call from Clay Decker.

Chapter Six

Ever since his visit to Deal's farm, Cliff's mind had been a whirlwind of thoughts and emotions. He couldn't shake the feeling that what he'd seen at Muddy Creek had something to do with what had visited Hank Deal. *Yet, what was it?*

He was nearing the end of his shift and returning to City Hall. He was surprised to see the Sheriff's SUV still parked outside. Bragg should have been gone hours ago.

With the offices closed, Cliff entered through the side alley door. Except for the janitor working his sloshing mop in the hallway, the place was quiet.

"What's going on, Sheriff?" Cliff asked as he walked into the Sheriff's office. Seeing Bragg at this hour meant only one thing: something must have happened.

Bragg was at his desk with pen in hand. "Clay Decker died this afternoon," Bragg said without looking up.

"What?" Clay's dead?" Cliff asked in disbelief. "What happened?"

"He was working under Anne's car when the jack gave out. The car crushed him. He never had a chance," Bragg replied coldly.

Cliff was stunned. He and Clay weren't close, but he was a friendly man. Everyone who knew Clay liked him. Cliff knew it would be a hard loss for a lot of people. Clay was the Zoning Board Chairperson; this group met across the hallway from the Sheriff's office.

The sight of Clay swinging happily down the hallway on his crutches was still an easy memory to reach.

"Wow," Cliff said, still processing the news. "I just talked with him before I went on vacation. It was the night of the Zoning Board meeting. He was a good guy."

"Good or bad, he knew better than to be working on a car without blocks in place." There was no emotion in Bragg's voice.

Bragg had a calloused nature. This served him well as Sheriff. However, at times Cliff found him incredibly insensitive.

"Got something that I'd like to run by you, Sheriff," Cliff said, changing the subject. He and Bragg were alone, and he felt like this was a good time to talk about what was on his mind.

"What's that?" Bragg asked without looking up, still buried in his work.

Cliff picked up a packet of mail that was in his pigeon hole and moved closer to Bragg's desk. "Remember on Monday when I went out to see Hank Deal? Well, he said that he saw a really huge…," he hadn't yet thought of the word he was going to use. "…person or animal prowling around his spring house. When he confronted it, it ran away."

"Did he get a good look at him?" Bragg asked. There wasn't even a hint of interest in his voice.

"Yeah, he did." Cliff paused and wondered how to continue the conversation. "And he believed it to be about nine feet tall and close to four hundred pounds."

"What?" Bragg growled. There was obvious irritation in his voice.

Bragg paused from his work and set his pen down. He then began to massage his temples in an effort to segue from one dilemma to another. The tremor in his hands was as bad as ever. "He's probably back on the bottle!" Bragg suggested sharply.

Bragg let his hands drop from his forehead and then leaned back in his swivel chair. His barreled chest swelled as he took in a full breath. Bragg was still an intimidating figure, despite how weathered he looked. Retrieving his pen, he began to tap out a rhythm on a stack of papers.

"No, I don't think he's drinking again. But that's what he reported seeing," Cliff said. "He showed me what looked like a single track in the ground. It was pretty huge, larger than any print I've ever seen. But it wasn't clear enough to really identify it."

"A shoe print?"

"No," Cliff replied, "it looked more like a foot print."

"Probably was a bear, Cliff," Bragg said. He accentuated Cliff's name slightly, as if to say that this was something Cliff should have already deduced.

"Could have been. But he said it walked off on two legs in a way that bears don't typically walk," Cliff returned.

"You're thinking it was a man?" Bragg asked with surprise.

"I'm not sure what to think. It just doesn't make sense to me," Cliff replied.

"Well, what other choices do you have? It's either a man or a bear, right?" Bragg was beginning to glare. His voice had a sharp edge. In the best of situations, he had a short fuse. But with a long day and the death investigation of a local official, there was no fuse. Cliff had made a mistake. This was not a good time to start talking about the similarities between what had happened to him in the woods and what had happened to Hank Deal. The infertile soil of Bragg's mood simply was not going to grow anything productive.

"Yeah, it's gotta be one or the other," Cliff compromised to end the conversation.

"Okay. If the thing shows up again we'll notify the Game Warden. If it's a rogue bear he'll need to look into it," Bragg replied as Cliff turned and walked to his own desk. He knew the best thing to do was let Bragg have the last word.

Cliff filed two affidavits on subpoenas that he had served earlier in the morning and then completed an accident report from a rear-end collision to which he'd responded. By the time the paperwork was completed, Bragg had left for the day, and it was already dark outside. Alone in the office, Cliff pulled out the county topographical map from behind an old filing cabinet. With the advancements of technology, the map didn't get used much. Cliff blew a film of dust off of it and laid it out on a table. He traced the twisting roadways until he found Hank's farm. He then located the Muddy Creek section of Pine Forest where he and Carly had been camping over the weekend. They were about twenty nautical miles apart, over some of the most rugged territory of Lycona National Forest.

As an investigator, he knew that he had to remain unbiased. But Cliff could not shake the feeling that whatever he'd glimpsed might be the same thing that Hank Deal had seen just over a week later. But even if they'd both sighted the same or similar things, Cliff still had no idea what it was.

Cliff's concentration was interrupted by the radio, which coughed to life just moments before the town's fire whistle sounded. "Explosion and fire with injuries at 1345 Willow Road." It was Carly's voice.

Although the Sheriff's office was not being summoned yet, Cliff sprang from his chair and moved quickly toward the door. He knew exactly how to get there–1345 Willow Road was Hank Deal's place.

////

It wasn't Clay Decker who called Sandy. It was his wife. Anne was frantic. Clay had been found dead; crushed beneath the weight of her car. With frantic urgency, she asked if Sandy could come immediately to their house.

In minutes, Sandy was hurrying through Lycona. Clay and Anne had a small farm on the outskirts of town. Clay was an elder at Lycona Community and sat on the Church Council. He was also one of Sandy's closest friends. It was Clay who had made the invitation for Sandy to visit Lycona. It was Clay who had happily announced to Sandy that he was unanimously voted in as their pastor. It was also Clay who always supported Sandy so strongly. But it wasn't just those memorable moments that made Clay stand out in Sandy's mind. Clay was a mentor to Sandy. He was a true man of God.

Some who attended Lycona Community were familiar with the Bible and basic Christian concepts. But Clay's faith wasn't like theirs. He didn't just know *about* God, he *knew* God. When Clay prayed, he really seemed to talk with God. Few people had impacted Sandy like Clay Decker.

Sandy pulled into the Decker's driveway well after dark. The ambulance and coroner were already gone. The cars of family members and close friends had filled the short driveway and spilled into the yard. As he approached the door, he could hear crying from inside. This was not going to be an easy visit.

Chapter Seven

As Cliff raced beneath the dark skies of Lycona, Carly was busy at work. Another call was lighting up her switchboard. Lycona was generally a quiet area during the day, but night sometimes changed things.

Carly answered the call, fully expecting it to be another report of the fire at Deal's farm.

"911, what's your emergency?" she calmly answered.

There was a frantic woman's scream followed by some unintelligible words. Sometimes prank 911 calls were made, but Carly instantly had a sense that this one was real.

"Calm down, ma'am," Carly responded. "What's your emergency?"

There was another scream, then some more sounds Carly could not discern. Finally, the voice broke through more clearly: "There's a freakin' monster on my porch!"

"A what? Did you say monster?" Carly responded as her fingers quickly worked the keyboard.

"Yeah! I went into my living room to open the curtains, and there stood this *huge* black monster with red eyes! He just stood there staring at me!"

A cold chill ran up Carly's back. She had never heard a call like this.

"Where is he now?" Carly asked, typing in the caller's address from the caller ID. Her voice did not betray the feeling of fear she felt.

"I don't know. I ran into the kitchen to call you. God, help me! Please get someone here fast!" The woman was hysterical.

"Is there anyone in your house with you?" Carly asked.

"No, I'm alone. Oh, God! Oh, God! Please! You've got to get someone here! I don't know what to do!"

The level of fear in the woman's voice was alarming. It was unlike any other call she had ever received. The absolute terror she heard was unsettling.

"Someone is on the way right now, Ma'am. You need to stay calm," Carly said as the Sheriff's office was alerted. "What is your name, honey?"

"Rita Brackenridge. I'm at 300 Cemetery Lane." The address matched the caller ID.

"Okay, Rita. Is there a safe place in your house where you can go?"

"I don't know. I'm so scared. Let me look to see if it is still on my porch."

"No! Just stay where you are, Ma'am!" Carly warned. "You need to be in safe place."

"Oh, my God! Oh, my God! He's still standing at the window looking right at me! *He sees me!* Oh, my G…"

Carly heard a loud bang and then the line went dead.

////

For the second time in a week, Cliff was making his way toward Hank Deal's place. His emergency lights were turned on, but his siren remained silent.

A fire and an explosion? Fires were known to occur at farms. But an *explosion?* That seemed unusual.

These thoughts were processed quickly as he pushed his cruiser through town. Then the sound of the radio split the air: "Dispatch to LS Eighteen."

The voice was that of Carly's co-worker, Lydia Wagner. Carly and Lydia were best friends, often working the second shift together. Lydia periodically dated a local man, whose name Cliff could never recall, and they had sometimes gone out as a group. Cliff liked Lydia, though she sometimes talked too much.

"LS Eighteen: go ahead, Dispatch," Cliff responded.

"We have a possible burglary in progress at 300 Cemetery Lane. 911 call made by occupant, Rita Brackenridge, but call was apparently terminated. Can you respond?"

Cemetery Lane was a rural road located outside of town in an old village known as Stanton. Cliff was already moving rapidly in that general direction. He wouldn't have to deviate far from his current course.

"10-4, Dispatch. I am en route."

"LS Eighteen: Be advised," the radio sounded again, "that female caller reported seeing subject on her porch, but ceased talking. Unknown if subject has entered home. Female caller claimed to be alone in her house. It is unknown if female caller is armed or if there are weapons in the house. The subject was not identified as either male or female. We are trying to reconnect with the caller."

"10-4, Dispatch," Cliff called back.

The fire at Hank's farm was being handled by the volunteer fire department. Although Cliff was interested in knowing what was going on there, this call took priority.

The few cars that he encountered in town quickly pulled off of the road, allowing him easy travel. He followed Rough Pike Road until he crossed Highway 23 near Stanton. As he entered Stanton, he called into the radio again.

"LS Eighteen to Dispatch. Can you give me a cross street for Cemetery Lane?"

"10-4," Lydia said, pausing. "Cross street is Chestnut Avenue."

Cliff slowed down and turned his emergency lights off. If a burglar was present, he wanted to catch him, not scare him off. It was when he passed the church that he saw Chestnut Ave on his left. Turning left, he followed to the first turn on the left: Cemetery Lane.

Cemetery Lane was a narrow road leading past the cemetery and through some open fields. Creeping slowly, Cliff hit his outside spotlight, sweeping the fields. He was not familiar with the Brackenridge home, but recalled that only a few houses were built off of the old road.

"Cliff," The radio blurted again. This time it was Carly, who rarely broke radio protocol. "I'm the one who took this call. It was pretty strange. The woman claimed that she saw a monster on her front porch. I cannot reconnect."

"What do you mean a *monster?*" he demanded into the microphone. A familiar twinge of fear gripped him.

"That's all that she said. She reported that a large monster with red eyes was on her front porch, looking in the window at her. She was really flipping out."

"10-4," Cliff replied, his headlights sweeping the mailbox of house number 300. "LS Eighteen on location."

"10-4. Be careful, Cliff," Carly said.

The house was well lit as Cliff pulled into the driveway. If someone was moving inside, this could work to his advantage. A rusting Pontiac Grand Prix was parked in the driveway. He quickly called in its license plate number. He then scanned the property with his spot light. Detecting nothing out of the ordinary he slowly eased open the door of his patrol car. He kept it as a shield between the house and himself. The palm of his right hand rested on the handle of his service weapon, still in its holster.

As soon as Cliff stepped into the cool night air, he was struck by an awful smell. A stench that was familiar to him. It was the same odor of rotting flesh that he had smelled at Muddy Creek. The twinge of fear doubled in intensity.

The headlights of his patrol car had lit up the front of the house. There was no movement from within or without. The house was a small, modular frame home with an attached garage. It was in poor repair, reflecting the general makeup of the small village. The rear of the house bordered a forested area. Everything else was open fields.

Cliff closed the car door and started to step toward the house; suddenly, the front door flew open. Instinctively, his hand gripped the handle of his weapon, although it remained unsheathed.

A heavy-set woman appeared at the door. Her hair hung over most of her face, and she was swaying. She slumped against the door frame as if she was going to fall, but managed to remain standing. Her left hand held the side of her face. Cliff could see her mouth moving, but he heard no sound.

"Ma'am, I'm Deputy Janowski of the Sheriff's Department," Cliff called out firmly. "We've received a call about a possible intruder at this location. Can you identify yourself, and are you okay?"

The woman tried to take a step, but fell backward against the door frame. She slumped down to a sitting position with her head falling forward. Her chin dropped to her chest. Cliff then saw a trail of blood leading down her blouse.

In one fluid movement, Cliff's right arm reacted. The smooth shaft of his semi-automatic broke free from its leathery home. He assumed a defensive posture with his left foot slightly in front of the other, the gun in his right hand pointing toward the ground. His head, as if on a swivel, scanned the area.

"LS Eighteen," Cliff called into his shoulder radio. "Send back-up, and get me an ambulance. I have a female victim down and bleeding."

"Ma'am," Cliff called out again. He kept a firm, non-threatening voice. "Are you okay? Is there anyone else here?"

No answer. Cliff cautiously began moving closer to the woman. His gun still pointed to the ground, he continued looking in all directions. The woman remained motionless in the doorway. As he stepped onto the porch, she stirred and raised her head. Her eyes were unsteady; seemingly unable to focus.

"Ma'am," Cliff said again, "are you okay?"

"No. My baby," she responded faintly.

"Where is your baby?"

"I think I'm having my baby," she said. Her chin dropped down again. Cliff now recognized her maternity blouse.

"Ma'am," Cliff asked, standing above her with his gun still aimed at the ground. "Is there anyone else in the house?"

"No," she said, shaking her head slightly.

"Where are you hurt?" he asked.

"I don't know," she replied groggily.

"Are you the one who called 911?" he asked.

She was quiet for several moments before answering, "I don't know."

"Can you tell me what happened?" Cliff asked, still trying to assess the situation.

"I fell down," the woman replied after spending some time in thought.

With one eye on the scene around him, Cliff crouched down. He saw that the blood had been streaming from the left side of her face. With one hand he pushed her hair back and saw a gash over her left temple. The wound was deep, but wasn't bleeding anymore.

"Do you live here?" he asked.

"Yeah," she said. She gripped her abdomen and let out a groan. Cliff waited for the pain to subside before continuing his interview.

"And you say that no one else is here?" he asked again, still trying to assess the scene.

"No, Ronnie's at work right now," she responded.

Cliff wanted to enter the house, but didn't want to leave the woman unattended on the porch. He still didn't know if there was an immediate threat present.

As he was scanning the perimeter of the house, he glanced down and saw a dog dish and water bowl near his feet. The dish was upside down, and the dog food was scattered across the porch. He knew that the female had not spilled the dish when she exited, and he had not disturbed it either. He looked around the front of the yard, but did not see a dog. He knew that dogs sometimes posed threats to lawmen.

"Ma'am, do you have a dog?" he asked.

She did not answer, but affirmed by nodding her head.

"Where is the dog now?" he asked.

She didn't immediately respond. Then she slowly looked toward the corner of the porch. Cliff followed her eyes to the corner post of the porch rail. There Cliff saw freshly splintered wood where it appeared two small screws had been ripped out. The woman, seemingly unable to hold her head up any longer, let it drop. She shrugged her shoulders in answer to Cliff's question.

Cliff saw the lights of a patrol car approaching along Cemetery Road, and then pulling into the driveway. Deputy Logan burst out of his

70

cruiser in the same way that his arms and chest were bursting from his tight uniform. As soon as Cliff had heard about the burglary, he'd known Logan would be enthusiastically on his way. Eagerness was written all over his face.

"What do we have?" Logan asked. When he saw Cliff's weapon in his hand, he quickly drew his own sidearm, keeping it low and pointing to the ground.

"Not sure yet," Cliff replied. "911 call indicated a burglary in progress. She's got a pretty nasty cut on her forehead and may be in labor. She claims that she's the only one at home. She doesn't know if she called 911 or not."

"What's that smell?" Logan asked, contorting his face.

"I need you to stand watch over her while I do a walk-through of the house." Cliff ignored his question.

"Go ahead," Logan replied, adrenaline pulsing, "I'll stay here." Cliff nodded and stepped through the open door into the living room. Nothing seemed out of order except for a small trail of blood between the front door and the next room. He followed the blood trail and stepped into the kitchen. There a pool of blood staining the floor. Near it was a cordless telephone, broken into several pieces. A writing desk was just inside the kitchen, where the phone's base was plugged in. A small spot of blood and a bit of flesh clung to the corner of the desk.

Taking in the scene, Cliff surmised that the woman's head had struck the desk. She had then fallen to the floor. From there, she must have stood up and walked out the front door.

Cliff made a sweep of the house and garage. There were no signs of forced entry from any of the windows or doors. Nothing appeared to be out of ordinary, except for the broken phone and blood stains. The last-minute interjection from Carly weighed heavily on his mind. She had suggested that a monster had been seen. Normally, he would not have given that report much credence. Coupled with Hank's recent sighting and his own history, however, Cliff was on high alert.

After concluding his search, he returned to the front porch with his weapon holstered. By that time the paramedics had arrived and were treating the woman's head injury. Her labor pains were coming at irregular intervals, and they were preparing her for transport to the hospital. He wasn't able to continue his interview with her.

After the ambulance had departed, Cliff and Logan walked the perimeter of the property. The smell in the air had abated. As they walked together, Cliff kept sweeping the ground with his flashlight, looking for tracks or any kind of evidence that might give him a clue as to what was going on. Logan saw the intent look on Cliff's face–his dogged scrutiny of the ground. He kept quiet and walked beside Cliff.

They had almost made a complete circle of the house when out of the woods trotted a black Doberman. Its head was hanging down, and it dragged a long chain. They watched it walk to the front porch. It sniffed around and then begin to lap water from the water bowl. It then curled up into the corner of the porch and looked up through sad eyes.

As Cliff cautiously approached the dog, it dropped its head and began to whimper. He picked up the end of the chain and found a grasping hook. It was still attached to a small, metal brace. Cliff crouched down and held the brace up to the porch post where the splintered wood was found. The two screws that held the brace were missing, but the brace perfectly matched the outline in the wood.

"Looks like he must have scared off our perp and maybe even taken off after him," Deputy Logan replied with a grin.

"Maybe," Cliff replied, "but this dog's cowering."

"Aw, he probably just knows he's in trouble for running off," Logan replied.

Cliff stood up and turned to Logan, "I'm going to head to the hospital to interview the victim. Can you secure the scene for me?"

Cliff drove back to town, heading straight to the Lycona Community Hospital. His shift was over, but he wasn't finished yet. At the Emergency Room, the doctor advised that his victim was being sedated in an effort to end the premature labor. The doctor asked Cliff to give her the night to recover. After one final stop at the Sheriff's office, he finally made his way home.

Chapter Eight

Eddie Law paused impatiently as the automatic doors slowly reacted to his presence. Hardly giving them time to part, he squeezed past and stepped into the Lycona Community Hospital. It was just after eight in the morning, and visitors were few at this hour. He knew no one would notice him.

He strolled confidently past the receptionist's desk. The silver-haired woman manning the switchboard barely glanced at him as he passed. He followed the hall past the elevators, turned left, and then made an immediate right. The chaplain's office door was plainly marked. He paused outside and listened. Not hearing any sounds from within, he turned the knob and found it unlocked, as he always did.

Eddie knew the hospital chaplain didn't arrive until eight-thirty. He still exercised caution as he opened the door slowly and stuck his head inside first. The office was empty. Stepping inside, he bent over the well-organized desk to search for what he knew would be there. He picked up the hospital census and quickly eyed the bottom of the page. The printer's time stamp indicated that it had been printed less than an hour ago. His finger skimmed down the list of alphabetically-indexed names. It slowed as it reached the B's, and then stopped as it came to Brackenridge, Rita. Room 313, bed A.

He gently opened the door and slipped back into the hallway. The nighttime cleaning crew had scrubbed the floors, leaving a heavily-sanitized smell. His Payless bargains clicked loudly as he made his way to the elevators.

Eddie started humming a tune that he had just made up. Rhythmically, he began spinning his car keys over his right index finger. He reached the twin elevator doors just as one dinged. The doors slid open and two aids stepped out. He smiled and nodded, but they were in a deep discussion over an unreasonable supervisor. They paid no attention to him. He was not surprised. No one ever paid attention to Eddie.

Eddie Law was not a remarkable man. He rarely caught anyone's eye. He was not handsome, yet he was not unsightly. He was neither tall nor short, heavy nor thin. His ears didn't stick out and his nose was not too big. His dull brown eyes didn't sparkle or inspire, and his dark hair never caught the sun. Brightly-colored, expensive clothing was something that he avoided. Instead, he selected dull apparel that was somewhere between fashionable and thrift-store-special. One could spend an hour talking with Eddie at the store or on the street corner, and a few minutes later be at a total loss to describe him. He was intensely mediocre.

Boarding the elevator, he pushed the third floor button and watched the first floor disappear behind the closing doors. As usual, he was in a good mood. He skimmed the elevator bulletin board as he felt the elevator lurch to a stop on the second floor. The doors opened, and a young, foreign intern with a stethoscope draped over his neck stepped on. Eddie glanced his way and nodded. The young man, however, only momentarily returned the look. The contents of his clipboard diverted his attention. He didn't smile in return. Even before the elevator stopped at the next floor, he had forgotten his short ride with Eddie Law.

Eddie was not offended. He knew that he was unremarkable; he even preferred to remain that way. He could have inquired about Ms. Brackenridge's room at the front desk. Instead, he chose to discover the same information in a way that would involve no one else. Doing things that way made his work easier.

Eddie was a reporter for the *Lycona Dispatch*. He enjoyed his work, and he was good at it. He probably possessed the talent to become a famous investigative reporter, but he lacked the charisma. What he did have, however, was a knack for being at the right place at the right time. He also had a good memory. It was because of that memory that he was going to visit Rita Brackenridge.

In a sense, this hospital trip had begun about five years ago. It had been a summer evening in August; he'd been leaving town for a weekend to visit his mother in Ridge Line. He'd been ascending one of the final hills surrounding Lycona when the timing belt in his old Pontiac had snapped. Not finding a cell phone signal, he'd hiked down the mountain in the driving rain. He eventually had come upon a local watering hole where loggers liked to gather. The moment he'd stepped in, he had sensed that it might be a difficult stay. In a room full of hard-cut men wearing plaid and denim, Eddie had felt, for the first time, as though he stood out.

Eddie had called for a tow truck and had then sat down to wait. Suspicious glances had been cast his way, and two men in particular had seemed overly agitated with his presence. To alleviate the tension, Eddie had bought a round of drinks for everyone. The gesture had worked, because no one had seemed suspicious of him anymore. However, it had left him without enough money to finish the trip to Ridge Line. All in all, it had been a fair exchange.

One particular logger, who had already consumed his legal limit, had filled the seat next to Eddie. He'd struck up a conversation, and Eddie had followed along, feeling like a little less of an outsider. He'd bought the man a few more drinks, hoping that the tow truck would soon arrive and save him. As he had gulped his beers, the old logger had started treating Eddie as though they had raised the flag together on some forgotten battle field. Eddie had been annoyed, but he'd felt a little more safe.

"I've got a story for ya!" the logger had yelled when he'd learned that Eddie was a reporter.

Eddie had raised his eyebrows in feigned interest. It was a line he had heard many times. Yet, he had never heard a story that was better than the last.

"You need to write a story about the Lycona Monster," the logger had continued, raising his beer for another swig.

"What's that?" Eddie had asked, glancing toward the door in hope of salvation.

"About a year ago, I was hunting at my cabin near Peak View. I was in my deer stand near the west edge when I heard all this noise in the underbrush. Two doe and a buck came running out of the thicket right beneath me. They were making tracks. I couldn't even get my gun to my shoulder before they was gone. Then it wasn't thirty seconds later that I heard this tremendous crashing comin' down through the woods. I couldn't imagine what kind of animal was making that kind of racket."

The logger had looked at Eddie to make sure he was listening. He really hadn't been, but Eddie had widened his eyes in mock surprise. Satisfied, the logger had continued.

"It kind of spooked me, ya know?" he'd said, displaying a rare moment of humility. "I just knew there was something wrong with this picture."

"What happened?" With nothing else to do, Eddie had grudgingly decided to join the conversation.

"Well, all of a sudden out of the brush steps this god-awful monster. It was huge and covered in hair, not fur, mind you–hair. It walked on two legs like a man, but it was no man! I saw it for a full ten seconds before it walked out of sight."

"What did you do?" Eddie had asked, amused.

"I got the heck out of there, that's what I did! And I haven't gone hunting since!"

Eddie would have dismissed the man's story completely if it wasn't for an incident that took place just seven days later. He had gone back to work and was responding to a vehicle accident. The car had been hanging precariously on a cliff. He'd known it would make a great photo, so he'd hurried to the scene before it was removed.

As suspected, the photo had been a good one. By climbing over the embankment and around some brush, he had been able to get a shot showing the rear end of the car hanging out over the guardrails. It had made the front page.

Eddie had gotten to the scene in time to overhear the driver being interviewed by the Sheriff's Department. The man had reported that he'd been coming down the mountain when a monster had stepped out on the road. He'd swerved to miss it and hit the guardrails. The rear end of his car had spun around and almost tossed him over the side.

Eddie had watched the driver fail the sobriety test and take a back seat in the Sheriff's car. He'd thought it was odd to hear two monster stories in one week. However, since both stories involved alcohol, he had decided they were imaginative stories fueled by dull living and hard drinking.

It had been six months later when Eddie heard another story. It had caused him to reconsider his opinion. This one hadn't involved alcohol, and in fact, originated with one of the community's respected citizens.

Lewis Marshall owned a financing company in Lycona. He was president of the Jaycees and served on the school board. He was not known to drink, and he was about as serious a man as Eddie knew. On the first day of bear season, hunters brought their kills to the newspaper office for photographs in the paper. Eddie didn't care much for photographing dead animals and the proud hunters who held their heads up, but this was life for a small-town newspaper reporter.

At that time, he had snapped a picture of Lewis standing over his 355 pound bruin and congratulated him on his kill. Lewis had thanked him and then coldly remarked, "if monster season was in, I'd really have a trophy."

When Lewis had climbed down from his pick-up truck, Eddie had asked him what he meant.

Lewis had closed the tailgate, turned to Eddie, and had said soberly, "'cause early this morning a huge, hairy monster walked into the clearing below me. I watched him through my scope for about twenty seconds. He was tall, walking on two feet, and covered with reddish black hair. He then seemed to sense me 'cause he looked right at me. I almost pulled the trigger, but his face looked like a man's face. I couldn't. Then he just walked off."

Eddie had tried wheedling Lewis for more information, but he'd had nothing more to add. Eddie's interest in the subject had grown, and over the next few years he had begun to pick up more stories. He'd casually dated Lydia Wagner, who worked at the county 911 office. She'd inadvertently leaked stories from strange calls. He had pieced enough of them together to form the opinion that something strange was indeed walking the mountains around Lycona. He had tried presenting the story to his editor once, but had been laughed out of his office. The *Dispatch* was not interested in stories that came from drunks and anonymous sources. Just in case, Eddie had started a digital file of notes on his laptop in a folder he named S*trange*. He added to them whenever something odd came up.

Last night something odd had certainly come up. Eddie had met Lydia for a late night bite after they'd both finished their respective shifts.

He often enjoyed her company, and always hoped it would lead to something more.

Lydia never intended to talk about the kinds of calls she took at work. Rather, she usually needed to unwind. Last night, unwinding had meant recounting everything that had happened from the time she'd gotten up until the present. In these venting sessions, Eddie often felt that it took longer for her to talk about the events of her day than it did for her to actually live them. Still, the calls she described were sometimes interesting to him, and he frequently picked up tidbits that gave him an edge at work.

Last night she'd shared with him the call that Carly had taken from Ms. Brackenridge. This seemed to be one of the most solid sightings that he had heard. It had piqued his interest enough to get him up in the morning to make an early run to the hospital.

Eddie really liked the tune that he was humming as he got off of the elevator. He hoped that he would remember it later. But he set the score aside as he counted down the hospital doors to Room 313.

The door was open as he cautiously walked in. Ms. Brackenridge was lying in bed with a breakfast tray in front of her. A bandage clung on the left part of her forehead, and her left eye was swollen. She looked up at him as he stopped, making sure to keep a comfortable distance from her bed.

"Ms. Brackenridge?" Eddie asked, catching her name on the dry-erase board above the bed.

"Yes?" she replied.

"I need to ask you some questions about last night; if you are feeling up to it."

Eddie purposely did not introduce himself. He had learned that if people did not know who he was, they would act on assumptions that they had devised about him. Others did not seem to care. In either case, he let the matter alone. If someone asked, he always told. But only if they asked.

Ms. Brackenridge looked at Eddie for a moment. He was wearing a white, short-sleeved shirt, brown dress pants, and a slightly-dated, striped brown tie.

"What do you want to know?" she asked, apparently convinced Eddie was someone she could talk to.

Eddie felt a tickling sensation somewhere deep within his brain. He felt it each time he was on an investigation and a chance that he took was going his way. The adrenaline started to flow.

"Tell me about the 911 call, please," he replied, taking a step closer to the bed.

Ms. Brackenridge dropped her head and winced as if in pain. Eddie assumed it was from her injuries. When the moment was over she looked back up.

"That was the *scariest* thing that ever happened to me," she said.

"I need you to tell me about it," he urged.

She took a deep breath before beginning. "My husband, Ronnie, was working late, and I was fixin' him supper. Sunshine, my dog, started going nuts outside. I never heard him bark like that. I knew something wasn't right. Before I could get over to the door I heard him take off through the yard. Since I had him chained to the porch I knew something wasn't right.

"I walked over to the front window in our living room and pulled the string to open the curtain. When I did, this... this *monster* just stood up in front of the window on my front porch!"

"What do you mean it 'just stood up?' What was it doing?"

"I don't know. I guess it was down on all fours or something, 'cause I didn't see it at first."

Ms. Brackenridge needed to pause to gain her composure. Eddie waited until she seemed a bit more calm, and then he asked, "What did it look like?"

Ms. Brackenridge looked directly at Eddie. "It was huge. It was maybe eight or nine feet tall; it had glowing red eyes." She shuddered, "I swear, it was the devil himself."

"What happened next?"

"I screamed and ran into the kitchen to call 911. I can't really remember much after that. I think that I passed out and hit my head on the kitchen desk. The next thing I remember is being loaded into the back of an ambulance."

"Any other injuries?" Eddie asked.

"No," she replied. "They were able to stop me from going into labor, and they think the baby will be okay. I also got six stitches in my head."

She spoke to Eddie as if he knew about her pregnancy. He did not, but he showed no sign of surprise. Evidently, she believed him to be someone who should know about it.

"Anything else you can tell me?" he asked.

"No, that's all. Do you have any idea what was on my porch?" she asked.

Eddie shook his head. "No, I'm afraid that I don't. But I'm working on it."

Ms. Brackenridge seemed relieved by the thought. Eddie thanked her for her time and wished her a swift recovery. He then slipped out of the room and walked down the hall, trying to remember the tune he had been humming. As the elevator doors closed behind him, the other set of elevator doors to the left opened. Cliff stepped out into the corridor and walked down the hall, looking for Room 313.

////

Cliff walked in and found Rita Brackenridge talking on the telephone. He paused and backed up in order to give her some privacy. She saw Cliff and waived him in, telling the caller that she had to go. As she hung the phone up, Cliff moved closer, politely taking off his deputy's hat.

"Good morning, Ma'am. How are you feeling today?"

"I'm doing okay, I guess. They were able to stop me from going into labor, and they think the baby is going to be alright. But I've got a splitting headache," she said touching her forehead.

"I'm glad to hear about your baby, Ma'am. You had me concerned last night."

"*You* were at my house last night?" she asked with a confused look on her face.

"Yes. I responded first and Deputy Logan came a bit later."

"Well, then who was the man who just talked to me?"

"I don't know, Ma'am. What man?"

"A man stopped in here just a minute ago to ask about last night. I thought he was one of you all. He left just before my husband called."

Cliff thought for a moment. "I don't know who that could have been. What did he ask?"

"He wanted to know about the 911 call, that's all. The way he talked he seemed to know what was going on."

Cliff didn't press the matter any further. He knew Ms. Brackenridge had suffered a head injury and he was not familiar with her mental history.

"I don't know about that," Cliff said, "I do need to ask you a few questions about last night, but only if you are feeling up to it."

Ms. Brackenridge recounted her story for Cliff. When she described the figure that she'd seen on her porch, he felt a chill of fear sweep over him. It was the same feeling that he'd had when he'd seen something at Muddy Creek. The general description of the figure that she was able to provide was strikingly similar to what he had seen. The cop in him struggled to keep an unbiased viewpoint, but his intuition told him they had seen the same thing.

Mrs. Brackenridge believed she had seen the "devil himself." Cliff wasn't ready to make that commitment, but he understood her fear.

"Did you say that that was your husband you were talking with?" Cliff asked, nodding toward the phone.

"Yeah, he came here straight from work last night and then went home early this morning. He'll be here in about an hour."

"Did he find anything missing or out of the ordinary at your house?"

"No. He said that I was bleeding in the kitchen, and he could tell where I walked to the door. But he said there wasn't anything else wrong."

"Alright, that's good. If you later find that something is missing, you need to give me a call." Cliff pulled a business card out of his breast pocket and set it on the table beside the bed.

Cliff rode the elevator back to the first floor and walked to the front receptionist's desk. "Do you have a Hank or Marge Deal listed as a patient?"

The receptionist consulted her computer. "There is a Hank Deal in room 250. He came in last night."

Cliff thanked her and took a step away. He then turned around. "One more thing: do you recall anyone this morning asking what room Rita Brackenridge was in?"

"Just you," She replied, smiling.

Cliff took the stairs to the second floor. Room 250 was at the end of the hallway. As he entered, he found Hank watching the morning news. He had several deep cuts on his face, and a bandage was covering his right ear. He glanced at Cliff as he walked in the room and gave him a friendly nod.

"I heard there was an explosion last night up at your place, Hank," Cliff said.

Hank turned the volume of the television down.

"You okay?" Cliff asked.

"Yeah, I'm a pretty lucky guy. I was welding the base on one of my manure tanks. The smallest tank was empty, but apparently had some methane gas in it. A spark from the welder set it off and blew the top off the tank off like a bomb. Lucky for me, the top of the tank was pretty weak 'cause the explosion went up instead of down and out. I was bending over right beneath her when she went off. It knocked me flat. I don't know how I lived through that."

"For Pete's sake, Hank! You're a lucky man," Cliff said. "Did you get hurt badly?"

"Nah, I caught a couple of pieces of metal, that's all. They kept me overnight 'cause it knocked me out. I should be outta here today."

"I heard the call come in last night and was heading out to see what was going on, but another call came in and I had to respond. I'm glad you're doing okay."

"You stopped in just to see if I was okay?" Hank asked curiously.

"Well, I had to stop in and talk with someone else." Cliff paused, considering what he was going to say next. "And it reminded me that I wanted to tell you something."

"What's that?"

"You know how you told me you saw something strange at your house?" Cliff continued without waiting for reply. "Well, someone else reported seeing something that sounded a lot like what you saw."

"Where?"

"About ten miles from your farm."

"What do you make of it?"

"I don't know, Hank. I just don't know."

Chapter Nine

The distinct smell of new carpeting greeted Sandy as he walked into the foyer of Lycona Community Church. Ten years ago, the congregation at Community had had the foresight to begin raising funds to add to the existing church building. Last year, just before Sandy had come on as pastor, Community finally had launched the building project. A large fellowship hall, a renovated kitchen, and several new classrooms were now added to the existing framework of the church. The sanctuary had also gotten a facelift. There was new carpeting throughout and comfortably padded pews. Consequently, there were big bills to pay. Some said it was Sandy's job to make sure the church and its offering plates were full every Sunday. This was a burden that he was reluctant to carry. However, it seemed to come with the job.

It was Sunday. A lot of people who liked to joke with Sandy told him it was "the only day that he had to work." Pastoring had never felt like work. Until recently.

Yesterday, he had buried Clay. The funeral had been just as difficult as Ardelle's. The loss of these two friends hurt him deeply. As if that was not enough, Sandy's own personal haunts had continued to provoke him.

Sandy made his way across the church foyer to his office, turning on lights as he walked. He pressed his key into the doorknob lock and felt the tiny tumblers reacting. Stepping inside his office, he turned on the lights and glanced at the clock on the wall. It was just after eight.

Sunday School would begin at nine-thirty, which meant that he had about an hour to pull himself together.

Sandy slumped into his office chair and sat staring at his sermon outline. Several weeks ago, he had begun a preaching series: "Heroes of the Bible." Today's lesson was based on the Old Testament story of Abraham and his son, Isaac.

How am I going to preach this? How am I going to tell everyone that when they pass God's test, they will be better and stronger Christians? I'm being tested; yet, I don't feel stronger or better. Ardelle, Clay, and my father are gone. I feel drained and alone.

Sandy glanced over the sermon again. He pressed his fingers into his forehead and felt the deep-creased furrows. *No wonder Abraham passed the test. He could hear God talking! How comforting that must have been to hear God speak. How different things would be for me if I could hear the voice of God! But all that I get is silence. No wonder Abraham had great faith. He was hearing God's voice! Me? I hear nothing. How am I ever going to preach this?*

Sandy recognized the self-pity in his inner voice, and it disgusted him. Yet, he couldn't seem to stop the flow. His father had hurt him profoundly. The hurt was emotional, but it was also spiritual. The injury had left an ugly scar across his soul. *Do I believe in God because I was taught to do so? Or, do I believe because I have chosen to believe?*

Sandy had hoped to go over his sermon, but he found that he simply didn't have the energy. As he turned on his laptop computer and waited for it to boot up, he dropped his face into his hands and slowly ran his fingers through his hair. He then closed his eyes, crossed his arms on the desk, and laid his head down.

For a while, he lost track of time. When he raised his head, he wondered if he had dozed off. He had intended to review some Biblical references in his notes, but instead began playing solitaire on his laptop. At least it occupied his mind with something other than self-indulgent thoughts.

Soon, Sandy heard noises throughout the church as members began arriving. Mark, the janitor, would be turning on lights in the sanctuary and adjusting the circulating fans. Nancy, the communion steward would be preparing the elements for the worship service. Several of the Sunday School teachers would be preparing for their classes. *Yet, here I sit. Playing solitaire while everyone is busy doing what they've been called to do.* Bitter thoughts raged through Sandy's mind. *The entire church is filled with saints while the preacher is a hypocrite.* His stomach tightened again.

A soft knock at his door jolted Sandy. "Come in," he called as he closed his laptop and turned toward the door. "It's open."

The door opened slowly. It was as if the person behind it was still unsure of the invitation. Children often stopped in to see Sandy before services began. They always brightened his morning, and today he needed some brightening.

"It's okay," Sandy encouraged. "I don't bite!" Sandy's voice sounded cheery despite the demons he had been combating.

"Well, I hope that you don't." The voice was not that of a child, but of a woman.

Before he could process the voice, Ellie stepped inside his office. He hadn't spoken with her since their dinner had been interrupted by

Anne Decker's frantic phone call a few days ago. His thoughts had drifted to her more than a few times since then.

Sandy was taken by Ellie's appearance. She was dressed nicely in a dark skirt and light, colored blouse. Her hair wasn't pulled back as before, but rather it hung down, dancing across her shoulders. She was even more striking than he remembered.

"Ellie–what a pleasant surprise!" Sandy proclaimed as he stumbled from his chair. He walked around the desk to greet her. He extended his hand, but feeling quite distracted, nearly missed hers. He made a feeble recovery, offering only a weak, embarrassing handshake that he absentmindedly let linger.

"Thank you," she replied with a smile. "I hope you don't mind me stopping in. A very nice gentleman in the church told me where I could find you."

"No, not at all," Sandy returned. "Please, come in."

Sandy stepped back to allow Ellie into his office. In so doing, he backed into a small table displaying a vase, nearly knocking them both over. He caught the vase before it struck the floor. He slid the table back to avoid doing it again.

"Thank you," Ellie said as she stepped in.

If she detected his inelegance, Sandy noticed that she graciously contained it to herself.

"It's great seeing you today!" Sandy exclaimed.

Sandy motioned for Ellie to take a seat that was tucked in between the door and a filing cabinet. She was about to sit when she looked at the office door she had left ajar.

"Oh, I'm sorry. Should I close the door?"

Thankfully, the question jolted Sandy back to reality. He knew that it was unwise to be alone in his office with a female. That's how rumors began, and rumors could end a minister's career. *A good name is more desirable than great riches,* Sandy recited to himself. As the scripture passage came to mind, he recalled their first visit at the parsonage. He made a mental note to be more careful about that in the future.

"No, that's not necessary," Sandy replied as he sat down behind his desk. "I'm so glad you came to church."

"Thanks," she said, straightening her skirt. She seemed to Sandy to be slightly uncomfortable in her attire. "When we were together last, you had to leave suddenly to visit Anne Decker. I heard you had Clay's funeral. I'm very sorry. How did he die?"

Sandy savored her use of the word *together.*

"Yes, it was sad," he said. "Clay was working beneath his wife's car when the jack gave out. He was crushed by it."

Ellie closed her eyes and shuddered.

"So, how are you doing?" Sandy asked, changing the subject.

"I think I'm doing okay. It's been a long, tiring week, but I'm getting along. Now that school is out, Caroline went to stay for a week with our other aunt. She seems to be doing better. That is a huge relief. But it's been hard to adjust."

"Well, give yourself some time," Sandy replied. He was slowly gaining control of his senses again and becoming more of a pastor.

"Everyone grieves differently," he continued. "There is no set timetable for getting over things. As a matter of fact, there is no such thing as 'getting over things.' We just learn to move forward in a different way."

Ellie paused, as if taking in what Sandy had just told her. She looked up and smiled at Sandy again. The smile warmed his heart.

Sandy glanced at his watch. It was almost time for Sunday School. "Come on, let me show you around before everything begins."

Sandy rose from the chair and walked to the door. Ellie also stood and straightened her blouse and skirt. Sandy pulled the door the rest of the way open, and they both stepped out of the office and into the foyer. Members of the congregation were starting to arrive. Some were hanging their jackets in the closet at the rear of the foyer, while others were engaged in friendly conversation with neighbors and friends. Little Justin nearly plowed into Sandy as he raced toward his grandmother, who had just walked through the front door. The sight of everyone interacting with each other lifted his mood even higher.

As they stepped into the foyer, Sandy remembered his sermon outline that still lay in the office. "Excuse me for a moment," he said, and then returned to retrieve it.

When he rejoined Ellie in the foyer, she was standing at the bulletin board, her eyes still skimming the many postings. Seeing her warmed his heart once more. He breathed a prayer of thanks for the much-needed grace that she had brought to his morning.

"This church seems busy," she said as Sandy reached her side. "You have a lot of things going on. I like that."

As Sandy looked over her shoulder, he caught the whiff of a delicate perfume. It catapulted his senses, and sent his mind whirling.

"Am I talking to myself, here?" she said with a light-hearted jab.

"Sorry," Sandy laughed as he tried to get back into the present. "Yeah, we try to offer things that appeal to everyone."

Sandy pointed out some activities that he thought Ellie might find interesting. He walked her to the Young Adult Sunday School classroom and introduced her to everyone.

Sandy had to hurry off to teach the teen class. After Sunday School, he took his usual spot near the front door to greet arriving parishioners. He kept an eye out for Ellie. As Worship Service began, he saw her enter the sanctuary and slip into one of the rear pews. Sandy couldn't keep from smiling.

Sandy felt that he preached a little better that day. He talked about being tested by God and passing the test, but didn't feel as hypocritical as he thought he might. He noticed a few stray looks, but most seemed to be tracking him. Ellie seemed to be listening the most intently. Sandy was glad she was there.

Chapter Ten

Spring rain clouds prematurely darkened the evening skies, sending damp shivers up and down the quiet river town. The cold rain conveyed the town's disposition. Like Ardelle's accident, Clay's death had come too suddenly. There had been no time for goodbyes or final thoughts. Within the span of two weeks, the town had lost two leaders. The church had lost two saints, and Sandy had lost two close friends. It was a lot of loss.

Sandy dug through his closet to find a light windbreaker to wear to the meeting at the church. With the camping program fast approaching, he needed to meet with his counselors and helpers to go over some details. Last year's camping program didn't go badly, but there had been a few glitches that he was hoping to fix.

He was also hoping that Ellie would show up. She had been attending church the past few weeks with Caroline, who had returned from visiting their aunt. After services, Sandy always stood at the doorway, greeting his parishioners. Ellie had made a habit of lingering in the sanctuary, giving them time to talk when everyone else had left. Sandy looked forward to spending this time with her each week. He was learning that there was a strange complexity about her. A type of sadness. Yet, Sandy thought he noticed the sadness lifting a bit recently. He hoped their conversations had something to do with that.

Sandy also kept reminding Ellie about summer camp. Though she hadn't yet committed, she had signed the form for the background check.

Sandy had mailed reminders out to everyone about this evening's meeting, making sure that Ellie's also went out. This morning he had left her a voicemail message expressing his hope that she would come to the meeting. He felt optimistic. Everyone loved her aunt, and he expected Ellie to be warmly received by the group.

Sandy picked up his jacket and was walking toward the door when he felt the vibration of his cell phone. He retrieved the phone and looked at the number. It was Harrison "Harris" Long, owner and director of Camp Atawanda. He answered the call while walking back to his home-office.

"Harris! Good to hear from you!" Sandy said as he searched his desk for a notepad and pencil.

"Hello, Sandy! How are you doing?" Harris said cheerfully.

"I'm doing fine, and you?" Sandy asked. He had met Harris the previous year through the camping program, and they had quickly formed a friendship. Harris loved two things: kids and the outdoors. He worked hard and had succeeded in bringing these passions together each year at the campground. In addition to offering camping to the Lycona Community Church, he filled the summer camping season with Boy Scout Troops, weekend retreats, an RV camping program, and plenty of primitive campsites for those wanting to retreat to the mountains.

"I'm doing okay, thanks. Did I catch you at a bad time, or do you have some time to talk?" Harris asked.

"You're timing couldn't be better, Harris. I was just about to leave for a meeting with my camping staff. We're going to go over assignments for this year's program. I'm glad you called when you did."

"Good, good," Harris said. For the next few minutes he talked about the water table levels, the new bunks that had been built over the winter, and the improved kitchen. Finally, Sandy interrupted.

"Harris, forgive me; I need to get to that meeting soon. Can we touch base later on camp conditions? Is there anything in particular that you think I need to address with the group tonight?"

Harris got quiet. Sandy heard him take a breath as if he was going to say something, but there was a hesitation. Sensing something, Sandy pulled his kitchen-office chair out from beneath his desk and sat down.

"What's wrong, Harris? Are you okay?"

"Yes, of course. I'm fine. There's just something that's on my mind, and I'm having a hard time talking about it."

"Well, I can't help you with it until I know what it is," Sandy replied, his concern growing.

"I know, I know." Harris grew silent again before continuing. "Some things have been going on up here that you may need to know about before camping begins."

"What things?" Sandy asked.

"Strange things. That's about all I can say—some pretty strange things."

"I'm listening," Sandy urged.

Harris took another deep breath and held it as if he were about to plunge under water. As he let it out, he began.

"Late last summer, we began working on the new hiking trails. With the grant money I was able to get, I hired some workers who really tore into things for me. They stayed here at the lodge during the week, and they would go home on weekends. They were a pretty good group of guys.

Near the middle of September, they started coming back to the lodge in the evenings with some pretty weird stories. They said they were hearing noises during the day. They'd be clearing timber all morning. At lunch time, they would be sitting around when they'd start to hear the strangest kind of noise. They said something would start to howl or make a whooping sound. At times it was distant, but as things progressed it seemed to get closer to the group.

I told them it was probably a coyote, and honestly, I didn't give it much thought. Then, one night they came back pretty excited. They said that the sound was a lot closer, maybe within fifty feet. They were pretty frightened, and a couple of them started carrying their guns to work."

"What made the noise?" Sandy asked. He didn't like the direction that the story seemed to be going.

"I don't know," Harris replied. "I guess at first I didn't pay too much attention to what they were saying. I've spent most of my life outdoors and have heard some pretty strange sounds over the years. I guess that I just figured this group scared easily.

Anyway, I told them it was probably a wild cat of some kind, and that it wouldn't cause them any problem if they stayed together. The two crews worked in groups of five, and they stayed pretty close to one another. I told them to make sure they made noises in the woods, so as not to startle the animal, and then I asked them to just go about their business."

"So, what happened?"

"About that time we got hit with some early snow, and I pulled them off of the trail work. I sent one crew to Sanctuary Rock, where we were building a new cabin. The other crew stayed down at the main lodge to help me with the kitchen repairs.

For about a week, everything went fine. Then sometime around the first part of October, the Sanctuary Rock crew came back at noon. I was surprised to see them so early; I suspected right away that something had happened. As soon as I saw them get out of the Suburban, I knew we had a problem. They were all badly shaken. I asked what happened, but it took a while for them to even calm down enough to talk.

From what they said, they were working inside the cabin when they heard a loud thud, as if something hit the outside wall. Two of them walked outside to take a look around. They found a large rock, about the size of a basketball. They said someone—or something—threw the rock against the cabin while they were inside. They couldn't see anyone around, so just they went back inside.

A few minutes later, another rock crashed into the cabin, followed by a third. They were freaking out by that time. Two of them had firearms, and they retrieved them from the vehicle to help alleviate everyone's fears a bit.

That's when the screams started. They said it was terrifying. They told me that it was so loud that it had to be just behind the treeline, about twenty feet from them. They all ran back into the cabin and locked the door. The screaming and rock throwing continued. They could tell that it was either circling the cabin or there were several of them. One of the guys panicked, opened one of the side windows, and started shooting into the woods. Whatever, or whoever, it was stopped at that point.

The silence gave them the courage to make a run for the Suburban, and they got out of there. They couldn't take the old logging road too fast, and while they were coming down the mountain they heard it screaming the whole way. They said it followed them to the blacktop road where they gunned it hard. They never got a look at it.

I told them to go to the kitchen and get something to eat, and to take the day off. Two of them decided to quit right there. They never came back. They were that scared!"

"Harris, what are you telling me? Do you have a mountain lion or bear up there running around scaring people?" Sandy asked incredulously.

"Like I said, Sandy, I don't know. I had Sheriff Bragg come up the next day. He and I drove up to the cabin. We found rocks at the side of the cabin that seemed out of place, and the Sheriff found empty shell casings near one of the windows. That seemed to back up their story. Bragg walked around the area and explored the woods inside the treeline. He said he didn't find anything unusual.

Bragg asked for the list of employee names. When he looked over it, he recognized the two guys who'd quit that day. He said both had had run-ins with the law and that he wouldn't put too much stock in what they had to say. He didn't say as much, but I think he left believing it was all a hoax. The three guys who stayed behind were pretty offended by that; they just clammed up and wouldn't talk about it anymore. They also refused to go back to the cabin."

Sandy leaned back and rubbed his forehead. He couldn't believe his ears. It all sounded surreal, like something out of a horror movie. Yet, here was a trusted friend telling him these strange things with complete sincerity.

"Anything else?" Sandy asked hesitantly.

"Yeah," Harris replied reluctantly. "There's more."

"Things seemed to quiet down for a couple of weeks," Harris continued. "I started thinking that everything was fine again. Then we had a break in the weather; I sent a crew back up to work on the trails some more. They said that they always felt like someone was watching them, and at times they heard strange knocking sounds. They described it as if someone was hitting a tree with a baseball bat. Then, from across the way, they would hear more knocks. They said that it was as if there was some kind of communication going on."

"Did you ever hear these things yourself?" Sandy asked.

"I didn't hear the knockings, but in late November I heard some howling and screaming coming from far off in the woods. We could hear it clear down at the lodge. Whatever it was sure had a set of lungs. It wasn't like *anything* I have heard before, Sandy. I don't know what it is." Harris sounded grim.

"What about the Game Warden? Did you ever call him?" Sandy asked.

"Yeah, I called Warden Flint after Bragg dismissed the whole thing. He came down during Thanksgiving break. All the workers were away, so he couldn't ask anyone any specific questions. He took a ride up to the cabin and then drove around some of the old logging roads. He said he didn't see or hear a thing, and I think he blew it off just like Bragg."

"So, no one knows what this is all about?" Sandy asked with increasing anxiety.

Harris laughed. "Well, Benjamin claims to know all about it!"

"Benjamin?"

"I guess you could say he's a drifter. I occasionally get them wandering into camp, looking for work or a place to stay. However, he's the first Native American I've ever had. Rarely does anyone come in so late in the year. He showed up in early December. He was on foot, carrying all of his belongings in a backpack. He asked if I had any work to give him. Having lost two guys in the fall, I jumped at the chance to hire him.

Benjamin is an interesting character. I haven't gotten a full day's work out of him since he started, but he's one of the most valuable guys that I have." Harris's voice sounded a little brighter.

"How's that?" Sandy asked, hoping for some light at the end of this darkening tunnel.

"Well, the crews started telling him about some of the things that had happened. I think they were trying to scare him. He just smiled and said, 'Must be Chiye-tanka.'"

"Chiye-tanka?" Sandy asked.

"He said that it has many names, but that's what he calls it. He said that it's an old Indian word meaning 'older brother' or something like that. Benjamin said Chiye-tanka is a being that's neither man nor animal. He's an 'older brother' to us and means no one any harm. As a matter of fact, he said that Chiye-tanka only appears when he has a message for us."

"You've got to be kidding me, Harris!" Sandy nearly shouted into the phone. "You're telling me that this guy thinks there's a ghost of some sort running around the woods wanting to talk with us?"

"It's not a ghost, Sandy," Harris's voice took on a serious tone again. "He says it's a real being that leaves us alone until there is something we need to know. It's then that it appears."

"You sound like you believe him," Sandy said with an accusing tone.

"Benjamin's not a kook," Harris said in his defense. "He's a very intelligent guy who makes a lot of sense. He's a little unorthodox, but he's a deep thinker. He even attended a seminary school in the midwest."

"Okaaayy," Sandy replied, not bothering to mask his sarcasm.

"Hey, you shouldn't knock him until you've heard him!" Harris replied defensively. "Besides, he's got a lot of good answers to questions that I've always had. Questions about life and faith. About a lot of things. In fact, he's been holding a little study class up here once a week. Just last night he was talking about how the New Testament writers took bits and pieces from other—I think he called them 'mystery religions'—and brought them into Christianity. I was amazed at how many tenets of Christianity were actually borrowed. Christmas, baptism, even resurrection, were ideas that existed in other religions *before* Christianity began. Benjamin showed us how, by removing those ideas from the Bible, we get to see the *real* Jesus; not the one made up by the Church! It made a lot of sense!"

Sandy's eyes widened in disbelief. He rattled his head as if the shaking movement could free him from the absurdity of the conversation. He didn't know what to say or where to begin.

"Alright, this is getting a little off track, Harris," Sandy finally replied, trying to force the conversation back to where it had begun. "What has Benjamin been doing about this animal?"

"Well," Harris continued, "he really has helped calm everyone down. I sent him out with the crews to clear the trails. Like I said, he's not a great worker. But most everyone likes having him along. When they get started in the morning, he usually sits down and starts praying. The guys say that he then sometimes chants or sings some Native American song. It spooked everyone at first, but—and here's the strange part—it seems to help! Whatever the thing is, it seems to leave everyone alone with Benjamin around!"

Sandy now closed his eyes and rubbed his forehead. None of this made any sense to him, and he was beginning to feel a little frustrated.

"Harris, in a few weeks I'm going to have a hundred children crawling all over your campground. I'm responsible for their safety. If some animal is prowling around the woods up there, and you think it's dangerous, you need to let me know. We'll cancel this year's program if we have to. But if someone's pulling your leg and playing a prank, you need to get to the bottom of it. There are a lot of families who have made a lot of plans for the summer. Canceling the camping program won't please anyone. Especially, if I tell them that it's because of some... ah, whatever!"

The sharpness in Sandy's voice surprised even him.

"Listen, Sandy, I don't know what to tell you. Something weird has been going on up here, and I don't know all the answers yet. I figured that the right thing to do was to let you know about it."

Sandy heard the defensiveness in Harris' voice again, and he felt badly for speaking to him so sternly. "I'm sorry, Harris. You did the right thing to call me, and it sounds like you're doing all that you can do." He then added in his own defense, "This is all just very strange to hear."

"I know, Sandy. Believe me when I say that I wish none of this was happening. I'm embarrassed to even talk to anyone about it."

"Well," Sandy asked, "what should I do? Should we go ahead with plans, or should we cancel the program this year?"

"The choice is yours. I'm running a business, so of course I want to see you use my facilities. But if you need to cancel, I'd understand.

We haven't had anything troubling in weeks. Even when things were happening, no one ever got hurt."

"We have a little more time," Sandy replied, "let's continue with our plans as they are. But if anything happens up there, I expect you to call me right away!"

After finishing the phone call, Sandy made his way out the door. He was running late for his meeting, but the church was only two blocks from the parsonage. As he walked down the sidewalk in the cold drizzle, he wondered how he could bring up his conversation with Harris. He also wondered how he would explain that they may have to cancel summer camp because of a mysterious ghost walking through the woods.

Chapter Eleven

In response to the wind and rain, Sandy pulled up his jacket collar and slipped his hands into his pockets. The chilling drizzle, however, was impervious to his efforts. A shiver raced through his body, causing him to quicken his pace. Sandy moved down the sidewalk and soon ascended the five concrete steps of Lycona Community Church.

Sandy sighed deeply as he pulled open the heavy door. He was running a few minutes late for the camp meeting because of his phone call with Harris. This meant that he would have to do a little explaining to Ardyth. At age sixty-seven, Ardyth Van Horten wasn't the oldest matriarch in the church. However, what she lacked in years she compensated for with attitude. There wasn't anything that happened in the church or the community that Ardyth didn't have her hand in. She had an opinion on everything and everybody, and she never labored under any burden preventing her from making that opinion known. Though she had always been a short woman, her golden years had not been kind. They were slowly robbing her of inches she could not afford to lose. Ardyth's stature, however, was not dependent upon the distance between her head and feet. Rather, her influence was measured by the level of control she maintained. And it was no secret that her control was connected to her personal wealth.

All three of her former husbands had been independently wealthy, and they had left her with vast resources. Only her first husband, however, had had the good fortune of dying. The remaining two had died a living death in divorce court. They had been forced to surrender half of their kingdoms to Ardyth and her team of three-piece-suit lawyers. Now, over half of the church's budget came directly from her giving. To say, however, that she was a generous giver would be more flattering than what the truth would allow. Her giving stemmed from her desire to be in control. Decades ago, this desire for control had driven her to secure the church treasurer position. Admittedly, it was a job no one else wanted. Now, it was also a job no one else would get. The next treasurer would have to stand at the casket and pry the checkbook from her bony, little fingers. Even then, Sandy believed there would be a fight. It was all about control. Everyone recognized it— especially Ardyth. And she was the one in control.

Sandy often wondered why Ardyth attended church. He never saw any spiritual graces about her, and she never talked about matters of faith. Lycona Community was the biggest church in the small town, so it became a natural hub of local contacts. Sandy believed Ardyth came for this reason.

If there was a positive side to Ardyth's presence in the church, it was the fact that she could get things done. Even Sandy would admit as much. From building projects to Sunday School picnics, Ardyth was usually at the center. She called the shots and moved people like chess pieces. Most of the time, people appreciated what she did. However, her overbearing nature often tested Sandy's patience. He felt that she didn't notice how she aggravated everyone around her. Or worse yet, Sandy feared, maybe she *did* notice. Perhaps this was what she *wanted*. Maybe it was what she sought. Clay Decker had been the only person Sandy had ever seen engage Ardyth and remain unscathed. Ardelle had also had her own way of managing her. Neither Clay nor Ardelle would be at tonight's meeting. Without these two close allies, Sandy knew things might be a challenge.

That Ardyth was even interested in the camping program was a surprise to Sandy. There was nothing about it that could possibly attract her. She was no fan of the outdoors and needed no prompting to proclaim her disdain for children. She usually made a small, annual donation to keep the program afloat, but had never offered any other assistance. Much to Sandy's surprise, Ardyth had stepped up to fill Ardelle's vacancy. She'd then sealed her intentions by making a sizable contribution to the camp. No one would object. That would only make her angry, and no one wanted an angry Ardyth.

What shocked Sandy even more was Ardyth's willingness to actually attend this year's camp as part of Lycona's staff. This defied every reasonable explanation and would greatly complicate the week. However, Sandy couldn't deny that a part of him relished the thought of seeing Ardyth roughing it for a week in the mountains of Lycona.

Ardyth would be critical of Sandy's late arrival. She would make certain everyone present learned just how upsetting it was to her. But even if Sandy were on time for the meeting, Ardyth would still find a reason to be critical. She liked only a few people, and Sandy's name wasn't on that list. When he'd first met her, he had tried to befriend her. She had kept him at a distance. Nearly every conversation had become a power struggle. Sandy had soon become disinterested in those battles, and he'd simply withdrawn from his attempts to smooth things over.

110

There were others in the congregation who needed his presence, so he had fixed his attention on them.

The evening meeting was to be attended by the counselors; those who would work directly with the children. Sandy had also invited four helpers who would come along to run errands for the counselors and assist where needed. Although Ardyth was not very agile and wouldn't lift a finger all week at camp, she would "serve" as one of the helpers. Missing from the meeting would be the youth leader, Jocelyn.

Walking quickly down the steps to the basement, Sandy's thoughts shifted to Ellie. He wondered if she would be present. His heart skipped a beat. He hoped to see her again.

Sandy turned at the bottom of the steps and made his way to one of the Sunday School rooms. He fully expected to find everyone chatting loudly. He was surprised, however, to be met with overwhelming silence as he entered. The excitement that he had been feeling about seeing Ellie became completely smothered by a serious intensity that seemed to be lying in wait.

Ardyth was sitting near the end of the table, tapping the eraser of a number two pencil against the tabletop in a frustrating rhythm. She glared at him with eyes that were perched just above the rims of her designer glasses. Sandy was expecting disapproval for his tardiness, but there was something about her look that forebode another problem.

The seating arrangement around the folding table immediately gave Sandy the first indication of what the deafening silence was about. Ardyth and most of the counselors were seated along one side of the table. Directly across from Ardyth sat Ellie. Several empty seats occupied the space between Ellie and the nearest helper. Two of the counselors had even taken chairs from Ellie's side of the table and moved them to the outskirts of the room. A tremendous effort was being made to avoid sitting near the unfortunate newcomer.

As Sandy entered the room and moved to the head of the table, he quickly scanned the faces of those present. The majority at the meeting were faithful members of the church. Only a few were there by special invitation, and these had been involved in the camping program during previous years.

As Sandy's eyes met those who sat around the table, he quickly recognized two different kinds of looks. Several had the same expression of indignation that Ardyth wore. They looked hard at Sandy; as if by a stern countenance their angry thoughts could be translated clearly. The remaining group of faces seemed to bear a look of compassion or pity.

He reached the head of the table and began pulling his chair out. It would not move. He looked beneath the table and saw that Ardyth's leg was slung over it, holding it in place. He looked at her in confusion.

"I'm having a lot of pain in my leg tonight," she said with a slight groan. "You know how my phlebitis has been acting up lately. I'm supposed to keep it elevated. You'll have to wait while I get it down."

No one in the room misunderstood what Ardyth was doing. She often played these games in order to maintain control over other people. While Sandy stood and waited, she slowly removed her leg from the chair. Everyone waited on Ardyth; *she* waited on no one.

When she had removed her leg, Sandy pulled the chair out and sat down. Most everyone was looking at Sandy, though a few were watching Ardyth. Sandy glanced at Ellie. Her eyes were cast down, but a pained look of embarrassment was scrawled across her face.

"It seems awfully quiet in here. Is something wrong?" Sandy asked.

Nearly every eye shifted to Ardyth. She would be the spokesperson. No one had the nerve to speak before her.

"Yes, there is something wrong, *Reverend*," Ardyth replied. She rarely called Sandy by this title, unless she was trying to make a point. Tonight she accented it with a biting sarcasm.

"You see, I was looking over the names of the counselors and helpers that we have this year," Ardyth continued, "and everyone is accounted for, but one." She finished her sentence by adjusting her glare from Sandy to Ellie, who had not moved since Sandy entered the room. "If I've missed this name, then please correct me. But if I haven't, then please explain why someone is here who is not on my list." Her eyes were fixed on Ellie, whose gaze remained downcast.

Sandy felt flushed with anger. Not because Ardyth lacked tact—which she certainly did. Rather, because she acted so calloused toward the hurt that she'd created.

"Ardyth, the list of names you have was prepared several months ago, and it is based on last year's list," Sandy replied tersely. "As chairperson of this committee, I have the liberty to amend the list as I see fit."

"I understand that, Reverend. But the issue is not *if* you can amend the list, but rather with *whom* you amend it."

Sandy felt his face getting hotter. Ardyth obviously had something to say about Ellie; a fact she was not attempting to conceal.

"Ardyth!" Sandy was having a hard time controlling his anger. "I can't believe that you would say such a thing!"

Ellie quickly stood up while keeping her face turned toward the floor. She muttered, "I really think that I should leave. Thank you, Pastor, for thinking about me."

"Wait a moment, Ellie!" Sandy called as he began to rise from his chair. Ellie did not pause. She made her way to the classroom door and closed it behind her as she stepped out.

Sandy followed her into the hallway. Ellie was already nearing the basement's exit door, walking very quickly. He called for her again, and this time she stopped. As he neared her side he saw her eyes were filled with tears.

"Hey, I'm really sorry about that," Sandy said gently. He hoped Ellie could hear the compassion he was feeling for her.

"I have no idea what's gotten into Ardyth," he continued. "She can be a little crass at times, but I've never seen her act like this."

"That's okay," Ellie responded. "She's right. I have no business being here, much less of joining the camping group. She said the things that she said because she knows me. You've invited me here because you *don't* know me."

Using the sleeve of her sweatshirt, Ellie wiped her eyes as she sniffed.

"Listen, Ellie," Sandy said, trying to come up with something to say.

"Please, just forget about it," Ellie interrupted. "It's okay."

Ellie very quickly turned and walked toward the door. Sandy called to her again, but she did not respond. Instead, she pushed the heavy steel door open and stepped out of the church.

Sandy stood quietly for a moment. He didn't know whether to chase after her or return to the meeting. Then, he remembered Ardyth. He wheeled around and marched into the classroom. Most everyone was looking down, their faces reflecting shame. Everyone, that is, except Ardyth. She sat scanning the minutes from the previous meeting. It was as if she was completely unaware of the turmoil that she had effectively orchestrated.

"Ardyth, could you please step out into the hallway? I'd like to have a word with you," Sandy said in a heated, but controlled manner.

"I'm afraid that my leg is hurting too badly to move right now," she replied innocently. "What is it that you want?"

From a lifetime of practice, Ardyth knew how to remain in control of a situation. It frustrated Sandy to feel like he was losing his patience while she seemed entirely at peace.

"Then I'm going to ask that everyone else please step out of the room so that I can have a moment with you," Sandy returned. He didn't consider himself an authoritative person, but the present moment seemed like a good time to change.

No one at the table moved. Instead, they turned to look at Ardyth for her reaction. She glanced around the room, satisfied with everyone's response, and then gave a slight nod. This gave them the permission they needed. They rose from their seats and filed past Sandy, who stood with folded arms at the doorway. When they emptied the room, he closed the door and moved back to his chair at the head of the table.

"What was that all about?" Sandy asked as he stood with both hands on the back of the chair. He remained standing to keep his body in a superior position.

"You don't know?" Ardyth asked in a snide tone. With no one else in the room, she no longer needed to feign innocence.

"The only thing that I know is that someone who came here to help us was treated very badly by *you*–and she is now gone!" Sandy replied, pointing in the general direction of the rear church door. It was strangely satisfying to hear his own voice sound so angry.

"You're right. That's the only thing you know!" Ardyth retorted with venom. "You had invited someone to a project involving little children without even knowing the kind of person you'd invited. I know that as a church we are supposed to reach out to others, but you wouldn't invite a drunk to guard the communion wine or a thief to take up the collection, would you?"

"A thief? What are you talking about?" Sandy's brow molded a perplexed look. The high road he was taking suddenly didn't feel so high.

"I'm talking about the kind of woman you invited here!" Ardyth shot back with force. "Ellie Lawson is a no good dope-head! Ardelle was a real saint to have put up with her. She took her in, gave her a good place to live, and then found out that Ellie was stealing from her. And when she couldn't steal, she would do whatever it took to get money to buy more drugs. You have no idea how much grief that woman caused

116

poor, old Ardelle! I walk in here tonight and who is sitting at this table, by *your* special invitation? That no-good tramp who drove poor Ardelle to her grave!"

Ardyth appeared delighted with the way her words changed the expression on Sandy's face. It was obvious that she had delivered information to Sandy of which he was previously unaware. She beamed with the intoxicating feeling of control that must have been surging through her.

Sandy remained standing above her, but he suddenly felt like sitting.

"No one drove her to her grave, Ardyth," he said. "She was killed when her car ran off the road. It was an accident." His voice had been weakened by her argument.

"She was out of town that weekend because she needed to get away from that niece of hers!" Ardyth said loudly. She apparently noticed how Sandy's voice trailed off and was taking advantage of the shift in power.

"If little-Miss-Lawson would have treated poor Ardelle in a respectable way," she continued, "she would not have had to leave her own home to get away from everything. She would not have crashed driving home so late!"

"But," Sandy said, still trying to find the right response.

"But nothing!" Ardyth snapped. She was clearly winning the argument. "The well-being of a lot of children rests with this committee. What do you think is going to happen to the camping program when everyone finds out the caliber of counselor you have invited?"

"Listen," Sandy's thoughts were finally beginning to form. "I didn't invite Ellie to come as a counselor, just as a helper. If she passes the background check, she will be running errands, helping in the kitchen, and being a support to the counselors. In that regard, she won't be any different than some of the on-site camping staff that Harris Long provides. You've never objected to them."

Sandy locked eyes with Ardyth. His voice began gaining momentum, "Our ministry is not just to the children, but to everyone, including Ellie. If even half of the things you said about her are true, then I would think that God would want us to be concerned for her. Don't you agree that being a Christian means we consider the needs of everyone?"

Sandy had beat Ardyth's hand with the ultimate trump card: God. She had recognized it coming too late to intercept the argument, and though she would be forced to capitulate, her rock-solid facial features remained unchanged.

"You better be certain of yourself, Reverend," Ardyth replied coolly. "If she comes along and something bad happens, it will be your head on the chopping block!"

////

Sandy decided against mentioning the call with Harris to the camping committee. Tensions were already high after the blowup with Ardyth, and he felt he needed more detail from Harris first. After the meeting, he drove across town to Ardelle's old place. His concern that someone might see him alone at her house at night was consumed by the need to be a pastor. As he pulled into the driveway, he saw her blue Jeep and a lamp glowing inside the house. Approaching the front door, he breathed a silent prayer for wisdom.

Sandy rang the bell twice, but he got no response. He then walked along the side of the house to the rear porch. Ardelle had often spent her evenings on the back porch. She never heard the doorbell from there.

Rounding the corner of the house, he found Ellie seated in Ardelle's favorite porch rocker. Caroline was sitting beside her. When Caroline saw Sandy approach, she shot him a sad, pleading look. Caroline then stood up and walked back into the house.

Ellie had evidently heard Sandy approach; she was looking up when he walked into view. She seemed relaxed. He felt relieved to find her in a such a composed condition.

"Your aunt loved sitting out here," Sandy said as he climbed the steps to the rear porch.

After Ardelle had been widowed, she'd made some badly-needed changes to the house. The old back porch had been replaced with a modern, deck-style landing. A new roof, extending from the existing frame of the home, reached out over the deck. This created delightful shade in the late afternoon. Potted plants hung from the porch roof throughout the summer, spouting colorful blossoms and creating a sweet-smelling wall around the deck.

"I know," Ellie replied, looking out at the back yard. "Every time that I come out here, I think of her. In fact—and you'll probably think I'm weird—this is where I come to talk to her."

"I don't find that weird at all," Sandy said. He paused to lean against one of the upright supports. Although it had stopped raining, the post was still wet. Sandy pulled back quickly, but already had gotten his jacket wet. He smiled shyly, and wondered why he always felt so clumsy around her.

"Please, have a seat," she said, gesturing to one of the chairs on the porch.

"Thanks." He sat down in a white, wicker rocker. "It's a beautiful evening, and you've got a great view of it."

Although the house was within city limits, it bordered a small grove of trees, giving it a rural feel. Sandy had stopped by Ardelle's place more than once to watch the deer wander into the yard to eat the small apples and acorns that fell. It was a place that Sandy found relaxing.

"Yes, I know. Aunt Dell really loved sitting back here," Ellie paused for a moment, and then continued. "And I sure do miss her."

Sandy responded by nodding his head. He had a sense this was a special moment for Ellie, and he didn't want to interrupt it with senseless chatter.

After a few more moments of silence, Sandy cleared his throat, "Ellie, I'm really sorry about what happened tonight. Ardyth was out of hand, and there's nothing that I can do but tell you how sorry I am. There's no excuse for the way she acted."

"Please, don't worry about it," Ellie interrupted. "It's not your fault." She kept her eyes fixed on the darkening backyard.

"No, I feel responsible for everything that happened," Sandy continued. "I'm not just the chairperson of the committee, but I'm the pastor of the church. That makes me somewhat responsible for what goes on there."

"Pastor," Ellie said.

"Please," Sandy interrupted. "Just call me Sandy."

"Okay, thanks," Ellie said with a slight nod. "Sandy, there's so much that you don't know about me. I really appreciate your kindness and desire to help, but there's much more to my story. Mrs. Van Horten knows a lot more about me than you do. She's right about everything. I'm not qualified to help with the camping program—or any church function for that matter."

"That depends upon what criteria you use to define 'qualified,'" Sandy replied, leaning forward to clasp his hands together. "You see, if we were 'qualified' to serve based on what kind of people we are, there wouldn't be anyone serving at all. All of us have done things we shouldn't have done. We all have our own skeletons hanging in our closets that we hope no one discovers. But church is not about who we used to be. It's about who we are now and who we can become."

"Oh, I'm sure you have some real nasty skeletons hanging in your closet!" Ellie said somewhat sharply. She didn't let him respond before she continued: "But the skeletons I'm talking about aren't J-walking or being late for Bible study. I'm talking about purposely doing things that are wrong. About hurting people close to you. About disappointing everyone who cares about you. I'm talking about being involved in the ugly things that you pray no one ever learns about you. I'm talking about what preacher-types like to call sin, the deep, dark kind."

Ellie slumped back into her chair as if exhausted. It was as if her monologue had been too taxing, too revealing.

Sandy sat staring at the floor. He had at first doubted the validity of the accusations made by Ardyth. He now knew they must have contained some truth. He lifted his head to find Ellie looking intently at him. He couldn't read all of the emotions that raged within her, but he could sense a very hurting soul. He didn't know what to say at first. Then he did the only thing he knew to do; he smiled gently at her.

Ellie seemed stunned to see his smile. Her eyes became moist with tears. To Sandy, her posture seemed to change. As if a great weight may have suddenly been dislodged, she relaxed. Tears loosened from hurting eyes began to roll down her cheeks. She started to rock softly back and forth. Sandy knew that their conversation was beginning to scratch the surface of something held very deeply.

Ellie began to talk. She told Sandy how hard it had been to grow up without her parents. She admitted to the hurt, confusion, and anger that she had felt daily. As a teenager, she had begun to lash out and run with "the wrong crowd." She had tried forgetting about life. The more she had tried to forget, however, the more damage she'd seemed to cause. What hurt the most was how she'd treated her aunt. Yes, she had taken money from her aunt's purse and had told lies about where she was going. But what had hurt the most was the shame that she'd caused. She explained that she'd been responsible for inflicting great emotional pain on the person she loved with all of her heart.

"Ellie," Sandy said when she had finished. "I really believe that God takes immense pleasure in showing us how great He is. And one of the ways that He does that is to take all of the wrong that we have done—no matter how bad it is—and forgive it. He just cancels the debt for us. It takes a tremendous amount of love and power to do that, but nothing pleases Him more."

"I know God can forgive me," Ellie replied. "And I believe He already has. It's just hard living with yourself when you know you became a source of pain for the people you loved."

"Ellie," Sandy said thoughtfully. "I believe that God's grace is able to not only forgive our past, but to repair the lives of those broken by it. He just wants us to trust Him."

Ellie wiped her eyes with her sleeve. As she stared off into the dark backyard again, she said, "Sandy, I want you to know that I don't live like I used to. I've changed. I *really* have."

When she looked back at him, Sandy replied, "I believe you."

"Thanks," she replied softly. The two sat in silence.

"I would still like you to go to camp," Sandy said breaking the silence. "I know things didn't get off on the right foot tonight, but please consider going."

"You saw how I was welcomed tonight, Sandy. How could I ever go? What about Mrs. Van Horten?"

"Ellie," Sandy began. "I believe that you are forgiven. That doesn't mean, however, that you won't have to face your past; or people who haven't let it go. Running from it won't do any good. Sometimes you just have to face it and trust God."

Ellie sat in deep thought for a few moments. She then nodded her head and looked up. "More than anything else, Sandy, I want to face my past."

Chapter Twelve

It was a crisp Lycona morning. Owen Kelly turned onto Church Street and slowed his rental car to a crawl. He'd been to Lycona only once before, when he had helped his son move into the parsonage a little more than a year ago. He had seen Sandy once since then, when he had come home for Christmas. It had been a good time; a nice family gathering. Two weeks later, his family had been changed forever.

Owen knew there would be no going back to his old life. He had tried calling Sandy a few times, but had felt so overwhelmed with emotion that he had never finished dialing. Finally, he'd sat down and written Sandy a letter. He had hoped for a reply. It hadn't come. Owen wasn't surprised; Sandy was too much like his father.

Owen scanned the homes on both sides of the street as he tried to get his bearings. Nothing looked familiar to him. He was beginning to understand that unfamiliarity was now his constant companion. So much had changed for him in the recent months that nothing appeared the same anymore.

Finally, he recognized his son's Honda parked in a driveway. He thought he remembered it being silver, not white. He was relearning so many things. Breathing a silent prayer, he pulled in behind the Honda. He thought to himself that maybe things would not go as badly as expected. The thought nearly made him laugh.

////

Sandy heard the doorbell ring. He glanced at the clock. It was just after eight in the morning. He had hoped to be at the church office by this time. Now, it seemed he would be running even later. As he walked from the kitchen to the front door, he saw the outline of a man's figure from just beyond the door's frosted glass. He glanced at the driveway and noticed a Ford Taurus parked behind his own car. He didn't recognize the vehicle or the form of the man at the door.

If he had been asked to name one hundred people who might have been standing on the other side of the door, Owen Kelly would never have made the list.

Sandy felt his eyes widen in disbelief as he opened the door. Shock surged over his face as the blood drained away in an instant. He didn't know what to say. He had no voice with which to say it.

"Son," Owen said. He rarely called Sandy by name.

"Father," Sandy replied in like-manner.

Suddenly, Sandy felt his face become hot with anger. The fire was being fed by multiple fuels. In particular, Sandy was angry because he had never prepared himself for this moment. He had not rehearsed how he would handle his father; or himself when this meeting occurred. His feelings and thoughts were still scattered. He was at a loss for words.

"May I come in?" Owen asked after an uncomfortably long pause.

"Ah, yeah. Okay," Sandy heard his own voice muttering.

Owen stepped in through the doorway and moved to his right as his son pushed the door closed. Sandy backed up and leaned a hand against the stairway newel post. His father looked different from when he last saw him. He seemed tired, and his face was much thinner. His clothing, which his mother had always made sure was cleaned and pressed, now hung loosely on his body. The sharp creases in his shirt that Sandy had always admired were painfully absent.

"I know you weren't expecting me, but I had hoped we could talk," Owen said.

"Well, I was just about to leave for the office."

"I understand, but do you have just a couple of minutes?"

Sandy glanced at his watch. He knew that he didn't have a tight schedule this morning, and that he could easily take some time to visit with his father. However, this unexpected appointment had filled him with an uncomfortable anxiety.

"I can take just a *couple* of minutes," Sandy replied, folding his arms in front of him.

Owen looked into the living room. "Can we sit down, please?"

Sandy grimaced and led the way into the living room. He nodded toward the couch as a way of inviting his father to sit, and then walked across the room to a rocker. The long gap he left between them was an obvious gesture.

"I've come to tell you that I'm sorry and to ask for forgiveness," Owen said as Sandy took a seat.

Sandy's temper suddenly flared as if a red-hot poker had been used to stir him. He could feel his face becoming hot, and he knew that his cheeks were turning red. An incredibly powerful urge to jump from the rocker and let loose a barrage of hateful words swept over him. It was only with great strength that he contained himself to rapidly rocking the chair back and forth.

"Why don't you tell *Mom* how sorry you are?" Sandy managed to say with a quiver in his voice. "She's the one you need to be talking to; not me!"

"I know, Sandy. In time."

"How could you do something like this?" Sandy interrupted loudly. The heat inside of him kicked up a notch. The feelings that he had not thought about started to boil to the surface.

"How could you walk away from Mom after all those years? How could you walk away from the church?" Sandy saw the pained look on his father's face. It grieved him to see his father hurt, but he couldn't stop. "How could you walk away from *God?*"

"You have every right to be angry with me, son," Owen said. "I know that I hurt you and your sister..."

"You have *no idea* what you did to our family!" Sandy interrupted again, his voice reaching a crescendo. Hot tears were beginning to form at the corners of his eyes. "And how dare you come here asking to be forgiven!"

"Believe me, Sandy, I know–."

"No, you don't!" Sandy was no longer in control. He jumped to his feet and pointed to the front door. "Just get out of here!"

He could feel the veins pulsing in his neck. Sandy felt terrible for having just yelled at his father, but anger had become his leader.

As Owen made his way to the door, he looked back once more at Sandy, who was still planted in front of the rocker. Tears were beginning to spill down Sandy's cheeks, and the anger was still burning on his face. Owen pulled the door open and paused.

"Just to let you know, I'll be in town until tomorrow. I'm staying at the Super 8. Room 104."

Sandy didn't move, but glared with an intensity that cut right through his father. Owen stepped out, closed the door behind him, and made his way to the car. Sandy heard the engine start and the car backing from the driveway. He walked to the front window, but remained far enough away that he wouldn't be seen. From this distance, he watched the car drive away.

Sandy stepped back to the center of the living room. He stood still for a moment and then collapsed to his knees. The tears that he had been fighting now flowed freely. He pushed his face into his hands to muffle the sounds of his loud sobs.

Chapter Thirteen

Eddie Law brought his Pontiac to a halt in front of the office at Camp Atawanda. It was mid-morning, and he was still on the clock. He'd been returning to the office from an interview with a retired football coach when he had decided to do some "digging around," as he liked to call it. He needed to get back to the newspaper office soon.

So far, his visit to the camp was not work-related. Mostly, it was conducted out of personal curiosity. During a late-night dinner with Lydia a few months prior, he had learned that the Sheriff's office had been dispatched to the camp to investigate a rock-throwing incident at one of the cabins. Normally, this would not have raised Eddie's interest. But Lydia had informed him that the 911 caller had also reported hearing strange screams and howling from the woods. Eddie had later made a note of the event and put it in his *Strange* file. With his interest renewed by his visit with Mrs. Brackenridge, he had now decided to follow up on the lead.

Camp Atawanda was an island of open space hemmed in by dense forest. Many years ago, it had been a logging camp and sawmill. At that time, there was nothing but space. The logging industry had scraped clean large sections of the mountain, leaving it desolate. Over time, the mountain had rejuvenated itself. The forest had returned to its former glory, leaving the old sawmill the perfect place for a campground.

Eddie banged on the front office door, but he got no response. He circled to the back and saw a light coming from an adjacent structure.

It appeared to be a gymnasium or recreation hall. Walking to the side of the building, he found the main entrance. There were two small cars and a white Chevy Suburban parked in front of it. Two steps up placed him on a very nice wrap-around porch.

Eddie found the door unlocked. He stepped inside and discovered that the building was actually a dining hall. Round, wooden tables were positioned about the room, each attended by eight very-worn chairs. Each table was crudely decorated with a wooden box, probably fashioned by a young camper. Each contained napkins, salt and pepper shakers, and an assortment of condiment packages. A massive walk-in stone fireplace took up most of the wall to his right, while antlered trophies adorned the wall on his left. A long serving window separated the far wall from the kitchen. The hardwood floors still shone from a recent mopping, and the room smelled like a hodgepodge of food, wood, and old varnish.

Two men were sitting at a table near the center of the room with their backs to the door when Eddie walked in. They were eating some overflowing turkey sandwiches that were falling apart on paper plates, and both were working through a large bag of potato chips. They turned around to see him step inside. It was apparent from the looks on their faces that they weren't expecting any visitors.

Eddie navigated through the maze of tables as the two men watched him intently. The walk was an uncomfortable one for Eddie; it made him feel as though he was on display. He smiled at them as he approached, but neither returned the gesture. To redirect their attention away from him, he began to talk before he reached the table, hoping that the conversation would distract them from watching him.

"I'm hoping that you can help me," Eddie politely said as he drew near. Since he didn't ask a question, neither man responded. They just watched him. "Is the camp manager or owner around?"

"That would be Harris Long, and no, he's not around," one of the men replied. "Can I help you with something?"

Eddie reached the table and unzipped his windbreaker, casually shoving his hands into his pockets. "Well, I was hoping to talk with someone about a 911 call that was made a few months ago."

"And you are ...?" the same man asked.

"My name is Eddie Law. I work at the *Lycona Dispatch*, and I'm following up on a story that might be related to something that happened here. I was hoping that someone might be able to help me."

"What exactly do you need?" Obviously, the man speaking was the leader of the two.

"Well, back in November someone called the Sheriff because of some rocks being thrown at a cabin nearby. I was hoping to talk with someone about that."

Eddie immediately knew that he had touched a nerve. The two men turned toward each other as if they were trying to silently communicate what should be said. Then, the same man who had been speaking looked back at Eddie, while the other one averted his eyes.

"What story are you working on that makes you think something is related to that call?"

The man's evasiveness revealed much to Eddie. First of all, he knew that he was onto something. Secondly, he knew that these men were going to be careful about what they revealed. But most importantly, he knew that he had to manipulate the conversation carefully or he might lose the opportunity.

"Someone I spoke with recently said that they had seen a very strange looking animal," he said. "They didn't know what it was, but it frightened them pretty badly. I think it is possible that what they saw could be related to what was behind that 911 call."

"I think you need to talk with Harris. He'll be in all day tomorrow," the man replied abruptly, returning to his sandwich.

Eddie knew he was on the right track. He also knew that at least one of the two men had enough knowledge about the incident to be curious about how much Eddie knew. And whatever the incident had been, it had apparently contained enough sensitive information to keep the two men from talking about it without their supervisor being present. Eddie was thrilled. He decided to try another route.

"Sure, no problem. I just know that something strange has been going on in these mountains and that no one has been able to offer an explanation for it. I know that you guys spend a lot of time in places that no one else would think of going, so I figured you could give me insight that no one else has."

Based on a glimmer he saw in both men's eyes, Eddie knew that their defensive edge was softening. He continued to work the angle.

"No one seems able to identify this animal, so I thought I'd come to the people who know the mountains better than anyone else. I figured if you couldn't help me, no one could."

"Benjamin says it's not really an animal," blurted the man who hadn't yet spoken.

Eddie had no idea who Benjamin was or what he had to do with the conversation. What Eddie did know, however, was that he had cracked the safe open just a bit.

"But what do you guys think? You two are the outdoorsmen," he said, still trying to get the right combination to unlock these two men's stories.

"I think Benjamin knows what he's talking about," the second man replied again. "He may have his crazy ways, but he knows what's out there."

The first man grunted angrily at the second in a way that was designed to hush him. Then he turned to Eddie. "Like I said, why don't you come back tomorrow and talk with Harris?"

"Sounds like a good idea," Eddie said, knowing that the conversation had reached its end. At least he had something that he didn't have when he had walked into the room.

Eddie stepped outside of the dining hall and looked around. Lined up beside it was an equipment shed, a storage unit, and a tiny camp store. Across a small yard stood a chapel. One of its doors was propped open. He decided to try and make another contact.

Eddie crossed the lawn to the chapel. As he neared the chapel, a man with long, dark hair stepped out. He saw Eddie approach and waited near the doors.

"Excuse me," Eddie said as he drew near. "I'm looking for Benjamin. Do you know where I can find him?"

"I'm Benjamin," the man replied. "What can I do for you?"

Eddie's brain tickled him. "I'd like to talk with you for a bit if you have some time," he said in an inviting manner.

"I have all the time in the world," Benjamin replied cheerfully.

Eddie extended his hand to Benjamin, who shook it firmly. "Some fellows in the dining room told me that you might be able to help me."

Benjamin released Eddie's hand and then placed both of his on his hips. Eddie began to admire him instantly. Benjamin was tall, well-built, and handsome by anyone's standards. He appeared to be of Native American descent, but probably not full-blooded. His teeth were perfectly lined and brilliantly whitened. But what impressed Eddie most was the air of confidence that he seemed to exude. It seemed to Eddie that Benjamin would probably be comfortable in any setting.

"Is there somewhere we could sit?" Eddie asked. He recalled his conversation with the two men in the dining hall, and he felt concerned that they might step outside and interrupt his time with Benjamin.

"Well, we could go in here," Benjamin replied, pointing toward the chapel door.

They made their way inside. There was a small room just inside the doors where coats were hung. They passed through that area and through some swinging doors into the main sanctuary. Hard wooden pews lined both sides of the main room, separated by an aisle that was barely covered by a well-worn industrial rug for muddy shoes. Benjamin gestured to the back pew. As Eddie sat down, Benjamin took up a folding chair from a stack kept in the back for overflow seating. Benjamin unfolded the chair, placed it in the aisle between the two rows of pews, and sat down.

"What can I do for you?" Benjamin asked.

Eddie couldn't help but admire the calm demeanor of the man before him. He had not asked who Eddie was, nor did he seem alarmed by the sudden approach of a stranger.

"I want to ask you about the strange animal that's been seen up here in the mountains," Eddie said.

Benjamin smiled and leaned back in the chair. He interlocked his hands behind his head.

"What do you want to know?" he asked.

Eddie's brain tickled him again. "Well, *what* is it?"

"First, why don't you introduce yourself to me and tell me what interest you have in this?" Benjamin said with a friendly gleam in his eye.

"Yes, I'm sorry," Eddie said. He really wasn't sorry. It was just a line he used when he was pressed for identification. "I'm Eddie Law, and I work for the *Lycona Dispatch*. I've been collecting reports for several years now of something that's been seen in these mountains, and I'm hoping that you can help me understand it."

"Are you writing a story about it?"

"I'm not even sure there's a story to write. My editor doesn't know I'm here. I guess you could say that I'm just curious."

"What will you do with what I tell you, Eddie?"

"What do you mean?"

"Well, a very wise man once said that we are not to 'cast our pearls before swine.' Do you know what that means?"

Eddie knew that he had heard the quote before, and though he didn't know what it meant, there was something about it that encouraged him to feel a little insulted.

"I'm not sure," he said truthfully.

"It means that it would be foolish to give something very precious, like pearls, to someone who cannot appreciate their value," Benjamin said.

"So, that makes me the pig?" Eddie said as he started to comprehend the illustration.

"Swine cannot choose to be anything other than swine. We, on the other hand, can choose to be respectful human beings; or we can choose to be pigs. Only one group gets the pearls."

Benjamin punctuated the last remark with a very disarming smile. Eddie might have been offended by the conversation, but Benjamin's demeanor had a way of preventing this.

"I will handle the pearls as pearls, then," Eddie confessed.

Benjamin nodded in appreciation of Eddie's response. "You asked me what it is. Well, it has many names to many people. My people call him Chiye-tanka. That means elder brother. He exists somewhere between man and animal. Not everyone, however, agrees on the nature of his existence; whether he is in bodily form or of supernatural makeup. He means no harm to anyone. We see him only when he has a message for us. Unfortunately, very few get to see him."

"So, there *has been* something up here?" Eddie replied, feeling somewhat astonished.

"Didn't you tell me that you have been collecting reports from others who have seen him?"

"Yeah, but I guess I had doubts about whether there was something to it." Eddie felt a little trapped, but tried to get Benjamin back on his track. "What other names is he known by?"

Benjamin shrugged his shoulders. I don't know them all, but many people from different faiths know him."

"For example?"

"Do you have a religious background?" Benjamin asked.

"I was raised Roman Catholic," Eddie quickly answered.

"Then your sacred scriptures speak of him," Benjamin said. Reading the surprise on Eddie's face, he continued: "He's known in the book of Genesis as the Nephilim. Your tradition differs a little from mine, but I believe it's the same. The Bible teaches that the Nephilim resulted from the union of mortal women and spiritual beings; or angels."

Eddie was stumped by that one. He wasn't terribly familiar with the Bible, and he had never heard of the word before. "Have you seen him? What does he look like?"

"I have not seen him," Benjamin said, shaking his head.

"So, how can you believe in something that you haven't seen?" Eddie asked. He was utterly perplexed.

Benjamin smiled again. "The same wise man I quoted earlier also said, 'the wind blows where it wishes. You hear the sound of it, but cannot tell where it comes from or where it is going.' You have never seen the wind, Eddie. But do you believe that there is a wind?"

"I believe that there is a wind because I see what it does. It bends the trees and blows things across my yard!"

"Exactly. You believe in it because you have seen what it does. I'm doing the same thing. If you think I am a fool, then you must consider yourself a fool, too. Because we are both accepting and believing things we can't see. You're not a bigot or a hypocrite, are you? That's like being swine; and they don't get the pearls."

Eddie was not sure what to say or think. Benjamin was not like anyone else he had ever interviewed. He was very philosophical, but in a simple, understandable kind of way.

"Where is he now? Can we go see him?" Eddie assumed that Benjamin's last question was rhetorical.

"We can look for him, but if he appears it's because he wants to appear. And if he appears, it's because he has something to share; something to say to us."

"If he means us no harm, then why have some of the people who saw him become so frightened of him?"

"Most people are trapped by their limited understanding of spiritual matters. They have taken a religion that has been handed to them and never asked of it any questions. They've never pressed it or challenged it. So, when confronted by something they've never encountered before, even if it is of spiritual origins, they become afraid. If they could learn to step beyond their spiritual confines, they would not be so frightened."

"You're saying we have no reason to be frightened of him?"

"Not of him. Perhaps the message he brings is frightening. But he is not."

Eddie considered this for a moment and then rose from the pew to extend his right hand. He had been hoping for a different kind of interview, but he was generally satisfied with what he had gleaned.

"Benjamin, thank you for taking the time to talk with me," he said. "I really need to get back to town. Can we talk again sometime?"

"Sure. I hold a Bible study here at the chapel on Wednesday evenings. Why don't you come next week at 6:30, join us for study, and then we can talk afterwards."

"You'll see me Wednesday at 6:30," Eddie said as he pumped Benjamin's hand.

////

Sandy was late getting to the church office after his visit with his father. He had composed himself the best that he could, but had still felt as though he looked pretty haggard. He was thankful that it was Beatrice's day off.

Sandy went directly to his office and closed the door. He fell into his office chair. It rolled backward on its casters until his head struck the corner of an oversized book sticking out from a bookcase behind him. He rubbed the back of his head. His head felt nothing like what was going on inside of his soul. He slid his chair closer to the desk, turning on his laptop. He saw that his hands were quivering.

A torrent of emotions swirled around inside of him like a vicious whirlpool. *I used to watch him preach from the pulpit and think that one day I wanted to be like him. He was the epitome of a Christian. He was brilliant, wise, and ... and ... and ...faithful! How could he do this to me? How could he turn his back on everything and everyone? I feel so ... betrayed.*

Sandy dropped his face into his open hands as he bent over the desk. He struggled to maintain his composure. The dagger that he felt sticking through his heart made this an impossible task.

Now he comes back into my life asking for forgiveness! Is he going to introduce me to this woman, as if she's my new mother? How could I ever forgive him after what he did to the family? He doesn't deserve forgiveness! He deserves to be in the same pain that he placed everyone else in. He deserves to hurt. I can get my revenge by withholding the forgiveness that he is now asking for. I'll make him feel the same pain that he made my mother and sister feel. I hate that man!

Sandy replayed his own thoughts. They repulsed him so much that he felt sick. His stomach tightened in knots, and he grabbed the garbage can as he almost began to heave in it. Returning the can beneath his desk, he leaned back in his chair and covered his face. *Here I am, the Pastor of Lycona Community Church, a preacher and teacher of righteousness, and I entertain thoughts of revenge and hatred!* As the realization of this thought sunk deeply into his mind, an overwhelming feeling of sick self-loathing began to emerge. *I am nothing but a pitiful excuse for a person. Maybe I am even worse than my own father! At least he left the church when he realized that his life was incompatible with what he preached. I, on the other hand, continue to be a fake ... a fraud ... a hypocrite.*

A knock at his office door startled Sandy. The last thing that he wanted right now was a visitor. He quickly took a tissue from a box on his desk and wiped his mouth and blew his nose. He then raked his fingers through his hair and straightened his shirt in a feeble effort to make himself more presentable.

"Come in," he said. His voice cracked. He had not spoken since the short visit with his father, and now his voice was hoarse from crying.

The door opened and Ellie leaned in, peering around the office door. Sandy's heart sank. *No, not Ellie; not now!*

"Wow, you look awful!" she said, not restraining her words with the reasonable bonds of decorum.

"Yeah, I'm not feeling very well today," Sandy muttered. At least he didn't lie. "Please, come in."

"Are you okay?" she asked tenderly. She entered the office.

"Yeah, I'm fine. Though, sometimes the pollen bothers me." Sandy scrambled for a plausible explanation as he took another tissue and blew his nose.

Ellie walked to his desk. She reached out with the back of her hand and felt Sandy's forehead. Then she moved her hand to each cheek. Sandy was startled by her forwardness. But when he felt her cool, soft touch, he silently wished that she would not stop. It felt like a soothing balm being poured out on a scathing wound. He savored the fleeting moments of the brief caress. Her touch brought relief, and he felt guilty for wishing she hadn't stopped by to visit.

"You don't feel like you're running a temperature," she said, pulling back her hand.

"I'll be fine," Sandy replied as he looked at Ellie and smiled. Even beneath the dull fluorescent bulbs of his office lights, her green eyes seemed to shimmer. He suddenly felt much calmer.

"What brings you in here today?" he asked, changing the subject from him to her. He then motioned for her to sit down on the small couch.

"Well, I wanted to talk with you some more about the camping trip," Ellie replied as she sat down across from his desk. "But if you're not well, we can talk later."

"No, not at all. This is fine." Sandy did not want her to leave.

"Well, I've given it a lot of thought, and I've been reading my Bible some more since we last talked," Ellie said. "I feel that God has really taken care of me and blessed me in so many ways. He gave me a wonderful aunt who loved me and provided for me, even though I rejected that care many times. I also see how God has protected me when I was in some very vulnerable positions. I feel like I need to start giving back. I know that there are people who think I should not be coming along, but I feel that I have a duty to start repaying God. Does that make sense to you?"

"Absolutely," Sandy replied as he fell into the role of a pastor again. "I was afraid that you were going to be too hurt by what happened at the meeting to consider going along. And if you had chosen

143

not to, I would probably have tried to persuade you with the very same argument that you came up with! I'm really glad, Ellie," Sandy beamed.

Ellie shrugged. "I figured that if God can overlook my past, then I need to do the same."

Sandy was overtaken by amazement; and guilt. Here was a woman who seemed new in her faith, yet she could do the great things of belief at which he, a trained clergyman, was failing.

"You told me something when we first talked," she continued. "You said that faith is doing the right thing even if it doesn't feel right; or something like that."

"That's right, Ellie," Sandy cleared his throat. "Feelings play an important part of our lives, but they can sometimes mislead us when it comes to matters of faith." A sharp, stinging sensation penetrated his heart.

"Well, when do we leave?" Ellie asked cheerfully, not understanding the convicting pain that the conversation was causing him.

"In one week. Do you still have the paper that I gave you with a list of what you'll need?"

"I have it right here," Ellie said as she pulled out a folded paper from her small purse. "I'm actually on my way to get a few things from the store that I'll be needing."

"Excellent!" Sandy exclaimed. "How about I call Jocelyn to pick you up on Sunday?"

"Sounds good!" she replied.

Sandy wished Ellie didn't have to leave his office. Though her presence challenged him, it also consoled and inspired him.

144

After Ellie left, he wheeled back in his chair to look out of the window. He strained his neck to watch Ellie walk down the sidewalk and out of sight. He was amazed at how he felt whenever he was with her. He brushed his hand on his cheek where she had touched him. He could smell the hint of her perfume. It was a fragrance he would always remember.

Sandy relaxed in his chair and thought about what he had told Ellie; that feelings should not get in the way of faith. Instead of feeling hypocritical over what he had said, he now considered his own words. The caustic anger that he had felt when he'd first arrived had subsided. They were just emotions. Sandy had let them champion his character and replace his faith. *Lord, forgive me for allowing my anger to control me. Give me the grace that I need to forgive.* Immediately, he felt a weight lifted from his shoulders. A peace came over him. *And thank You once again for sending Your grace to me through Ellie.*

The vibration of his cell phone interrupted his prayer. He glanced at the number. It was Harris Long. He had not heard from him since the night of the camping meeting and had nearly forgotten about their strange conversation. He suddenly realized that this was a call that he needed to take.

"Hey, Harris," Sandy said after touching the answer key on his cell phone.

"Hey, Sandy. How are you doing?" Harris replied.

"I'm doing fine, thanks. How are things up there at the campground? Any problems?"

"Well, that's why I called. No, I'm thankful to say that we haven't had any problems since the end of winter. Things seem to have quieted down around here. Whatever that thing is, I think it's gone."

/ / / /

Eddie squeezed his Pontiac into the last remaining space beside the chapel at Camp Atawanda. It was a beautiful evening in the mountains. Vivid greens surrounded the campground. The days were getting hot now, and even the evenings could be stuffy. Summer was finally here.

With difficulty, Eddie crawled out of his car. The small lot was filled to overflowing, and the cars were parked so closely that there was barely enough room to get in and out of vehicles. Eddie had arrived later than he had wanted. However, he had not been expecting a crowd this size to gather in such a remote location on a Wednesday evening.

He slipped through the chapel doors and into the small sanctuary. Seating was packed. Benjamin saw Eddie enter and flashed him a broad, whitened smile.

"Mr. Law, it's very good to see you tonight! Please have a seat and make yourself comfortable. I'm just going over some questions that were stirred by tonight's study."

Every head turned in Eddie's direction. His hopes of remaining an unseen observer had just been dashed. He slipped into an empty space in the back pew as quickly and quietly as he could. He was surprised to see so many faces from town. He even saw two in the pews wearing clergy collars.

146

Benjamin wasn't behind the pulpit as Eddie would have anticipated, but rather stood casually in front of the rows of pews. In his hand he held a thin book that looked to Eddie to be a Bible.

"Alright," Benjamin said, looking back to the congregation, whose collective eye was trained intently on him, "let me answer the question that was just asked: 'Where are the Gospel discrepancies?'"

Benjamin set down the Bible he had been holding.

"Does someone have a King James Version?" Benjamin asked. After a hand was raised, he asked, "please read from Matthew 24:36."

After the passage was read out loud, Benjamin asked someone to read the same passage from another version. Someone had a more modern version and read the verse.

"Did you notice the difference?" Benjamin asked.

A clergyman near Eddie raised his hand and replied, "the modern version records that Jesus doesn't know when He'll return. However, the King James Version doesn't include that part."

Benjamin flashed a satisfied smile. "Exactly," he said. "The newer version of the Bible is actually based on the oldest and best manuscripts. The *real* Jesus didn't know everything. Later, after the church started making up things about Him, they got real uncomfortable with the way the Gospels read. Therefore, they dropped the phrase about Jesus not knowing about His return. It better fit the doctrine of Jesus that they wanted. After discovering the older manuscripts, we are finally getting a glimpse of the *real* Jesus."

Eddie saw a number of heads nodding in agreement. Others were pouring over notebooks that were already filled with notes. Each

147

answer he gave stirred more questions. Eddie was impressed with his responses. They were unorthodox, yet sounded reasonable.

The study lasted well into the night. Eddie had come hoping to talk with Benjamin about the Creature. But after the gathering had concluded, the people milled about to talk with him. Eventually, Eddie had to leave. Although he was disappointed in not being able to talk in depth with Benjamin, there was something he liked about the controversial teaching that he had just heard.

Chapter Fourteen

Cliff couldn't shake himself free from his wonderings. He was now convinced that whatever he had seen at Muddy Creek was the same Creature that Hank Deal and Mrs. Brackenridge had also seen. *But what was it?* He was dumbfounded. *Was there some new animal prowling around the mountains? Or, as Mrs. Brackenridge claimed, was it the devil himself?*

These questions plagued him, and he had no answers.

"Sheriff, I need to run something by you," Cliff said as he pushed open the Department door. He was halfway through his shift and had returned to the department office to file a report.

Bragg was crouched at a metal filing cabinet. He was leafing through a drawer stuffed with files. As he pulled one free, it cut him beneath his thumbnail. He reacted by jerking his arm back and striking a nearby chair with his elbow. It seemed to Cliff that Bragg grew clumsier by the day.

Bragg cursed and pushed his thumb into his mouth while he massaged his elbow. The sight of the Sheriff sucking his thumb amused Cliff, and he let out a chuckle. That was a mistake.

Bragg grunted as he struggled to raise his aging, overweight frame from its crouched position. He turned to face Cliff with a deep scowl. Bragg's mood could easily be swayed by minor things like paper cuts. When this happened, it was best to tread lightly.

"What is it?" Bragg growled after he pulled the injured digit from his mouth. He tried looking at his thumb, but his eyes wouldn't focus. In search of his eyeglasses, he patted himself down and cursed again

149

when he failed to locate them. Not only was he getting clumsy, but he was also becoming forgetful. He made his way back to his desk. Cliff followed at a safe distance.

"Do you remember last week when I responded to a call at Hank Deal's place, and I told you that he had reported seeing something standing about nine feet tall?" Cliff began as they both entered Bragg's cramped office.

"Yeah," Bragg muttered as he retrieved his reading glasses from his desk and put them on to inspect his wound.

"Well, the other night I responded to a call out in Stanton. A woman there reported seeing something on her front porch. It sounded a lot like what Hank Deal saw. I think there's some kind of strange animal walking around."

Bragg peered at Cliff over the top of his glasses. "Exactly what kind of animal do you think this is?" His tone wasn't welcoming.

"I don't know, but now two people have reported seeing it in very close proximity; and both were pretty frightened by it."

"Like I told you before, it was probably a bear," Bragg said, his voice dripping with impatience. "They live around here, you know."

"Yeah, I know. But about two weeks ago, Carly and I were camping at Muddy Creek, and I saw something, too. It was very strange. And it *wasn't* a bear."

"What was it?" Bragg asked, falling into his chair.

"I couldn't tell. It was on two feet, stood pretty tall, and had a bad odor."

"Sounds like someone is fooling with you, Janowski. A couple of months ago I responded to a call up at Camp Atawanda. A few clowns were working on a cabin up there when they claimed that something started throwing rocks and screaming at them. I looked around, but I didn't find anything. As it turns out, a couple of those fellows had been picked up for shoplifting or vagrancy; I think they were just trying to scare everyone else."

Bragg forced a chuckle. Cliff knew it wasn't because he thought anything was funny. Rather, he laughed because his thumb hurt, and he was annoyed with Cliff.

"And," Bragg continued, "what do you think we should do about this? We don't have the manpower to be going on a ghost hunt through thousands of acres of forest. If something else comes up, we'll handle it."

Cliff decided it was time to let the subject drop. These days Bragg was becoming too easily agitated and angry. Too many years of seeing the worst of people were catching up to him.

As Bragg busied himself, Cliff remembered the topographical map. He retrieved it once more and found Hank Deal's farm and the Muddy Creek campsite. Then he added a third coordinate: the Brackenridge house in the village of Stanton. These three points formed an uneven triangle. He printed a copy, outlined the triangle, and tucked it into his pocket. When he returned to his patrol, his plan had already begun to formulate.

Back on the road, Cliff called Carly. She was working the second shift and would still be at home. Cliff was just ending a four-day work week, which left him with three days off. He and Carly's rotating shifts often made it hard to spend time together. Therefore, what he was about to ask could get a little tricky.

"Hey, honey," he said as she answered. "I didn't get you out of bed, did I?"

"No, I've been up for a little while now. What's going on?" Cliff didn't often call Carly during the day. He noted the surprise in her voice.

"I'd like to do something," he started. "But first a question: what would I have to do to make it up to you if I took the next three days off to do some backpacking?" Cliff asked, holding his breath.

"Aww, Cliff!" her tone was not promising. "You mean you want to spend your time off without me? Why? What's with the sudden hike?"

Cliff felt that it wasn't a good idea to tell her that he really wanted to go look for a mysterious monster.

"I just want to do some exploring, that's all. Just name your price, baby. I'm good for it, you know that!"

Cliff sounded as light-hearted as he could. He knew, however, that fooling Carly would be next to impossible. She read him like a book.

"In four weeks we have the same weekend off," she began. "There is a little bed and breakfast near the outlet mall in Waterford. We go all weekend, we shop all weekend. and you make all the arrangements."

Cliff swallowed hard. He would rather have had her ask that he fly her to the moon. "Okay," he muttered.

They talked for a few more minutes. Cliff noticed that Carly's voice sounded happier; despite the fact that the luster in his own had vanished.

Cliff then called Game Warden Flint's office. When he was patched through to the Warden, he asked if there had been any recent rogue bear or unusual animal sightings. Flint could only recall the report from Sanctuary Rock from last November.

At the next stop light, Cliff pulled the map from his pocket. He found Sanctuary Rock located on the private property of Camp Atawanda. That was the place Bragg had talked about. Sanctuary Rock was near the center of the triangle he had drawn. The light turned green, and he continued driving.

After getting the number from dispatch, Cliff called Camp Atawanda. As he dialed their number, his phone battery light began to blink. He fumbled through the glove box for the car charger and plugged it in just as the phone was answered. He made a mental note to replace the battery with a new one.

The camp's secretary took Cliff's call. He introduced himself and asked permission to backpack onto their property. He explained that he hoped to hike to Sanctuary Rock, spend the night in the area, and hike out the following day. He was warmly welcomed, but was asked to make no fires on their property.

Cliff next scrolled through the list of his contacts and dialed Mason Carter. While he waited for the phone to ring, he pulled his patrol car over and backed into a concealed vantage point where he monitored traffic speeds.

"Mase! How's it going, buddy?" Cliff said excitedly.

"Hey, Cliff, it's going good. What's up with you?"

"Want to get away for a couple of days to the woods? I've got three days off, and I'm going to do a little hiking. Can you free yourself?"

Cliff and Mason were close friends. They had done some extensive hiking together before they each had married. However, when Mason had begun raising a family, much of his focus had been turned toward his electronic repair business. Their outdoor trips had become fewer.

"Aww, come on, Cliff! You know that I can't just take off anymore! My wife would kill me if I left on such short notice. Plus, there's no one to watch the shop.

"Well then, I've got a little project for you, old buddy," Cliff replied with a coaxing smile that Mason couldn't see.

////

The cell phone on Sandy's desk rang. It startled him to see Ardelle's home phone number on the screen.

"This is Pastor Sandy," he said as he answered.

"Hi, Pastor. This is Caroline," the young voice chirped.

"Caroline! How are you doing?"

"I'm doing okay, thanks," she replied. "Everything is still kind of strange, though. Some days I feel pretty good, but sometimes I really,

really struggle. You never know how much you miss someone until they aren't there."

Sandy was impressed with how easily Caroline opened up about herself. She was so unlike her sister.

"That makes sense to me," Sandy replied. "I'm really looking forward to having you at camp next week. It will probably be a very good distraction for you."

"Well, that's why I called. I'm afraid that I can't go this year."

"What?" Sandy exclaimed. "You love Camp Atawanda! Why can't you go?"

"I know. This wasn't an easy decision. After Aunt Dell's accident, I had to get a car. I used the insurance money for that, but now I need money for gas and insurance. That's why I got a job waitressing at the Timber Creek Cafe. I just started and I don't want to ask for time off right away."

Sandy was disappointed. He knew Caroline really enjoyed camp, and he suspected she really needed to get away. He also knew one of the reasons Ellie had agreed to go to camp was because of Caroline.

"It's disappointing, but I understand," he replied. "Ellie just told me that she is coming. I hope this doesn't change her plans, too."

"I don't think so," Caroline said. "I'm not the *only* reason she's going this year."

Sandy sensed a teasing smile in her voice.

////

Carly was already at work when Cliff got home. He immediately began packing for his trip. The thrill-seeker in Cliff was revving up. A keen sense of adventure was coursing through his veins, giving him a natural high. Although he had hoped Mason could go, it didn't bother him to hike solo. He had always felt at home in the woods.

So Carly wouldn't notice, Cliff buried his service weapon, holster, and several loaded magazines of ammunition deep in his backpack. His encounter at Muddy Creek had unnerved him. This time he vowed he would be prepared.

Carly was still in bed as Cliff left early the next morning. His plan was to spend the first night at Muddy Creek, and then hike the next day to Sanctuary Rock. He would spend the second night there, hike back to his vehicle, and possibly visit the bluffs behind Deal's farm.

After stopping for gas and coffee, Cliff made his way out of Lycona. Just out of town, he came upon a stalled vehicle partially blocking the roadway. He stopped to talk with the driver, and then set out some traffic cones that he kept in his Blazer. Cliff called for a tow truck. His coffee was still hot when Jack "Hubcap" Harcom pulled up in his flatbed.

"You're lookin' like you're off-duty today!" Hubcap hollered as he climbed out of the cab. His smile was checkered by the results of poor dental care.

"Yep. Off for a few days of hiking," Cliff replied.

"There's some weather movin' in on ya," Hubcap warned as he walked past Cliff to the stalled car.

Cliff froze. There it was. The smell. The same odor he had detected at Muddy Creek. The same stench that he'd smelled at the Brackenridge house. It was faint. Very faint. But its scent was unmistakable.

Cliff followed Hubcap, who had crouched behind the disabled car. Cliff drew in a breath.

"Hubcap, what's that smell?" Cliff asked.

"What smell?"

"You. I smell something on you."

Hubcap stood up with a puzzled look and then sniffed his jacket sleeve. His face flashed with embarrassment as he silently mouthed a curse word.

"I thought it was gone. I guess I'm so used to it that I can't smell it any longer," he offered apologetically.

"What *is* it?" Cliff asked.

"Have no idea," Hubcap offered. "Remember when that councilwoman was killed? Well, I had to get her vehicle up over that bank. The whole place reeked. Her car stank, too. My wife made me get undressed before she'd let me in the house! I have no idea what it was, but it was bad."

When the disabled car was finally moved, Cliff continued on his way. The turn of events probed him. *Is it possible that this beast is somehow involved in the wreck and death of Ardelle Bingham? What kind of animal is this? Did it get in her car?* That last thought frightened him. He needed to follow up on this when he returned to work.

Muddy Creek Trail was situated at the farthermost point of the triangle on Cliff's map. It was found in a section of Pine Forest, which was part of the larger Lycona National Forest system. Upon arrival, Cliff registered his visit with the park office and parked his Blazer in the trailhead lot. Within minutes of arriving, he was on the trail.

It was a pleasant day to be hiking despite the foreboding rain clouds that threatened from above. Cliff's spirit, however, would not be dampened. He was being fueled by adventure and a sense of danger. It was exhilarating.

Soon the rain began. Cliff donned his rain gear and walked the remainder of the day through a steady drizzle. Just before dinnertime, he reached the Muddy Creek camping area.

There was no one else present when Cliff arrived; which didn't surprise him. Although the trail was popular, the campsites were quite primitive. They were attractive only to the more serious hiker.

Judging from the thin layer of ashes in the fire ring, Cliff surmised that only a few visitors had been at the site since his last visit. He set up his tent on the same tenting platform as before. The rain eventually subsided, giving him a chance to build a fire and dry out.

After making camp, Cliff scouted the area. He found the large black oak where he had last seen the Creature hiding. Not only was there no evidence from that night, the new growth of underbrush and ferns had completely covered the forest floor. The scene looked remarkably different.

After returning to his camp site, Cliff replenished his water from a spring and cooked dinner. When dusk fell, he withdrew from his backpack the project that he'd given Mason. It was an electronic, trip-wire system that Mason had designed when they'd backpacked sections of Nunavut Park in Canada.

Polar bears had been a constant threat during that arctic trip. Erecting the alarm system had become an essential part of their nightly routine. The system consisted of small nylon poles that Cliff staked in a circle around his campsite. From a small spool, he extended a double strand of wire around the poles and back to his tent. Just as it was beginning to rain again, Cliff attached the wires to a separate control unit. He connected that to a six-volt lantern battery. He had asked Mason to alter the system by removing the loud siren and replacing it with a small electric motor. If the wire was tripped during the night, the little motor would begin to run. The running created a whirring sound and a vibrating motion. Cliff also set out his semiautomatic sidearm. The presence of the gun gave him a tremendous feeling of security; one that he didn't have the last time he'd camped at Muddy Creek.

Cliff listened to the rainfall from inside his tent. He would have preferred to sleep in the open, but the weather was not cooperating. He sent a text message to Carly letting her know that he was doing fine and that he missed her. A few minutes later, she replied. After checking the weather report from his phone, he turned it off.

Cliff lay listening to the forest around him. The patter of a million raindrops was the only sound he could hear. Its inviting, repetitious noise soon made him drowsy. He pulled the alarm closer and set his service weapon next to his pillow. Sleep came upon him quickly.

////

"Can you connect me to room 104, please?"

The only response was the clicking of the front desk switchboard. Sandy sucked in a long breath. His short visit with Ellie had transformed his attitude and thinking. Her strength and character amazed him. The ease with which she could forgive someone she barely knew was inspiring. *How much easier*, he thought to himself, *should I forgive someone whom I love! Thank You, Lord for speaking to me through her.*

His prayer was interrupted by an unfamiliar female voice. Sandy paused. *Why would a woman be answering my father's motel phone?* He felt the blood drain from his face. *Oh no! This is her! This is the woman my father ran off with!*

"Hello?" the woman asked again. She sounded very young to Sandy, and he could detect the slight strain of a foreign accent.

I'm not prepared for this. I can't face her; not yet! Breathlessly, Sandy held the phone to his ear. He wished that Ellie was with him; sitting beside him. He remembered her delicate touch across his cheek, and he longed for it once again.

"Hello?" The woman repeated. "Are you calling for Mr. Kelly?"

Sandy could not reply. He was handicapped by too many thoughts. The line clicked as the woman hung up the phone.

////

Cliff awoke to a rousing chorus of birds. He could feel the sunlight as it was already filtering through the trees, drying the ground from the previous night's rain. He looked at his watch. It was already after eight in the morning. He laughed for falling so completely and soundly asleep when he had intended on keeping a vigilant watch. He glanced at the alarm control unit. The green light glowed softly. The system had not been tripped.

After breakfast, Cliff gathered the wires around his campsite and packed his belongings. The bright sunshine promised a lovely day of hiking. He felt lighthearted. At the moment, it didn't matter if he found anything at all. He was simply glad to be out in the woods.

After putting on his sturdy pack, he examined the map. Today's hike would eventually take him off the well-worn trail and through some dense forest. His GPS would then lead him to Sanctuary Rock.

The hiking became more difficult as he moved along the trail. The few descents that he encountered were quickly engulfed by longer and more difficult climbs. Slowly, he was gaining altitude. The climb, however, did not bother him. He was ably fit and superbly ready to accept the challenges of the steep hills. Small critters of the forest often crossed his path, giving him reason to pause and savor the walk. He had to remind himself not to forget the reason why he was making the trip.

It was around noontime when he intersected a logging road. He decided to stop at the juncture and have lunch. He checked his voice mail and the weather report. He sent a text message to Carly. She soon replied, and while he ate they chatted in short electronic bursts.

When he resumed his hike, he left the marked trail and began to follow the logging road. He had never hiked this section before, and he didn't know how the terrain would be. It was easy at first. The road was wide and easy to follow. However, it soon began to narrow. Eventually, the road faded and he was in the woods. He now had to rely solely on his GPS.

Movement became much slower as he pushed through the unmarked woods. He found no evidence that anyone had previously walked this section.

Eventually, Cliff began to feel fatigued as he cut his way through the woods. He had to stop and rest much more frequently. It was during one of these breaks that Cliff began to experience a strange sensation. He was starting to get jumpy. He also found himself constantly scanning the forest. Soon, a strange feeling of anxiety began to wash over him. It was something that he had only felt once before; when he had his encounter with the Creature. He first attributed the anxiety to walking alone through unfamiliar territory. However, exploring new areas was something that he often did; and enjoyed. This was different.

By the end of the afternoon, he had finally reached the foot of Sanctuary Rock. The uneasiness that he was feeling was building to a crescendo. Cliff could not shake the feeling that he was being watched. He had not seen or heard anything that gave him that impression. However, he couldn't dismiss the sensation. His "gut" had warned him of dangerous situations while on patrol, and he had learned to follow it. He knew it was rarely wrong.

Sanctuary Rock was a knobby, rotund hill. Its seclusion and peacefulness made it feel like a sanctuary. It offered an outstanding, unbroken view of the area. To enjoy that view, however, required a difficult climb.

Cliff circled the small hill until he found the best passage to the top. Before climbing, he paused to eat something and regain his composure. This, however, was difficult. The strange feeling of anxiety was not easy to govern.

At the top, Cliff discovered a small, level clearing with a newly-built log cabin tucked near the forest's edge. The sight of the cabin made him feel slightly connected to normalcy. It brought a touch of relief.

He inspected the cabin and found it locked. It appeared to be a simple, four-bedroom structure with a kitchen and open living room. To the left of the cabin, he discovered a small dirt road that led down the hill and presumably toward Camp Atawanda.

Cliff made camp in the open field. The weather was clear, so he decided to sleep on a ground tarp in place of his tent. He fixed his dinner and rested from his long hike. He calculated that he had walked roughly fifteen miles. His feet felt heavy. There was also an ache in his neck and shoulders. At first, he assumed it was from carrying the heavy pack all day. However, he wondered if it wasn't from the tension that he had been feeling. He popped some pain medication and stretched his legs to rest. He found it almost impossible to relax for the continued sense of paranoia he felt.

As it was beginning to get dark, Cliff began stringing the trip-wire system. Driven by a sense of uneasiness, he decided to double the size of the perimeter. He kept the wire off of the ground by two and a half feet, so no small animal would startle him by tripping it. Once installed, he tested the system several times to make certain it was operating. He then retrieved his cell phone and tried sending a text message to Carly. He had hoped for some conversation. However, the reception was very poor. It was difficult to tell if the message reached her. He kept his phone turned on, waiting to see if she would respond.

When the sun set, his anxiety spiked. He yearned for a fire, but Camp Atawanda had requested that he not make one in the open. For the first time in his life, he regretted coming to the woods alone.

Eventually, Cliff crawled into his sleeping bag. He withdrew his sidearm and placed it in a ready position near his small pillow. He was strangely cheered to hear some coyotes howling on a distant mountaintop; at least he did not feel so alone.

Eventually, Cliff dozed in a fitful sleep. His odd dreams continually jolted him awake. He would then reassure himself by checking the glowing green light of the alarm and by feeling the cold steel of his gun next to him. As he drifted off to sleep the disruptive cycle continued to plague him.

Cliff dreamt that he was on duty and responding to a robbery. He had his service weapon drawn and was approaching the front door of a bank. He was about to burst through the front doors when he felt his cell phone vibrating. He feared that the buzzing would reveal his position to the perpetrators. He tried covering it with his hand. The pulsing vibration only got louder. In his dream, he withdrew the phone and tried to turn it off, but the power button wouldn't work. He

164

removed the back cover and tried prying the battery out, but his fingers seemed too large to conduct fine manipulation. He became frantic. He tried smothering the phone in his hands and even stomping on it. Nothing would stop the phone. Fear and panic rose up inside of him as he tried to leave his phone and run from it. His feet wouldn't move.

Cliff suddenly jolted from his dream. He was covered in sweat and panting loudly. Then, to his horror, he realized that something was indeed vibrating. It was the alarm system. The wire had been tripped!

////

It had been as if an anvil was strapped to his back. Owen Kelly had walked from Sandy's front porch to the car in the driveway still shouldering his burden. He had known the meeting with his son would be difficult. However, he had never expected it to go that badly.

Owen had backed his car from the driveway and pulled away from the house. A weakened hand had run across his partially balding scalp. He had sighed heavily through his nose and put on his sunglasses. Owen had felt surprised that he'd not cried. Oddly, he had felt at peace.

Owen had then returned to the hotel. As he had pushed open the glass doors leading into the hotel lobby, the manager behind the desk had looked up. He was a thin gentleman of middle-eastern descent who had very kind eyes. He'd recognized Owen and had swallowed hard before calling out to him.

"Mr. Kelly?"

"Yes?" Owen had replied as he'd redirected his steps to the front desk.

"Excuse me, but there seems to be a problem," the manager had said with a thick accent. "When you checked in last night my clerk made an imprint of your card. We received a call today from our credit agency indicating that your card has been reported lost or stolen. I'm very sorry, but we cannot accept it."

Owen had pulled out his wallet. He'd guessed what had happened; his wife had closed the account. This would be a great inconvenience to him, but he'd felt no anger.

"I'm afraid that I don't have another credit card," Owen had replied. "Can you tell me how much my bill is going to be?"

The manager had nodded thoughtfully and stepped behind his computer. He had tapped a few keys and given Owen the amount.

Owen had slowly run his hand down over his face while he'd thought. He hadn't enough money to stay for another night and then fill his car with gasoline for the drive out of town.

"What time is check out?" he'd asked.

"Eleven o'clock."

"Okay, let me pack my things and I'll pay cash for my stay. I'm very sorry if this has been an inconvenience to you."

The manager had smiled and shook his head. Owen had walked down the hall and entered his room. He'd sighed heavily as the door had closed behind him.

He had packed his things in a worn, black duffle bag that he had bought at a thrift store, and then he'd sat down at the desk. His tattered

Bible had lay beside the phone where he had left it earlier this morning. He'd opened it to the fifty-first Psalm and had begun to read. Occasionally, he had looked up at the phone; as if by staring at it he could get Sandy to call. The phone had remained silent in its cradle.

At eleven o'clock, Owen had slung his bag over his shoulder and had tucked his Bible under his arm. Reluctantly, he had walked to the front desk where he'd paid his bill. Minutes later, he had been driving toward the interstate highway.

Within moments, a young cleaning woman had pushed her cart to Owen's old room and opened the door with her master key. As she'd entered the room, the phone had rung. She had never answered a guest's phone before. However, Mr. Kelly had just checked out, and he'd seemed like a nice man. She had answered the call, but had heard only silence. After trying again, she had shrugged her shoulders and had hung up.

////

Cliff had been driven to a state of panic by his terrifying dream. Being awake, however, brought no relief. Instead, he was only catapulted from one nightmare to another. Only this one wasn't a dream.

He had been holding his breath in his sleep. When he sat up in his sleeping bag, he was gasping for breath. He jerked his head wildly around, scanning the tiny opening where he was camping. He tried to see what had tripped the alarm. But the night that had enveloped him was formidably deep, offering only the slightest glimmer of starlight by which to see. Each time that he turned to look in a direction, he felt a sudden fear that something unknown was creeping behind him. He would then swing frantically in the other direction. The fear was rising to an irrational level. The peculiar groans and grunts coming from his own throat startled him. Self-control was beginning to slip away.

Although he did not know if he was actually facing any danger yet, he knew that survival in any situation hinged on remaining calm. His training as a deputy eventually began to take over. He took several deep breaths, letting each one out very slowly. He realized the alarm was still running, and so he turned it off. In doing so, he discovered that his sidearm was already in his hand. He couldn't remember picking it up.

The night seemed exceptionally black. His eyes struggled to focus on anything. His ears strained to hear. The sheer quietness of the whole scene nearly overwhelmed him. The rhythmic pounding of his heart seemed to be the only thing breaking the silence.

With stealth, Cliff moved out of his sleeping bag and to his knees. With his gun following his gaze, he began to sweep in a circle around him. His eyes started adjusting better to the poor lighting that was available, and he could make out the tall trees that surrounded the opening. He then reached into one of the pockets of his backpack, which was beside his sleeping bag, to retrieve his headlamp.

The headlamp would not immediately dislodge itself from the pocket. He gently shook it until the snap of a twig to his right caught his attention. Cliff froze. He quickly moved his eyes in that direction. His right arm followed more slowly, bringing the weapon to the same bearing.

"I'm Deputy Janowski of the Lycona Sheriff's Department," Cliff called out. "I need to warn you that I am armed. Please identify yourself!" Cliff was surprised by how calm his voice sounded. It completely masked what he was feeling inside.

The only response that he received was more snapping, as if something was moving along the treeline. Cliff followed the noise it made with the barrel of his sidearm, straining to see the author of the sound. His left hand was still poised in the backpack when he remembered the headlamp. He redoubled his efforts to release it, but the strap had become snagged on something.

Suddenly, the most terrifying sound Cliff had ever heard erupted from the woods. It started as a rumbling growl, but quickly escalated to a high-pitched shriek that carried for what seemed an eternity to Cliff. He dropped the headlamp with his left hand and moved it to the handle of his weapon, pointing in the direction of the sound. He had never heard anything like this in all of his life. The sound was so loud that if he wasn't holding his gun, he would have clapped his hands over his ears. Cliff quickly brought his left leg out and planted his foot on the ground, keeping his right knee still bent beneath him. Both legs were quivering uncontrollably.

"Get out! Get away from here!" Cliff shouted as he fired a warning shot high into the trees.

The scream was so inhuman that Cliff was no longer treating the intruder as a person. He had chased bears from campsites by yelling at them. He didn't know what he was facing, but he prayed that the same tactic might work.

In response to the shot and Cliff's yelling, the scream erupted once more. Again, it began with a low growl and quickly grew in volume and intensity to a high pitched scream that lasted for nearly fifteen seconds. It was the most savage, feral thing Cliff had ever heard. He was completely shaken by it. He struggled to hold his gun steady, but saw the barrel of the sidearm tracing tiny circles in the cold, night air. He fired off two more rounds into the trees. *That's three rounds*, his trained mind counted as the muzzle of his weapon flashed brightly in the deep darkness. The two loaded magazines he had brought were still stowed in an outside pocket on the backpack, just out of reach.

The Creature screamed again; and if it were possible, Cliff thought it was even louder than before. He also heard something in the scream that he had not heard the first two times; anger. That caught him completely off guard. He had never heard such raw, hot, fierce fury come from an animal.

Cliff knew the anger was directed toward him. The volume of the scream told him that it came from an enormous set of lungs. Suddenly, he felt very small and insignificant.

There was movement again. A branch snapped, and then there was some rustling of leaves. Cliff followed the movement for a few feet with his gun barrel and fired off another warning arch above the trees. Then the forest became silent. Another noise sounded to Cliff's right. He spun his body and weapon in that direction, noting that the Creature had been able to move about twenty yards without making a sound. His sidearm barked again. *Five rounds.* The forest was quiet again. The crack of a branch turned Cliff even farther to his right. Bang! *Six rounds.* He was being circled by the great Beast, who could pass almost noiselessly through the woods.

"Go on! Get out of here!" Cliff warned, aware that he sounded pathetic. Just as the words passed by his lips he was hit by an overwhelming odor. Instantly, the smell took him back to Muddy Creek. There was no doubt in his mind that he was dealing with the same thing as that night.

A grunt. Cliff followed the noise with his pistol, his finger tensing on the trigger. Silence. Then another movement to the left of the last sound. Cliff moved his weapon. *Don't shoot until you see a target.* Silence again. He waited, not knowing if the Beast was standing still or moving.

Cliff was kneeling in the soft dirt with gun raised, searching for a target. He listened but could not hear a sound. His heart was pounding wildly as he fought to remain in control of his senses. Then, as quickly as his mind could register it, Cliff heard—no, he *felt* the swift pounding across the open ground behind him. Even as he began spinning around he knew that the Creature had circled undetected and was bolting across the tiny opening in his direction. He turned to see a darkened, massive form almost completely on top of him. He squeezed off a round from his gun as the Creature was already beside him. Something hard and heavy glanced off his left shoulder throwing him violently from his knees. A black blur, barely distinguishable from the night itself, passed by him so fast that he couldn't track it. It was so close, however, that Cliff felt heat from its body. The putrid odor of rotting flesh filled his nostrils.

171

The blow to Cliff's shoulder had sent him spinning wildly. He felt the gun sail from his hand as he fell backward. His shoulders collided with the ground causing his head to snap back and strike the hardened dirt like a hammer. The Beast bellowed. Another long, frightful scream. Far off in the distance, Cliff thought he heard a similar scream in reply.

The adrenaline pumping through his system kept Cliff from feeling any pain. He tried to move, but his body would not obey his mental commands. As he lay on his back looking at the night sky, the tiny stars above him began to swirl and dance. *I'm in trouble now,* he thought.

There were noises about him, but he could not react. The stars continued to spin. They began to dim. Cliff's world then went very dark.

Chapter Fifteen

Benjamin awoke with a start. He looked at the glowing, red numbers of the clock near his cot. It was just after three in the morning. The other men in the dorm-style bunkhouse were snoring peacefully. They were apparently unaware of what had stirred him. Benjamin swung his legs out from beneath the thin blankets and crept across the creaking wooden floor. As he slipped out of the front door, he grabbed his jacket from the coat tree.

The night air was cool. He pushed his hands in the pockets of his jacket and stood in the dark, looking and listening.

The door behind him creaked. Benjamin turned to see his blond-headed friend step out.

"Mitch," Benjamin whispered, "did I wake you?"

Mitch was a skinny, young man with buck teeth and a shuffling, defeated gait. He had quit school and run away from home two years ago, hoping that life on the road would be easier than with a drunk father. It was. Mitch was a good-hearted, talkative kid who needed to feel that he belonged. Harris had hoped to keep him on summer staff. However, funds were depleting quickly, and his future now seemed uncertain.

"I don't know, dude. *Something* woke me," he replied sleepily.

"It woke me, too."

"You mean it was *him*?" disbelief filled his voice. He suddenly seemed very awake.

"Yes," Benjamin replied as he looked back toward the dark. "He is restless tonight."

The shiver that ran through Mitch's body had nothing to do with the cold. "Why? What's going on?"

"I don't know," Benjamin said. "But something is happening. He's trying to tell us something."

Mitch studied Benjamin's face, ready to mirror its expression. He idolized Benjamin. The guys would be jealous tomorrow when they learned that he and Benjamin were out listening for the Creature together. This pleased him.

"What's he trying to say?"

"I'm not sure, but I think there's trouble."

Mitch's eyes widened.

////

The earliest rays of sunlight were just finding their way to earth as Cliff began to gain awareness of his surroundings. He shivered in the cold and tried to pull the sleeping bag to his shoulders. But there was no bag. It felt like he was recovering from a bad dream, one whose details were still beyond reach. A hangover-like headache made his head throb.

A cool breeze blew over his body, causing his eyes to flutter open. Strands of colored light were reaching their eerie hands across a large, empty sky. It was morning.

In pieces, memories of a crazed night began to seep back into his mind. Cliff tried lifting his head, but was rewarded with a stabbing pain

174

that shot down his neck and back. A powerful frontal headache then surged across his skull, and he felt nauseous. He let out a gasp and gently placed his head back on the ground.

Cliff's mind continued to replay the events of the preceding night. At first, it seemed as though they had happened to someone else. It felt like he was only hearing about them. His thoughts continued to merge into larger pools and began connecting with one another. He began to remember how he had been at the center of something frightfully traumatic.

Instead of trying to lift his head again, Cliff rolled to his left side and slowly raised himself to a seated position. He reached to the back of his head and felt a fleshy knot with his fingertips. He examined his hand, but found no blood. He glanced at his watch. It was just after five-thirty. He shivered again as a breeze passed through the tiny opening of Sanctuary Rock. He wrapped himself in a hug and vigorously rubbed his arms to get the circulation going.

Sitting even more erect, Cliff looked at his camp site. His sleeping bag was in place, but his backpack was not. He scanned the small field until a swab of green caught his attention near the treeline. His backpack had been moved. This was evidence that it had not been a dream. He felt a cascade of fear ripple down his body. He quickly scanned the treeline. He saw nothing.

As Cliff crawled to his feet, he instinctively reached to his hip for his sidearm. He then recalled that the gun had fallen from his hand. He peered around and saw the steel piece just feet from where he had been lying. He picked it up, wiped it clean, and gripped it tightly in his right hand, his index finger hugging the trigger.

Cliff recalled getting a shot off at his attacker. When he found several shell casings near his feet, he was perplexed. He only remembered squeezing off one round. Entire pages of his memory seemed to have been ripped from their bindings.

Cliff began to search for signs of blood from his attacker. An immeasurable wave of relief swept over him when he found no evidence that any of the bullets had found their mark. A beast of its size and temperament would not have taken kindly to being wounded.

Cliff stumbled to his backpack. It was open and on its side. Its contents were partially spilled on the ground. He uprighted the backpack and gathered things together. He slung it over one shoulder and carried it to his campsite. He then grabbed his sleeping bag and dragged everything to the tiny cabin. Sitting down on the small front porch, he emptied the contents of the backpack. He attached his holster to his belt and replaced the spent magazine with a loaded one. An inventory of his belongings revealed that everything was accounted for.

Cliff unzipped an outside pocket on his backpack and retrieved some over-the-counter pain medication. Downing the maximum dosage, he chased it with water and put on a heavy sweater. He then leaned back against the cabin to gather his thoughts. That's when he felt it again: terror. Like a wave driven by wild winds, it struck his body. He felt it so forcefully that he dropped his head and curled his legs to his chest. His heart hammered wildly. He tried to reach for his sidearm, but his hand was shaking so violently that even when he found the holster he could not immediately release the weapon. He felt as though he was unraveling inside. He had no control over himself. Wildly, he scanned the opening of the field. He saw nothing.

He withdrew his sidearm. His right arm was shaking so badly that he knew he could not use it effectively. Holding the pistol brought no comfort. In terror, he huddled near his backpack. He felt his chest getting tight, making it harder to breath. Then, as quickly as it had come, the fear began to subside. Normal sensations began replacing the out-of-control ones that had ravaged him. With the adrenaline in his veins beginning to wane, he was left feeling exhausted. He stretched out on the cabin porch and closed his eyes. Within seconds, he fell asleep.

When he awoke, Cliff checked his watch. He had slept for more than thirty minutes. He knew, however, that he couldn't stay where he was. He needed help. He retrieved some bagels from his backpack and spread on some peanut butter. Cliff felt the knot on the back of his head. It was still swollen. The pain medicine was beginning to kick in a bit, and the knot didn't feel as tender as it had been.

Clumsily, Cliff stood and walked to the outskirts of his camp. He began retrieving the trip wire and poles. Halfway around the circle, he found where the wire had been pulled from the nylon post. He examined the ground and found several large footprints. The previous day's rain had softened the soil, making the impressions quite clear. Cliff was stunned. The shape roughly resembled that of a bear's hind paw, but was *at least* twice the size of any bear print he had ever seen. He found no front paw print, suggesting that the Creature had been moving about on two legs. The size of the print warned him that this was the most massive living thing he had ever encountered.

It was still hard to shake the feeling that this was all just a dream. Everything seemed surreal. At times, Cliff felt that he was watching himself move at a distance. He felt disconnected from himself and his surroundings.

Returning to the cabin porch, Cliff finished packing his things. Sitting on the porch, he suddenly remembered his cell phone. He couldn't believe that he had not thought of it right away. *I'm definitely not thinking right,* Cliff told himself. He reached into his pocket and retrieved it. As soon as he began to dial, the battery icon began blinking. *No, the battery!* The phone went dead. Cliff thought back to when he'd used it last: he'd been trying to text Carly the night before. His heart sank. He couldn't remember turning the phone off. The cold night air had drained the already weakening battery. He would have to walk out of this.

Cliff studied his map. The road leading to the cabin had been recently built and wasn't on the map. Using his GPS and the paper map, he calculated that Camp Atawanda was about three nautical miles away. Although he didn't know if the road traveled directly to the camp, he felt that it would be his best chance of reaching help. The painful headache made him suspect that he had suffered a concussion.

Cliff loaded all of his things into his backpack and strapped it to his back. When he stood up to leave, he felt it again. A bolt of terror-filled anxiety struck him like a battering ram. He staggered to the ground. The added weight of the backpack seemed to crush him. Tears filled his eyes so that he could not see. His hands shook again so violently that he didn't even try to reach for his sidearm.

Then, as suddenly as it had come, the terror lifted. *What is happening to me?* He wondered. *I'm really losing it. I don't feel like I'm in control of myself anymore. It's like I'm a puppet on a string being pulled at will by someone else. This doesn't make any sense.*

He was tired from the emotional attack, so he remained on the ground for a few more minutes. Finally, he was able to gather himself. It took a tremendous amount of energy to pull himself to his knees while wearing the backpack. Using his trekking poles, he then pushed himself to his feet. He was sweating profusely in the cool morning air, and he shivered in the light breeze. This was going to be the longest few miles of his life.

Cliff turned toward the rocky road leading out of Sanctuary Rock and began to walk. He descended the road to the bottom, where it began to level off. By the time he reached the first ascent, he was beginning to feel ill. He slowed his pace and began to climb the small hill. When he reached the top, his stomach began churning wildly. He grabbed a small hemlock at the road's side and held tightly as the forest began to spin. He bent over and coughed twice before his stomach emptied on the ground before him.

Cliff stumbled forward again. His head was pounding like an African drum, while his stomach danced without rhythm to it. He knew that he had to press on. Carly wasn't expecting him home until tomorrow, and she wouldn't be overly concerned if he didn't make contact today. The last thing that he wanted was to spend another night alone in these woods.

Cliff got sick again at the bottom of the next hill. After the retching ceased, he pushed on. The road leveled off, so he kept walking slowly forward. When he reached the next ascent, he knew that he had to stop for a rest. With no comfortable place to sit, he dropped his backpack against a friendly maple. He sank gratefully onto it, allowing his body some rest. His eyes felt heavy, and though he struggled to stay awake, he couldn't resist the temptation to close them for just a moment.

/ / / /

Mitch fought the steering wheel on the big Suburban as he guided the craft along Cabin Road. The surface of the road, gutted by the recent spring rains, tested the springs of the old vehicle and the skills of its inexperienced driver. The vehicle slammed into a large pothole and then heaved upward like a breaching whale. Mitch glanced at Benjamin in the passenger seat, who reached out a hand to steady himself.

"Slow it down, Mitch, we don't have to hurry," Benjamin said. "I just want to have a look around."

Mitch eased his foot off the accelerator and slowed the craft down. Because Benjamin was looking around, he too glanced into the woods that surrounded them on both sides.

Their early morning meeting on the bunkhouse porch had lasted about twenty minutes. They had stood listening and talking before finally retiring. Mitch had tried to fall asleep, but had mostly lain awake, listening for the Creature to say something to him. When he finally had crawled down from his top bunk, Benjamin was already gone. He had caught up to him leaving Harris's office with the keys of the Suburban in his hand. Benjamin had wanted to make a quick run to the cabin to look around before breakfast. Mitch had nearly burst with pride when Benjamin had tossed him the keys and asked him to drive.

"Watch it!" Benjamin's warning reminded Mitch that he needed to be watching the road, not the woods. It was too late to avoid the kettle-sized hole in the road. Mitch's hat struck the ceiling of the vehicle during the upswing. After he recovered from the wave, he reached one hand to the brim of his cap and pulled it away from his eyes.

As the vehicle rounded the top of a small knoll, Mitch saw something ahead of them in the next dip. He glanced at Benjamin, who already was squinting with his dark eyes.

"What the...?" Mitch exclaimed.

"Slow down," Benjamin said. "It's someone sitting along the road."

////

The sound of the approaching vehicle woke Cliff. Through dazed eyes, he looked up to see a Suburban slowly approaching. As the vehicle coasted to a stop beside him, the driver cranked his window down.

"You okay, Mister?" he asked.

"No, I'm not," Cliff answered. "I fell and hit my head last night."

"Anyone with you?" the driver asked.

181

"No, I'm hiking by myself. I could sure use a lift."

"No problem. Climb on in," he said as he jumped out to give Cliff a hand. Then he caught sight of Cliff's holster.

"That thing loaded?" he asked, nodding toward Cliff's firearm.

"It's okay. I'm a deputy with the Lycona County Sheriff's Department."

There was no place for the Suburban to make a turn on the narrow road. Mitch drove to Sanctuary Rock, where he could wheel it around. Cliff glanced out of the window at the scene. A chill ran over his weakened body. Cliff felt his hands shaking slightly. He dropped his head and took a few short, gulping breaths. As the vehicle started descending Sanctuary Rock, Cliff opened his eyes again.

The ride to Camp Atawanda was not three miles, as Cliff had estimated, but nearly five. The road rolled over two very steep hills. Cliff knew that he never could have made it alone. Even riding in the rear of a vehicle made him feel weak and disoriented. The constant jarring kept him feeling on the edge of nausea. He focused his energy to not getting sick in the back seat.

Cliff glanced at the two men in the front seat. He didn't recognize either of them. The younger of the two, Mitch, as he had introduced himself, was talkative and tried to engage Cliff in conversation. His questions were probing, suggesting that he knew something extraordinary had happened. This made Cliff feel uneasy, so he remained aloof.

Near the end of the road was a steel gate with a heavy, combination padlock. Mitch got out to open it, while the passenger

182

remained in the front seat. He was older than Mitch, and possibly of Native American descent. He occasionally glanced back at Cliff, but made no conversation. For some reason, he made Cliff feel uneasy.

Within a few minutes, they reached Camp Atawanda. It was unanimous that Cliff needed to get to a hospital. He didn't want an ambulance called and was relieved when Mitch agreed to drive him to the emergency room. After a quick stop at the camp office, they were on their way.

In the Emergency Room, Cliff was finally able to use a phone. Carly had worked the night before and was still in bed. He left her a message. He also phoned Sheriff Bragg and left him a message.

Cliff was ushered to a bed. He was soon examined by a physician who seemed interested in Cliff's injuries; not any details. Cliff reported that he had fallen, but decided against discussing the attack with the doctor.

After some tests, Cliff was informed that he may have sustained a concussion, and that he would be admitted overnight for observation. He soon found himself in a sterile bed on a quiet wing of the hospital floor.

"How ya feeling?" Bragg asked as he stepped inside Cliff's hospital room. It was Sunday, and though Bragg wasn't scheduled to work, Cliff wasn't surprised to see him in full uniform. He had made this a professional visit.

"Head still hurts," Cliff said as Bragg positioned his large frame at the foot of his bed.

"What happened?"

Cliff decided it was time to talk. He had been attacked by a Creature that had approached several other people, and he now had reason to believe that it had had something to do with the death of Ardelle Bingham.

"Sheriff," Cliff started, "I think we have some kind of animal running around these mountains. I don't know what it is, but it attacked me last night while I was camping up at Sanctuary Rock."

"What kind of animal?" Bragg asked, his tone matter of fact.

"I don't know, but it's *big*; and it isn't a bear. I think it's the same thing that Hank Deal saw, and the same thing that the Stanton lady saw on her front porch. I also think it is the same thing that I saw once before. Those mountains will get busy with campers and hikers during the summer, and we may need to do something about it."

Bragg stroked his mustache while listening. "Okay," he said. "We can take a look into it."

"There's more," Cliff continued. "Whatever this animal is, I think it is somehow related to Ardelle Bingham's car crash."

Bragg stopped stroking his mustache. Instead, he folded his arms and furrowed his brow. "What do you mean?" he asked. His interest was clearly piqued.

"Everyone who has seen this thing has smelled a really bad smell," Cliff began his case. "I smelled it; Deal smelled it, and the lady in Stanton smelled it.

I ran into Hubcap Harcom two days ago, and I could smell the same smell on him," Cliff continued. "When I had asked him about it, he told me that Bingham's car smelled like it when he pulled it out from the woods. Whatever kind of *thing* this is, it was at her car. Based on the way it attacked me, I feel that it may have had something to do with her death."

"The coroner said she died of internal injuries sustained by blunt force," Bragg said sternly. "And he said the blunt force was consistent with a car accident."

"Yeah, but I just *know* that this thing that attacked me had something to do with it."

"Because you smelled something?" Bragg asked sarcastically.

Cliff paused for a moment, and then spat, "Yeah, because I 'smelled something!' Listen, I just want to take another look at that accident. I want to inspect her car. What's wrong with that?" He winced as the rise of emotions caused the back of his head to throb.

"Listen, Janowski," Bragg lowered his voice so that no one else would hear. "Bingham was a councilwoman. Her death rocked this town. And now you want to open old wounds and do some *monster* investigation about the way she died? News like that will go national, and our department will be the laughing stock of the world."

Cliff blinked his eyes in disbelief. He wasn't following the Sheriff's logic.

"But there's no harm in just looking ..."

Bragg interrupted: "I handled that investigation; it's over. She fell asleep at the wheel and crashed. There was nothing fishy about it, and I didn't *smell* anything. Leave it alone, Janowski."

"Sheriff, I just want to go over her car. It's probably still being held. There's no harm in that, is there?"

"Let it go, Deputy." Bragg unfolded his arms and placed them on the foot of Cliff's bed as he leaned his bulky frame forward. His eyes narrowed to two sharp squints.

"What's the problem, Sheriff? Why can't I just take a look?" Cliff persisted.

"Did you lose your hearing when you fell?" Bragg lowered his voice to a growl. "I said leave it alone. When the town hears that the Sheriff's Department is chasing some sort of monster through the woods, we'll lose our credibility and support. Do you understand that?"

Cliff had known Bragg would be skeptical, but he was shocked over this kind of resistance. He softened his voice and tried again. "Sheriff, I'm not second-guessing you. All that I'm suggesting is that this animal that attacked me had something to do with Bingham's accident, and I just want to check it out."

"Janowski, you either let this drop right now," Bragg paused for effect. "Or Mrs. Janowski and this town learn what happened in Clinton a few years back. Do you hear me?"

Bragg's last words reverberated from his chest like a pit bull's growl. His narrowed eyes had locked onto Cliff's like heat-seeking missiles. It only took a moment for his words to sink into Cliff's consciousness. Suddenly, his world began to collapse. His stomach began tightening like a knotted rope, and he felt himself becoming ill.

Bragg stared at him. His unblinking eyes now set ablaze. "I asked if you heard me, Janowski."

"Yes, sir," came the weak reply. "I hear you."

Chapter Sixteen

It was Sunday; camping day. The week had passed quickly for Sandy. He had not heard from his father, and Sandy had made no more attempts to reach him.

Preparations for camp had been completed. Sandy had breathed a sigh of relief when he'd received Ellie's clean background check. He had been harboring some concerns.

The group had had their final meeting on Wednesday night. Ellie had come with Jocelyn. Jocelyn had a solid reputation in the church. Seeing them together had seemed to improve Ellie's standing in everyone's eyes. Ardyth, however, had refused to acknowledge her.

With the exception of Ardyth's attitude, the meeting had gone well. Jocelyn had shared some ideas about new crafts. Sandy had been glad when she was talking. It had provided an opportunity to look at Ellie beside her. She'd been dressed comfortably in jeans and a light T-shirt. While Jocelyn had been speaking, Ellie had looked up at Sandy. They had smiled at each other. Ardyth had seen the smile and had tightened her lips.

Camp registration had begun on Sunday afternoon. A steady flow of excited children had arrived with parents and grandparents. They'd formed a line in front of Sandy and Ardyth, who had sat together at a picnic table beneath an ancient butternut tree. Sandy had checked names off a master list, while Ardyth had kept careful track of who had paid and who had not. It was over this latter group that Ardyth had made extra fuss. She'd sighed loudly and shifted papers, as if finding the third paper in a stack of five was difficult. She had checked her math three times before announcing rather loudly the amount that each camper still owed. With great difficulty, Sandy had maintained his composure. He was really beginning to dislike this woman.

////

Cliff lay on the hospital bed, staring at the ceiling. The knot at the back of his head couldn't compare to the emotional bruise he was nursing. Without warning, his world was suddenly imploding.

The incident at Sanctuary Rock, the mystery surrounding the Creature, the questions over the death of Ardelle Bingham; all of these had lost their significance. Pushed to the forefront of Cliff's mind was a matter that he thought that he had buried forever. He had so rarely thought of it that if it came to mind, he felt as though he was thinking of someone else.

Cliff was stunned that Bragg knew his secret. It had been carefully guarded. Cliff had never shared even a shred of information with anyone. However, if his experience as a policeman had taught him anything, it was that no crime, no sin, is ever completely hidden. Every person has a history, and every history leaves a trace.

Cliff's own history had left a blemish, and it had unexpectedly returned; with a vengeance. It had the power to destroy everything he loved; everything he cherished. It had the power to destroy him. Demons that he had once wrestled were back for another fight. He wasn't ready. Not here. Not now. Too much was going on. Too much was happening. He felt ill-prepared.

His thoughts were suddenly interrupted. As unprepared as he was to handle his past, he was just as unprepared to handle his present. Like a warm and gentle breeze which carried the promise of a brewing storm, Carly rushed into the room.

"I just woke up and got your voice mail!" she exclaimed as she moved quickly to his bedside. Though she'd only had a few hours of sleep, her eyes were wild with excitement. Her face was flushed with a deep look of concern.

As soon as he saw his wife, the great love Cliff felt for her surfaced. He felt startled by the feelings. They surprised him. He knew that he loved her, but it was overwhelming to actually come in contact with that love. To feel it. To *really* feel it.

The past few years were happy ones with Carly. She had been diagnosed with leukemia years ago, and he had almost lost her. She was so strong, and her faith was so deep. With these, she had overcome the disease. Her recovery was nothing short of miraculous. Since then, they both had lived life to the fullest, savoring the time they had together.

Cliff's eyes pooled with tears. He was not a man who cried, and he fought to keep the tears from spilling.

"Cliff? Are you okay? What happened?" Reacting to something she saw, Carly's face furrowed with concern.

Cliff struggled to maintain his composure. He couldn't let Carly know there was a struggle inside. She would try to find it. She would try to wrestle it free. She would try to heal it. However, Cliff felt she couldn't heal this. He steeled himself as she drew near.

Carly's eyes reacted with sympathetic tears as she bent down and wrapped her arms around him, laying her head against his chest.

"What's wrong, honey?" she asked in a soothing manner. "What happened?"

Cliff blinked hard and steadied his thoughts. "I fell backwards on my head while I was hiking."

It was all that he could say at the moment. He didn't have the strength to talk about the attack. He didn't have the energy to tell Carly that he hadn't been completely truthful about why he had gone into the woods. He certainly didn't have the resources to talk about a much deeper wound that he was now nursing.

Carly pulled away and searched Cliff with her thoughtful, brown eyes. He knew that she felt his pain. She was now searching for its source.

Fearing that she might penetrate him too deeply, Cliff dropped his own eyes to the bed sheet, now stained with sweat.

"Are you okay?" she asked with obvious worry.

"The doctor told me that I might have a concussion. He wants me to stay overnight. Just to keep an eye on me." Cliff heard the mumble in his own voice.

"Is there something else wrong?" she inquired. Her instincts had been alerted.

"No, baby. I'm just glad to see you." Cliff pulled her into a hug so that he could avoid her eyes.

Chapter Seventeen

Cliff had been discharged a day after his admission. With deliberate belligerence, he had badgered his doctor for permission to return to work. It was a hard fight, but he had won.

Carly was still working nights, so Mason had volunteered to give Cliff a ride home. Having been silenced by Bragg, Cliff had refused to talk; even to Mason. It wasn't that he didn't want to talk. He did. In fact, he needed to talk. But he couldn't. Too much was at stake. Too much was riding on his silence. He had to remain quiet to keep his life together. He had been attacked by a frightful, mysterious Creature. He now believed it was somehow connected to the death of Ardelle Bingham. But instead of being able to investigate, he was being blackmailed by his superior with a terrible secret that he thought he had buried. Talking about what had happened would result in flushing out the secret. If that secret came to light, so much of what he loved would come to an end. Cliff felt as though he was being forced into a prison with no hope of escape. Silence would become his cellmate.

Mason had given him a ride to the Muddy Creek trailhead, where Cliff had found his Blazer in the lot. He had returned home and unpacked his camping gear. Carly had slept most of the day because of her shift. Before it was time for her to get up for work, Cliff had lain down on the couch. The throb in his head had been replaced by a low-grade headache. He hadn't been lying down as much to rest as to avoid Carly. After she'd left, he had gotten back up and turned on the TV.

He'd soon discovered that television was not enough distraction to rob him of his anxiety.

Before Carly came home from work the next day, Cliff left for his first day back on the job. He was on the daylight shift and was hoping for a busy day. However, the daylight shift also meant that he would have to face Bragg. As he entered the office building, he met two deputies who were also coming to work. They walked in together. Bragg was at his desk. He glanced up from his work, and then back to his desk.

"Good morning, gentlemen," Bragg said. "Welcome back, Janowski."

"Thank you, sir." Cliff replied.

"Feeling better?" Bragg asked without looking up. There was no concern in his voice.

"Yes, sir," Cliff said. "Headache is gone now."

"I assume that you have a signed release to return to work."

"Yes, sir," Cliff said, handing him the document. "Got it right here."

Bragg was all about business. He went through his morning routine without acknowledging a hint of his last conversation with Cliff. However, Cliff noticed a steady gleam in Bragg's eye. He seemed confident. The shaking in his hands was gone. This both perplexed and bothered Cliff. He knew Bragg flourished when he felt he was in control. But why Bragg needed him to keep quiet about the strange Creature was not making any sense. It was remarkably odd how this information seemed to soothe Bragg's nerves.

////

Camping thrilled Sandy. He had many fond memories of church camp from his youth. Introducing it to others was something that he genuinely enjoyed. This year, he'd been especially excited about introducing it to Ellie.

Running a camp was busy work. It wasn't easy to keep so many excited children on task and out of mischief. They had planned well, though. Sandy's staff was experienced and knew how to handle the energy of so many children.

The weather couldn't have been better. The brilliant sunshine that welcomed each day reflected everyone's cheery attitude.

Ardyth quickly proved to be of no value. Her phlebitis "flared up" each morning after breakfast. She would then restrict her activities to the air-conditioned camp office. Sandy learned that Ardyth had been periodically leaving the grounds. Jocelyn saw her getting into one of the campground vehicles and being shuttled off by one of Harris's staff members. Sandy didn't care. Her absence only lightened the mood.

What became the most exciting for Sandy was the time he got to spend with Ellie. Though it was only moments here or there, he treasured each brief, magical interlude. Occasionally, they walked together from chapel service or sat with each other for meals in the mess hall. Once, after some nighttime games, Sandy got the opportunity to walk Ellie back to her cabin. She'd never seemed so happy. For the first time ever, Sandy saw her acting carefree and spontaneous. Ellie seemed to be stepping free of her former self and toward someone Sandy was finding even more beautiful.

////

Thursday afternoon's plans at camp promised to be exciting. Harris had provided a bus to drop everyone off at Sanctuary Rock. They began with a picnic near the cabin, and then played games in the open field. As darkness was settling, Sandy led some of the older kids on a hike. Plainly-marked trails provided easy going for the group. Ellie came along. They made a long loop and were returning to Sanctuary Rock. The moon was nearly full, and the sky was clear. They didn't even need their flashlights.

Ellie was walking with a young girl a few paces in front of Sandy. The girl bolted from Ellie as a newly-made friend called to her. Sandy took advantage of the opening and quickened his pace to reach her side.

"Are you enjoying yourself?" he asked.

"Very much," Ellie replied. "I'm having such a great time. I can see why camping meant so much to Aunt Dell."

"She'd be proud to know you're here."

"Oh, I think she knows," Ellie replied with a satisfied sigh.

Ellie's face was illuminated by the moon. Sandy saw her soft smile and relished the moment. He remembered when he had first spoken with Ellie after Ardelle's funeral: how her swollen eyes and blushed cheeks had concealed her natural beauty. Now, in the soft moonlight, her face was radiant. Sandy felt as though he had never seen a woman look so beautiful. He felt a strong desire to take her hand. He wanted to pull her close. He wanted to touch her. He wondered if her skin was as soft to touch as the pale light made it appear. Though he resisted these overt desires, he moved a bit closer to her as they strolled along the path.

They walked together, talking about nothing in particular. Sandy loved hearing Ellie's voice. Every syllable sounded like singing. His feet felt so light with each step that he thought he might tumble upward. *This must be what it feels like to be in love.*

Sandy could hear the children's voices off in the distance. They were playing in the field. However, for the moment, he began to feel disconnected from everything around him. It was as if his mind could only process one thing at a time. And that one thing had become Ellie's sweet voice. Sandy wasn't even sure he understood the words she was saying. He only heard her voice.

Suddenly, and without warning, Ellie slipped her hand into Sandy's as they walked together. This small act catapulted his world. His heart leaped and his mind ceased all communication with his body. He felt dizzy. He felt out of touch with reality. His mind couldn't even process her voice any longer. The only thing he felt was her soft, warm skin against his. Sandy had never *felt* like this before, and he loved it.

As they neared the opening at Sanctuary Rock, Sandy regained some of his composer. He turned and playfully said to Ellie, "Come on, let's go this way!"

He turned off the rutted path and climbed a steep, short bank. Ellie tried keeping up with him, but she wasn't able to hold his hand at the same time. Sandy felt her hand leave his, and for a moment he regretted the detour.

They climbed the bank and followed the treeline. A large rock protruded through the trees, offering a perfect vantage point over the field beneath them. Sandy climbed on top of the rock and patted a spot beside him for Ellie. Ellie smiled and sat down. Sandy could feel the warmth of her body in the cool night air. When she sat down, Sandy placed his hand over hers.

They sat on the rock together and watched the children playing below. Ellie motioned to the children and asked, "What's this game?"

"They call it Night Patrol," Sandy replied. "It's like playing tag; but at night!"

Sandy and Ellie watched as a counselor spotted a young boy and began a wild chase. He took off with the staff member on his heels and scurried around a large stump just beneath the feet of Sandy and Ellie. He disappeared into the woods. The same chaser spied another teenager, whose back was turned, and wheeled around to catch him.

Sandy withdrew his cell phone and snapped a picture of the scene below them. Then he turned to Ellie and motioned for her to lean toward him. She placed her head on his shoulder, and he squeezed off another picture.

"You really enjoy being up here, don't you?" Ellie said as Sandy tucked the phone in his pocket.

"Do you mean this rock?" Sandy joked.

"Yes, Sandy, I know how you just love rocks," she replied, rolling her eyes.

Sandy laughed and turned to catch Ellie's glance. Their eyes met. She didn't look away.

"I enjoy it very much," he said. "But mostly I enjoy it because you are here."

Without premeditation or plan, Sandy leaned toward Ellie and kissed her softly on the lips. He opened his eyes to see her looking longingly at him. They both smiled, and Ellie moved her face closer. Their lips met again. This time the connection lasted longer. When they pulled back, Sandy felt as though their gaze continued the kiss. Ellie's eyes shimmered, and she placed her head against Sandy's shoulder. Sandy wrapped his arms around her. It felt like a dream; one that he hoped would never be interrupted.

They both sat looking at the scene below them. A young girl darted from the treeline into the open field. She saw Jocelyn approaching her, so she began running toward the large stump. She drew near the stump and appeared to be planning on hiding behind it when suddenly she froze in her tracks.

Sandy and Ellie were watching the young girl. They saw her stop just ten feet from the stump and remain motionless. In the bright light of the moon, the young girl's face was plainly visible. The playful smile was suddenly replaced by a confused look. In a matter of moments, it gave way to a look of terror. Sandy suddenly felt a terrific sense of foreboding.

His eyes followed the girl's horror-stricken stare to the stump in front of her. To his absolute shock, the stump began to move. It happened slowly at first, but then the movements quickly accelerated. Sandy watched in disbelief as the large, darkened stump suddenly transformed right before his eyes. It wasn't a stump. It seemed to take the shape of a man. Sandy's mind quickly ran through possibilities. At first, he assumed that it was one of the counselors. However, the sheer magnitude of the figure made that unlikely.

When it fully unfurled itself, the figure stood at least eight feet tall. It was completely dark, making it difficult to note its characteristics. However, its muscular arms could be seen hanging to its knees. The waist was narrow, and the shoulders were exceedingly broad; like a football player in his pads. In the available light, Sandy could see and feel the incredible strength of the darkened figure before him.

The young girl did not–could not–move. Jocelyn had stopped behind her and froze like a statue. For a brief moment, everything on the open field came to a halt. Pandemonium then broke out. Terrified screams erupted. Children and staff members began running toward the cabin. Jocelyn seemed to find her feet. She cautiously approached the young girl, while keeping her eyes focused on the figure. When she reached the little girl, she took her by the hand. She pulled her away and they slowly walked backward. Finally, they both broke out into a run.

Sandy realized that he was now standing. Ellie had risen as well; she was gripping him tightly. Sandy's eyes remained fixed on the Creature that stood just fifteen feet away. He was mesmerized by it. He felt both terrified and enthralled. He saw its chest rising and falling with each massive breath. Steam seemed to rise from its body in the chilly night air.

After standing, the figure had remained motionless. Suddenly, almost violently, it wheeled its head around. Sandy felt the blood drain from his face and his knees grow weak as he found himself staring into the Creature's flaming red eyes. It had sensed their presence.

Time stood still for Sandy. He had no sense of anything around him, but could only take in the sight of the Creature. Sandy felt its eyes appraising him. He had a sense that the great Beast was trying to determine if Sandy and Ellie represented a threat.

As if the Creature sensed Sandy's thoughts, it reacted. It cocked its head as if in contemplation. It held it there for a moment. Suddenly, it opened its mouth in what first appeared to be a deep yawn. The silence, however, was shattered by a long and freakish scream that poured out like bats scattering from a cave. The hideous sound reverberated around the small clearing and echoed off the surrounding mountainside. Several campers clapped their hands over their ears. Sandy not only heard it, but *felt* its impact in his chest.

The Creature closed its mouth as the echoes continued to bounce off the distant hillsides. It then cast one more look at Sandy and Ellie, turned to its side, and took three causal steps into the waiting woods. Sandy heard terrific crashing as it forced itself through the underbrush. He followed the sound as it seemed to be walking in a straight line away from the clearing. The breaking of sticks and the crunching of leaves seemed to weaken in intensity, as if the Creature's sudden emotions were subsiding as it walked away. Then the sound altogether disappeared.

Sandy suddenly became aware again of Ellie's tight grip. He pulled her with him as he climbed down from the rock. They scurried across the opening toward the cabin where everyone was gathering. Sandy could feel Ellie looking at the treeline behind them as they ran.

Some of the children saw Sandy approaching and began running to meet him. Others began to cry. The little girl who had approached the Creature was sitting on the cabin porch, her arms wrapped around her knees. Jocelyn was huddled over her.

"What was that?" Ellie's question sounded more like a plea than anything else.

"I have no idea," Sandy quickly replied. "We just need to make sure everyone is here and get them inside the cabin as quickly as we can."

Ellie took his cue and began helping Sandy gather the children. This wasn't a difficult task since everyone was already closely herded together.

Sandy felt numb. It was though he was outside of his own body watching the activity. Without emotion, he listened to himself instruct the counselors to quickly gather all of the children. When they were accounted for, Sandy closed and locked the cabin door. The children, huddled in the center of the cabin, were in various stages of shock. Some were crying, some were just staring blankly. Ellie appeared calm, yet was visibly shaken. Sandy felt admiration. Her demeanor encouraged him to maintain a sense of order in an otherwise chaotic room.

"Okay," Sandy said with hands extended to hush the crowd. "We need to keep calm. Everything will be okay. I'm not sure what is going on here, but we'll soon find out." Looking at Ellie, Sandy asked, "What time is it?"

Ellie glanced at her watch. "Almost nine," she replied.

Sandy thought for a moment. The bus wasn't supposed to come back until nine-thirty. He withdrew his cell phone. He scrolled to

Harris's phone number and hit the send button. Holding the phone to his ear he heard a frustrating tone. Glancing at the reception bars on his phone, he saw the dimly lit words: *No Service.*

"Does anyone else have any service?" Sandy asked.

Phones began appearing. Many of the kids, who weren't supposed to be carrying them, pulled them out and began checking. No one could get a call out.

"Alright, no problem," Sandy hoped he sounded convincing. "We'll just have to wait right here until the bus arrives."

One of the young girls began to sob very loudly. This caused a chain reaction, and soon the collective crying began to intensify. Sandy quickly motioned to the counselors to move in and comfort the most frightened. They responded, but he could tell that even some of the adults were badly shaken.

Sandy then thought he heard an engine. He raised his hand to get everyone's attention, and soon a frightened hush enveloped the room. Sandy strained his ears as hard as he could. Several children held their breath.

"The bus is coming!" Sandy said, breaking the silence. Everyone let out a collective breath of relief.

The camp bus had returned earlier than anticipated. Sandy heard the gears grinding at the bottom of Sanctuary Rock as the driver downshifted. The engine began to whine as it climbed the steep ascent. Moments later, the headlights of the bus swept the front of the cabin as it wheeled into the clearing.

The sound of the bus made Sandy feel calmer. Fear's sting was still intact, but its poison was beginning to dilute.

When the bus stopped in the field, Sandy unlocked the cabin door and swung it open. The cool night air rushed in to meet the stale air created by terror. Sandy felt relief as he saw two camp employees step off the bus. Sandy knew one of them as Mitch.

"Everyone ready to go?" Mitch asked as Sandy stepped to the cabin porch.

"Yes, we are. Let's get out of here as soon as we can, please," Sandy replied.

"Is everything okay?" Mitch replied to the terseness in Sandy's voice.

"Not really," Sandy replied. "We've had a bit of a scare this evening."

"What happened?" Mitch asked as he dug a hand beneath his ball cap to scratch his scalp.

"I'm not really sure," Sandy said. "We were playing a game here in the field when we suddenly saw something."

"What did you see?" Mitch asked with a flash of interest.

"Not sure. We saw a ..." Sandy paused, realizing that he did not have a word to describe what he had seen. He started over. "We saw some type of animal or something in the field with us. It was incredibly huge. Kind of looked like a ... but," Sandy paused again. He just didn't have the words.

"But what?" Mitch asked, clearly excited for more information.

"I don't know," Sandy said, shaking his head. He didn't know how to finish his thought. "It doesn't matter. We need to get everyone back to camp as soon as we can. These kids are pretty scared. Can you move the bus closer to the cabin?"

Mitch nodded and jumped back onto the bus. He backed it close to the cabin door. After the bus was moved, Sandy and Mitch stood between the cabin and bus to form a barrier between the kids and woods. In single file, they moved out of the cabin and loaded onto the bus, filling the front seats first.

Ellie filed past Sandy with each of her hands on the shoulders of two young girls. Ellie's eyes met Sandy's for a brief moment. It seemed to Sandy that she was hoping to find an explanation in his gaze. He tried to exude confidence. Deep down inside, though, Sandy was frightened.

When everyone was on board, Sandy took another head count and confirmed that everyone was present. He bounded off the bus to lock the cabin. As soon as he stepped back on, he closed the door and nodded to Mitch, who lurched it forward.

Sandy stood while Mitch wheeled the bus around. Its headlamps swept the treeline. The prospect of having the headlights illuminate something in the woods was incredibly frightening to Sandy. Yet, it was impossible for him not to look.

Chapter Eighteen

It was exceedingly dark as the old school bus pulled into the Camp Atawanda parking lot. Its riders were quiet. The crying had subsided. Counselors wrapped their arms around as many children as they could gather. Many of the older campers sat holding hands. Heads were bowed. No one dared look outside into the dark.

Sandy remained standing near the front doors of the bus. He had been holding so tightly to the grab bar that his hand had become cramped. When the bus ground to a halt, he released his grip. As he watched his fingers slowly straighten out, he had a vision of the strange Creature slowly unfurling itself in the field below him. A shiver shook his whole frame.

Sandy didn't know what to do next. The bus had parked in front of the mess hall. An ice cream Sundae bar waited inside, but he doubted anyone wanted to eat. He felt the need to keep everyone moving; to keep everyone occupied.

"Let's all move into the mess hall," Sandy announced after turning toward the muted passengers.

Sandy was the last to enter the mess hall. The ice cream bar was laid out near the serving window, but no one had made a move toward it. Instead, everyone had taken a seat around the varnished dining tables. They seemed lost and were earnestly looking to Sandy for leadership.

Ardyth was waiting in the mess hall. It didn't take long for her to find out what had happened. She appeared furious.

Sandy held up both hands as if to gain silence and get everyone's attention. It was a needless act. No one was speaking a word.

"I'm not sure exactly what happened, but let's be thankful that everyone is here and that no one is hurt," Sandy began. He had not formulated a plan and had no idea what to do next. Having an encounter with a monster was not anything for which his seminary training had prepared him.

"I want to go home," a young teenage girl said softly from one of the tables near Sandy. The silence in the room allowed her voice to carry throughout the cafeteria.

"Yes, I want to leave, too!" another voice cried.

Suddenly, a rush of voices sang the same kind of chorus from all over the room. Demands to see their mothers were made. Requests to leave immediately were raised. The younger children, encouraged by the thought of seeing their parents, began to cry loudly. Counselors and aids moved in to comfort the children, but they were overwhelmed by the multitude of tears. Some of them looked at Sandy as if to say that they also wanted to leave.

As Sandy struggled to find something to say—something to do— the doors of the mess hall suddenly swung open. Mitch, the driver of the bus, walked in. He glanced in everyone's direction and then turned behind him as if introducing a guest. From out of the darkness stepped a tall man of Native American descent. Sandy had seen him around the campgrounds, but did not know him.

"My name is Benjamin," the tall stranger announced to everyone as he raised a hand to gain attention. His voice was confident, and his presence seemed soothing. Instantly, the room quieted. Everyone seemed anxious for someone to take control, and this stranger seemed to offer that hope.

"I understand that something happened out at Sanctuary Rock," he said in a matter-of-fact tone.

Sandy remembered Harris telling him about Benjamin and how he was helpful in calming the workers. Feeling hopeful, Sandy stepped aside to allow Benjamin the floor. But Benjamin had already wound around Sandy, assuming a position of leadership.

"You having nothing to be afraid of," Benjamin continued as he moved to the center of the room. He flashed a wide, easy smile that contrasted the mounting stress. He glanced around the room, making eye contact with as many children as he could.

"What you've seen will not harm you. He is our friend." Benjamin's voice was as placating as his smile.

Sandy saw that there was something about Benjamin's presence that stilled the crowd. His confidence and words seemed to bring a sense of normalcy.

"What was it?" came a question from one of the counselors.

"His name is Chiye-tanka," Benjamin replied, looking first at the counselor who posed the question and then to his audience as a whole. "He is what we Native Americans call our 'older brother.' He wishes no one any harm and is always on a mission of peace. You can consider yourself very fortunate to have met him tonight, as he does not often seek us out."

Having a name to call the Creature seemed to turn a sense of dread into a sense of awe for some.

"He was very scary to look at," came a reply from a young girl.

Benjamin smiled in appreciation of the remark, but then shook his head.

"He's not scary; he's just a little different. When you learn to know him you find that there's no reason to be frightened."

Sandy couldn't tell if Benjamin's thoughts actually calmed everyone down, or if it just confused them into silence. In any event, the atmosphere, though still tense, seemed more manageable.

Just then, Sandy felt his cell phone vibrate. He glanced at it and saw a number that he didn't recognize. With Benjamin taking charge of the situation, he decided to step back and take the call. Benjamin continued talking.

"Pastor Kelly," Sandy said, answering the call with his left hand while a finger from his right hand closed off the other ear.

"This is Don Bowman," a male voice barked. "My daughter, Alyssa, is there at the camp with you. She just sent a text message saying that the camp had been attacked by some monster! What is going on?"

"No one has been attacked," Sandy said in a controlled voice. He then stepped from the cafeteria floor to an adjoining rec room.

"Well, what happened?" The voice was more demanding than inquisitive.

"We're not sure yet. We were playing some games at Sanctuary Rock, and some big ..." Sandy hesitated, "...animal came out of the woods. It didn't hurt anyone. Everyone is okay, I assure you."

"Well, my daughter is terrified, and we're coming to get her; now!"

Sandy didn't have a chance to respond as the caller suddenly hung the phone up. As he was making his way back into the cafeteria, his cell phone vibrated again. Another number that he didn't recognize appeared. He answered the call and found another distraught father calling to say that he was on his way to the camp to get his daughter.

Before Sandy ended the conversation, his phone beeped with another incoming call. Soon, the calls began piling up. Frightened or angry voicemail messages were left. Everyone was coming for their son or daughter. Apparently, the campers had been texting their parents with reports of the evening's events as soon as they'd gotten within range. The news had then begun spreading uncontrollably. Many of the reports were greatly exaggerated, making some parents quite angry. Those that weren't exaggerated contained enough information to cause a great deal of alarm. Sandy was too confused with all that was taking place to think of a way to hold everyone off and salvage the camping week. He wasn't even sure if that was the right thing to do.

Harris Long suddenly walked into the rec room where Sandy stood. As soon as Sandy saw Harris, he finished the call he was on and dropped the phone to his side. He ignored its vibrations. He needed a break.

"I heard there was a problem," Harris said pointedly.

"And it's only getting worse," Sandy replied, holding up his vibrating phone. "Everyone is on his or her way up here right now to get his or her kid."

Harris sighed and looked down at his feet. Sandy studied him, hoping that he would say something that would erase everything that had just happened.

"Obviously, we can't stop parents from taking their kids home," Harris said, finally looking up at Sandy. "And we can't run a camp if everyone's gone away. So, I guess we got to do what we got to do."

"I don't even know what to say right now, Harris. All of these parents are frightened, and some are angry. *Very* angry. It won't be pretty when they get here. I'm going to need your help."

"Of course," Harris said nodding. "Benjamin is in the cafeteria right now talking with everyone. He will be glad to help, too."

"I guess this is the little *problem* that you had when you called me a few weeks back?" Sandy asked.

Harris nodded.

"I thought everything was resolved. I thought you had it all taken care of!" Sandy continued. The exasperation in his voice was obvious.

"Listen, I told you everything that I knew, Sandy," Harris replied defensively. "I didn't make any promises, and I didn't tell you that the problem was resolved."

Harris was not accepting the blame, and Sandy knew he was right. Harris had never told him that the problem had been fixed. Because of the sudden death of Clay Decker, the arrival of his dad, and his interest in Ellie, he had pushed this issue into the background. Sandy had a sense that a lot of blame was about to fall heavily on his shoulders. He wondered how he would bear it.

It didn't take long for the normally quiet Camp Atawanda parking lot to look like a city beltway during rush hour. At first, Sandy made an effort to keep camp going. But he could gain no ground with his weak arguments. The tide was just too powerful to stop. Parents walked into the cafeteria and children rushed into their arms. Soon, there was no turning back. They all wanted to go home. Camp was over. Chaos ensued as everyone demanded answers. Sandy felt lost in a sea of confusion. He was being surrounded by a mob who wanted answers to questions that seemed as surreal as the answers he gave.

Just as Sandy was finishing negotiations with an angry mother, he glanced to a corner of the cafeteria. Benjamin was standing with his back to Sandy. And just beyond Benjamin, facing him in close conversation was Ellie. They were standing remarkably near one another. Then Benjamin leaned forward, and Sandy saw him whispering in her ear. He then placed his hand on her forearm. Sandy felt confused. Then he felt threatened. *What are they talking about? And why are they touching?*

While watching Benjamin and Ellie, Sandy suddenly felt the presence of someone nearby. Turning, he discovered Ardyth standing with arms folded in front of her. She had followed his gaze from Benjamin and Ellie and was looking at him as their eyes met. Sandy found something very menacing in the way she was leering at him.

"Thank you, Pastor, for a wonderful camping program!" she said. Sarcasm was dripping from her tongue. "You've managed to take something meant to be so wholesome and happy for children and turn it into a horror movie."

"This is not my fault, Ardyth," Sandy pleaded. "I had no idea any of this was going to take place."

"Do you realize how traumatized you have left these children?" She ignored his every word. "They will need years of counseling to get over what you did tonight!"

"I didn't *do* anything!" Sandy words were defiant, but he was beginning to doubt himself.

"That's right, Pastor, you didn't do *anything*." Sarcasm again.

"Listen," Sandy knew this conversation was becoming a waste of his time. "Let's just get through this night, and we'll work through everything tomorrow step by step."

"Tonight is only the beginning of your troubles." Ardyth ended the conversation by turning and stomping quickly away. Sandy noticed that her phlebitis was not flaring up tonight.

Sandy turned back to see Ellie. The corner was vacant. They were both gone. He quickly scanned the room. Nowhere. *Where'd she go?*

"Pastor?" It was Jocelyn who got Sandy's attention this time.

Sandy turned to her. Her eyes were red from crying, but she seemed composed.

"How are we going to handle this? No one is packed to go home, and everyone is demanding their stuff from the cabins."

Sandy was on overload. His emotions were drawn taut and were near breaking. Confusion reigned everywhere about him. He closed his eyes and bowed his head in a silent prayer. When he lifted his eyes again he felt slightly better.

"Go find Harris," Sandy thought out loud. "Have him rouse as much camping staff as possible. Then, let's have counselors and camping staff accompany parents and their kids to their respective cabins to help them pack. Also, we need to get a signup list. I want signatures for every camper who is leaving. *Everyone* has to be accounted for!"

Jocelyn turned to follow Sandy's instructions. Sandy wanted to look for Ellie, but he had more important business to handle. To prevent a complete disaster, he had to orchestrate a proper exit plan. He gathered paper and pencil and then began to account for campers. He needed to know who was leaving and who was not. He knew that some of the campers did not have cell phones. Their parents had not been reached. The results of his census soon revealed that they would be spending at least another night at Camp Atawanda. The thought of going to sleep in the mountains so close to where they had just seen the most hideous Beast was an incredibly frightful thought to Sandy. But even more troubling was the fact that Sandy couldn't find Ellie.

Chapter Nineteen

Under Sandy's leadership, the counselors retrieved sleeping bags and cot mattresses from the cabins. The campers and camping staff were instructed to sleep in the cafeteria. At one point, Sandy saw Ellie carrying things from one of the cabins. He was relieved to see her, but felt confused when it became obvious that she was ignoring him. He eventually drifted into a fitful, short sleep.

As Sandy woke a few hours later, he looked to what had been designated as the girls' section of the cafeteria. Ellie's tousled red hair could be seen peeking from her sleeping bag. Sandy felt guarded relief.

Eventually, noise from the busy kitchen staff woke everyone. The light of the new day seemed to bring a sense of renewal. It created distance from the memories of a crazed night. Sandy even saw a few smiles. As everyone moved to the tables for breakfast, Sandy led them in one of their morning camp songs. It seemed strange at first, but with each chorus their voices increased in volume. Sandy then prayed, and they ate their breakfast. While they ate, Ellie looked at Sandy once and smiled. But the smile seemed too impersonal; too formal. It didn't reflect the level to which their relationship had ascended the night before. Sandy wondered if Ellie was also blaming him for this disaster.

Within hours, more parents rushed into the cafeteria. Sandy found himself answering the same questions with the same feeble answers as the night before. However, the few hours of sleep and the passage of time that separated him from the events had been helpful. He was a little more composed and ready to respond to the worried and frightened questions.

Eventually, a decision was reached to transport the few remaining campers to the church. They would remain there until they could be picked up. By noon, everyone was packed and ready to go. Counselors and camp staff helped the children pack. Everyone then waited in the cafeteria. Sandy watched the children talk and interact. They seemed to be in better spirits.

While everyone waited to leave, Benjamin came into the cafeteria for a few minutes. He moved about, talking with the campers and staff. Most everyone seemed encouraged by his presence. Sandy watched him hold a long conversation with Ardyth. She seemed especially impressed. Benjamin then stopped at the table full of girls where Ellie was waiting. Benjamin soon had the girls laughing. Ellie didn't talk with Benjamin directly, nor did she ignore him, however. Sandy felt a jealous hurt rise within his chest.

Harris didn't come to the cafeteria. Sandy asked about him, but was told he was tied up in his office. Sandy hoped to talk with him before they left. However, Harris never showed. Eventually, the small convoy of vehicles wound its way off the mountain and began the drive into Lycona. Sandy had hoped he could sit with Ellie, but she was in another van with Jocelyn and some children.

////

As each new day came, Cliff found it increasingly harder to manage the tormenting thoughts that ravaged his mind. He continued avoiding Carly. He knew that she noticed. He told her he wasn't feeling well; however, he knew that he couldn't keep that charade going. He had to do something. He had to talk.

As Cliff wound his patrol car through Lycona, he aimlessly turned down Church Street. Passing Lycona Community Church, he saw the church van in the lot. *Pastor Kelly. Why not talk with him?*

Carly went to Lycona Community Church as often as her work schedule permitted. If Cliff wasn't working, he attended with her. Carly went because she had a strong faith in God. Cliff mostly attended because Carly wanted him there. It wasn't that Cliff didn't believe in God. He did. He just didn't know exactly how to make that belief a part of his life. Still, he liked attending when he could. He especially liked the pastor. He was young, energetic, and had a style of preaching that Cliff could appreciate. Cliff didn't have trouble staying awake in church like he did with the old preacher. Pastor Kelly held his interest.

Cliff turned his patrol car into the church parking lot. He saw a Honda Civic parked at a sign marked "Pastor," and hoped that this meant he was available. If the pastor was in, maybe they could just talk a little. Maybe he could get someone to listen objectively. Maybe he could get his troubles off of his chest. Cliff was lifted by hope as he walked to the front of the church.

The doors were unlocked, so he stepped inside and made his way to the office door. Cliff was about to knock when he heard a voice from behind him.

"Can I help you?"

It was Beatrice. She was standing behind Cliff, halfway out of a fire exit door. She had a cigarette pinched between her fingers. She took one last drag and blew the bitter nicotine out the door. Dropping the cigarette to the concrete step, she crushed it with her flat shoe. She knocked it off the step to a pile of cigarette butts that had accumulated behind an evergreen bush.

"Is the Pastor in?" Cliff asked, turning in her direction.

Beatrice walked past the deputy to her desk. It seemed to Cliff that she needed to be seated properly at her station before continuing the conversation.

"Yes, he is," she answered, leaning forward over her desk. "What is this about?"

Cliff didn't know Beatrice well. He didn't know that her mind was a gossip-gathering machine. He didn't know that she had arrived back from lunch to find the pastor in his office. He didn't know that she had immediately begun an intense interrogation as to why he'd returned early from camp. He didn't know that Beatrice had been told that "something had happened."

"I just need to speak with him, please," Cliff replied. He didn't intend for his voice to sound so formal, but he was taken aback by the secretary's intrusive attitude.

Beatrice cocked an eyebrow as she appraised Cliff.

"Will you be needing to speak with me as well?" she probed.

The question puzzled Cliff. Then he realized that even though this was a personal visit, his uniform might be conveying a different message.

"No, Ma'am," he replied with a smile. "This isn't official police business. I would just like to speak with the pastor."

His response didn't seem to relieve her suspicions.

"I'll see if he's available," she said, still eyeing Cliff.

Beatrice stood up and walked to the closed door of the pastor's office. At the same time that she opened the door, she gave it a quick knock. It seemed to be more of a warning than a request for permission to enter.

Cliff heard her announce that the Sheriff's Department had come for a visit. She turned to Cliff. With a jerk of her head, she motioned for him to enter. Cliff wondered if she was always this friendly.

Cliff entered Sandy's office. The pastor was seated behind his desk. His laptop was turned on, and it appeared he was working on something. After saving his work, he closed the laptop and stood to welcome his guest.

Cliff was a little surprised to see the pastor dressed in shorts and a T-shirt. This seemed a bit informal. However, this was the first time he had seen the pastor on a weekday. He had no point of reference. More surprising than his attire was his appearance. The pastor looked tired; perhaps exhausted. His hair either hadn't been combed, or he had constantly been running a hand through it. He had also missed a shave. This wasn't what Cliff had been expecting.

"I hope I'm not disturbing you," Cliff said, shaking the pastor's outstretched hand.

"Not at all, Cliff," Sandy replied. "Please, have a seat."

Sandy motioned to a chair near the desk. Cliff sat down and then looked up. It seemed the pastor was waiting to see if he would sit or not. When Cliff had taken a seat, the pastor seemed to take this as his own cue to sit. He appeared nervous. Cliff knew his uniform made a lot of people nervous.

"Please don't worry," Cliff said, holding up an empty palm. "I'm not here on police business. I just want to talk with you if you have some time."

Cliff expected the pastor to relax a little. Instead, he seemed as rigid as before. He didn't recline in his chair, but remained sitting erect. His hands were folded unnaturally on the desktop.

Sandy nodded and then motioned for Cliff to hold his thought. He got up from behind his desk and walked to the open door. He pushed it shut and returned to his desk. Cliff then heard some movement from the secretary's office.

"What can I do for you?" the pastor said as he returned to his seat. He still sat rigid and appeared to be on edge.

Something didn't seem right to Cliff. The pastor's dress, appearance, and the way he was acting was odd. Cliff didn't feel comfortable enough to start baring his soul.

"Are you sure that I'm not stopping at a bad time?" Cliff avoided his pastor's previous question and decided to fish around first. It was hard to stop the cop in him.

"No, this is fine," Sandy replied. "I'm not even scheduled to be in today, so I have no other appointments."

"Are you on vacation?"

"Not really. I was supposed to be at camp this week with the kids, but..." He stopped.

Cliff saw the pastor trying to figure out what to say next.

"Things changed for us, so we came home early," Sandy finished his thought.

"I hope things are okay," Cliff replied.

Instead of answering, Sandy looked at Cliff as if he was trying to size up the situation. Cliff had seen the same look in criminals who were about to confess. Sandy ran his hand through his hair, leaving a lock standing straight up. Something definitely was not right.

"Actually, things aren't okay," Sandy finally responded, letting out a long breath. "We had an incident at camp this week that has rattled everyone pretty badly. In fact, I'm guessing that that's the reason why you are here."

"I haven't heard anything about what happened," Cliff said shaking his head. The pastor studied his face for a few moments and then finally relaxed a little.

"Actually, I had stopped by for personal reasons, but now I'm curious to know if I can help you with anything," Cliff replied.

He watched Sandy glance to his side as if weighing his options. His eyes then drifted upward as he leaned back in his chair. A hand shot through his hair again. The lock of hair fell back down.

"I don't know if you can help or not," Sandy finally responded. "We had a pretty bad incident up at Camp Atawanda this week."

Cliff froze.

"What kind of incident?" he forced himself to ask.

"I don't even know how to tell you," Sandy replied, shaking his head. "I doubt that you would believe me; I doubt *anyone* would believe me."

"Try me," Cliff said confidently.

"We saw some kind of animal that frightened the heck out of everyone," Sandy blurted. "We have no idea what it was, but it was the most terrifying experience I've ever had."

"Was anyone hurt?"

"No, thank the Lord."

"Can you describe to me what you saw?" Cliff asked.

"It was…" Sandy paused. His eyes then dropped to the floor for a moment, as if searching for words.

"It was a monster," he finally said. "I know that sounds crazy, but that's the only way I can describe it. It walked on two legs and had long hair and flaming red eyes."

Sandy's eyes met Cliff's. Cliff sensed that they seemed to be searching him; looking for help.

"When and where did this happen?"

Sandy closed his eyes and sighed. He began with the call from Harris. He told Cliff about the camping program and their trip to Atawanda. He described the excursion to Sanctuary Rock, the encounter, and how the whole camping program had fallen apart. He

220

talked about the trip back to town earlier that morning and how the campers finally had been sent home. His explanation provided Cliff with a very good reason for his disheveled look.

Before Cliff could respond, a knock at the office door interrupted him. Beatrice's head pushed into the room. She glanced at Cliff and then at Sandy. Her deeply scowled face bore an even heavier look of concern.

"Pastor, there are some people out here to see you," she said, gesturing with an unlit cigarette.

"Can it wait?" Sandy replied.

"I don't think so," she answered.

Chapter Twenty

Sandy stood from behind his desk and apologized to Cliff for the interruption. Then he made his way out the church office and followed Beatrice into the foyer. She opened the swinging doors and let him walk past her. Sandy felt on edge. The events of the preceding night had placed him on high alert; now he was filled with a sense of foreboding. Something didn't feel right.

As he entered the foyer, Sandy's feeling of dread was confirmed. Standing inside the front doors of the church were five members of the church council. They watched him as he approached. There were no smiles. Each face was somber.

Sandy knew these people well. He considered them partners in ministry. They had shared dinners, picnics, and long, intense meetings. They had prayed together and had bared their souls to one another. As Sandy entered the room, he felt the presence of a thick emotional wall. These people had daytime jobs and weren't typically available for weekday meetings. Furthermore, Sandy had not been alerted to a council meeting. None of these were good signs. Oddly, what *didn't* surprise him was seeing Ardyth standing there with arms crossed and a determined look on her face. Somehow, that made sense.

"What's going on?" Sandy asked as he walked into the foyer.

Jim McNair cleared his throat. After Clay had died, he'd been promoted to chairperson of the council. McNair was a small-time attorney in Lycona who had barely kept his business afloat with property issues and wills. Not long after he'd joined the church, Ardyth had hired him to handle her business affairs. She'd soon become his most valued customer. It hadn't been the volume of work she'd provided that had made her so important. Rather, she had been, and still remained, the only customer willing to pay his full rate. Sandy liked McNair, but he lacked the deep spiritual sense and leadership qualities that Clay had possessed.

When McNair had become chair of the council, Sandy had experienced concern over how much influence Ardyth may wield through him. He'd feared these flaws might become a lever in Ardyth's hands. At the moment, he had a sense that that leverage was about to be leaned upon.

"Sandy, we just heard about what happened at camp and we need to hear your side of the story," McNair said.

"My side of the story?" Sandy repeated. "I didn't realize that there were *sides* to what happened!"

McNair shifted awkwardly from leg to leg, then folded his arms across his chest before continuing. Although he had the smarts to be a good trial lawyer, McNair lacked the strong presence needed to impress others.

"Is it true," he asked, "that you had been warned that this animal had been a problem long before you got there?"

Sandy shot a glance to Ardyth. The meeting was making sense. Ardyth must have had spoken with Harris while at camp. He apparently had revealed to her his earlier conversation with Sandy. This interrogation was being orchestrated by her.

"Harris called me a few weeks before camp," Sandy admitted, his eyes drifting back to McNair. "He explained that they had heard some weird noises and there had been some strange things happening. However, right before camp began, he told me that they had had no more problems."

"Did you share this with anyone?" McNair asked firmly.

Sandy quickly scanned the faces of the council members. Two looked at the floor; two were staring at him with furrowed brows.

"I had planned on it. Then Clay died and..." Sandy paused. He had not told anyone about the stress he was going through with his father. Obviously, he was not about to share with them his interest in Ellie either. "But," he continued, "things just got a little crazy, and I forgot about it."

"So, you didn't tell anyone?" McNair was pushing for an answer.

"No!" Sandy said defensively. "If that's what you came to hear; I did not tell anyone!"

The stern look on Ardyth's face gave way to a smug smile. She locked eyes with McNair and gave him a slight nod.

"Pastor," McNair said with his arms still crossed. "We are very concerned about the fallout that is to come from what's happened. When, and not if, the public learns that this church knew of the possibility of danger, but failed to act responsibly, we will face a very serious situation. Our phones are already beginning to ring with questions; to which we have no good answers."

Sandy felt the rug being pulled out from beneath his feet. He suddenly felt very alone. Very vulnerable.

"Do you understand?" McNair asked when Sandy failed to respond.

"Yes, I do," Sandy said quietly.

"Pastor," McNair continued, "the council just held an emergency meeting to discuss the matter. A decision was reached: if you had taken the children to Camp Atawanda without telling anyone of the danger, then we would be left with no choice but to activate the Inappropriate Conduct Clause of our contract."

"You're *firing* me?" Sandy asked in disbelief.

"Please understand," McNair continued. "To protect this church and its ministry, we feel that it is in the best interest of everyone to terminate our relationship at this time." His voice reflected his sterile, legal language.

"But," Sandy interrupted, "the Inappropriate Conduct Clause is only to be activated if there has been gross inappropriate behavior. I may have erred in not discussing a phone call with anyone, but I haven't even come close to doing anything that would fall into *that* category!"

McNair kept his arms folded in front of him, but he let his eyes drop to the floor. This was a sign to Sandy that McNair wasn't completely behind the decision.

"Come on, Jim," Sandy pleaded. "What's going on? The Inappropriate Conduct Clause is to protect the congregation if I fall into some unrepentant sin. Forgetting to tell someone about a phone call isn't exactly sinful, and if you think it is; then give me a chance to repent!"

"I'm sorry, Pastor," McNair said, looking up again. "We've reached our decision because we feel it is the best thing for the life of this church."

"Not to mention the fact," Ardyth suddenly interrupted, "that while the children were being attacked, you and dear Miss Ellie were sitting nearby, making out like a couple of teenagers!"

"What?" Sandy shrieked. He felt his face flush.

"Ardyth," McNair said, extending his arm in front of her as if to keep her from physically engaging. "We agreed that that report was unsubstantiated and that we would not take it into consideration."

Ardyth's posture relaxed, but the smile on her face widened. She had made her point.

"Jim," Sandy said sharply, "that's not what happened."

"Whether it's true or not is of no concern," McNair replied, raising both open palms toward Sandy. "We based our decision on the report that you had prior knowledge of a danger, and by your own testimony, failed to report it to anyone."

"Okay, I think we're rushing things a bit," Sandy cautioned, softening his voice. "We don't even know if there will actually *be* a problem. No one was hurt, and everyone made it safely home. Not even twenty-four hours has passed; don't you think that firing your pastor is a little premature?"

"Sandy," McNair replied, also lowering his voice. "This wasn't an easy decision to reach, and I can understand the way you must feel about it. However, the council has made its decision, and we feel it is best for everyone."

It was painfully obvious that McNair had stopped calling Sandy 'pastor.'

"In other words, you need someone to take the fall. You want someone to blame. And you'd rather have it be me than you!" Sandy retorted.

"Sandy," McNair said sternly, "you've made your choice, which has forced us to make ours."

"Was this a unanimous vote?" Sandy prodded.

With lips pursed, McNair nodded thoughtfully.

"There are nine members on the council. Five could make the emergency meeting; two could not," McNair said. "We were able to get two more by conference call. The vote to proceed with activation of the Inappropriate Conduct Clause was carried by a vote of five to two. Even if the remaining two had been present and voted against the motion, it would have carried. As you know, the council has the authority to act on the contract without a congregational vote."

Sandy closed his eyes and shook his head. This moment hadn't even been on the radar. He didn't know how to react or what to say.

"What's next?" Sandy finally asked.

"We are terminating the contract immediately. However, we're not just throwing you out, Sandy. Your salary will be continued for thirty days, and of course you can continue to live at the parsonage during that time." McNair's voice reflected concern, yet Sandy could not tell if it was genuine. "We will have someone fill the pulpit on Sunday morning,"

"May I address the congregation on Sunday?"

"Sandy," McNair flashed an uncomfortable smile, "there will be no need. We will announce your departure graciously and without any mention of the contract details. This is the best way to handle it."

"May I at least come to church on Sunday to say goodbye?" Sandy asked.

"We've talked about that, and we've decided that that would not be a good idea," McNair said. "We must stay focused on the best interest of the congregation. Having you in church on Sunday will just confuse everyone and make it very uncomfortable."

"Are you telling me that I can't come see my own church family?" Sandy asked incredulously.

"Sandy," McNair's voice took a firm tone. "You need to look past your own hurt and try to see what's best for the whole church. This is not about you. It's about Lycona Community!"

With these words, the meeting came to an abrupt end.
When the council had left, Sandy stood speechless. He knew that he had made a mistake by not reporting the phone call. A huge one. However, he still believed it was an honest mistake. Not one fitting the punishment just meted out.

Finally, he turned around. Beatrice was standing just inside the swinging doors. At least he didn't have to explain what had just happened; she had heard the whole conversation.

"I'm sorry, Pastor," Beatrice muttered. She seemed just as surprised. "That wasn't fair."

"Thanks, Beatrice." Her support made him feel a little better.

"Here, you need this more than me," she said, extending the cigarette she had carried from the office.

"If ever there was a time I needed a cigarette, it would be now," Sandy responded with a weak smile. "Maybe later."

"Suit yourself," she replied curtly. "But I'm stepping out for one."

Suddenly, Sandy remembered Cliff. He walked back through the church. As he stepped into the office, he blew out a long breath. *This day could not possibly get any worse!*

////

If Sandy looked bad when he stepped out of his office, Cliff thought he looked worse coming back in. Sandy seemed pale and thoroughly shaken.

"Are you okay, Pastor?" Cliff asked as Sandy made his way behind his desk.

"Not really," Sandy replied, easing himself into the large, black chair.

"What's wrong?"

Sandy stared at the desk for a few moments.

"The church council decided to fire me after the incident at camp," Sandy abruptly said, looking up at Cliff. "I'm no longer the pastor here."

"How can they do that?"

Cliff listened as Sandy walked through what had just happened. Sandy explained to him about the contract that he had signed and why the council decided to act on it. Cliff saw the hurt in his pastor's face and genuinely empathized with him. Cliff had always felt a lack of interest in the business affairs of the church. To him, it all seemed so political; so removed from what he thought a church should be. He was revulsed having seen it close up.

"Is there anything I can do?" Cliff asked when Sandy had finished.

"No, thanks. I appreciate your kindness, but there's nothing that anyone can do right now." Then Sandy added, "Cliff, I feel terribly. You never did tell me why you wanted to see me."

Cliff studied Sandy's face. It didn't take him long to make a decision.

"It can wait," Cliff replied. He rose to shake Sandy's hand. "You have more important things on your plate right now."

As Cliff slumped into his squad car, he felt deflated. He had hoped to open himself up to Pastor Sandy. Not only was he still carrying the same weight he had arrived with, but he was now feeling a greater pain. Had Cliff told someone about the Creature, none of this would have happened. *Did my silence just cost a good man his job?*

Cliff pulled out onto Church Street and eased his patrol car into traffic. His radio then blurted, "Dispatch to LS Eighteen."

"LS Eighteen. Go ahead, Dispatch," Cliff replied into the microphone.

"We have a disturbance at Camp Atawanda on Atawanda Lane. Game Warden is present and is requesting back up. Can you respond?"

////

Sandy sat quietly in the church office chair. He was numb; barely able to feel anything. Lycona Community was the first full-time pastoral appointment he had ever had. The thought of being fired from his position was too difficult to absorb.

When he had signed the contract, he hadn't given a second thought to the Inappropriate Conduct Clause. He'd felt that he had taken every possible precaution to protect his ministry. When he had learned of his father's fall, he'd made an even stronger resolve to prevent something like that from occurring with him. He'd taken even greater care to prevent any of his actions from being misconstrued. He had been careful about where he'd gone and how he'd handled himself. He'd thought that he had insulated himself from an attack like this. How could he have let this happen? His father had left the ministry because of an inappropriate action, and now he had just been fired on the same grounds!

Sandy sat with his head buried in his hands. He needed to reach out to someone. *Ellie!* He had not seen her since they had piled into the vans at camp this morning. Sandy's van had dropped two children off at their respective homes before reaching the church. When he'd arrived to the church, she had already gone.

Sandy picked up the office phone and dialed Ellie's cell. Her voice mail kicked in. Sandy left a message. He figured that she was probably in bed. No one had gotten any good rest at camp. Sandy was also very tired. What he craved more than sleep, however, was companionship; someone to talk to.

In the short time he had known Ellie, he had really appreciated the moments they'd had to talk. As a pastor, he was surrounded by people all day. However, it was hard to form the kind of relationship that fed his own soul. He was always in great demand, and he did his best to serve others. So often, however, he just wanted someone to listen to him. Ellie was the only person with whom he could talk about himself. She seemed to be the only one in his life who really cared.

His thoughts were interrupted by a sharp rap at the office door. Sandy looked up to see Beatrice standing in the doorway.

"I'm supposed to keep an eye on you," she offered abruptly.

"What do you mean?' Sandy replied.

"I mean I'm supposed to keep an eye on you," she said, as if by repeating herself things became clearer.

"I'm still not sure I understand."

Beatrice rolled her eyes and took a step into the office. "Jim McNair just called and asked me to help you gather your things and make sure you don't cause any problems."

Sandy lowered his face in hurt and anger. It wasn't enough that he was being fired over a misunderstanding. He was now being treated like a common thief to be escorted out of the courtroom. There was, however, a small amount of consolation: McNair most likely hadn't told

232

Beatrice to let Sandy know what she was doing. It was her way of letting him know that she was on his side. He considered thanking her, but he knew that would just get awkward.

"Do they really think that I'm going to go berserk and trash the office on my way out?" he asked.

Beatrice leaned her head to one side and shrugged that shoulder as if the idea was completely plausible.

Sandy sighed. He asked for some cardboard boxes to pack his belongings. Beatrice disappeared for a few minutes and then returned with a couple of boxes from the janitor's room.

"Let me ask you a question, Beatrice," Sandy said while going through his desk drawer. "What just happened out there? Why was I just fired?"

"Because Ardyth Van Horten doesn't like you," she replied simply.

"And why doesn't she like me?" Sandy asked as he pulled open another drawer.

"Because she likes to be the one in control," Beatrice said. "Ever since you moved into town, she has tried to put you under her thumb. But you were all fresh-out-of-college and had big ambitions for the church that she don't care nothing about. She had her goals; you had yours."

"Yeah, but why get me fired?" Sandy paused while considering Beatrice's words.

She shrugged as if the answer should have been obvious.

"That's easy," she said, bending over to pick up an empty box. When she straightened, she began to hack and cough in an unsanitary and grotesque way. When Sandy had first met Beatrice, he'd been repulsed by her coughing fits. Eventually, he'd become as used to them as she was.

"Dell and Clay were always against her," Beatrice continued after spitting something into a Kleenex. "With them gone, you were her last threat. She gets you out of the way, helps put in a preacher she can run, and then she controls this church."

Sandy took a few moments to mull these thoughts over. "Do you seriously think that she was able to get me fired? She's not even on the council!"

Beatrice placed a book in an open box and stopped to look at Sandy. It was one of those "don't-be-so-naive" stares that he had seen numerous times. They had always annoyed him; now he didn't care.

"Jim McNair is in her back pocket," Beatrice began. "He makes so much money from her that he can't afford *not* to do what she wants. I guarantee you that the first thing she did when she got home from camp was to call him and tell him that she wanted you fired. All he had to do was round up a few council members. He impressed them with some legal dance about how the church was going to get sued, or he cashed in on a few favors. There ain't too many people with college degrees in the church, you know. Most common folks are intimidated by college-educated people like McNair. Getting that vote from the council was probably the easiest job he's ever done for her."

////

Cliff radioed his location to Dispatch and increased his speed through town. When Pastor Sandy had told him about what had happened at camp, he'd had a sense that the Sheriff's Department may get involved. He was also interested in talking to the Game Warden about the animal. Oscar Flint had been the Game Warden for as long as Cliff could remember. His love for the mountains surrounding Lycona eventually had landed him the Warden's position. But the stress of the job and its sedentary administrative duties had slowly robbed him of the health he needed to enjoy it. He was now an overweight, out of shape man who got winded using the drive-through at McDonalds. Still, Flint knew the woods and its creatures better than anyone else.

As Cliff made his way to the mountains, he wondered how this recent turn of events might complicate matters. Bragg had seemed completely disinterested in doing anything about the Creature when Cliff had been attacked. Now the same animal had just threatened the safety of a group of young children at camp. It wouldn't be so easy to turn the other way. Cliff knew, however, that he still had to tread lightly around Bragg; who was holding the ultimate trump card right now.

Before long, Cliff found himself winding up an old logging road now known as Atawanda Lane. Over a week before, he was being shuttled on it in the opposite direction toward the hospital. That seemed like a long time ago.

When Cliff pulled into Camp Atawanda, Warden Flint's green and white Ford Explorer was parked near the office door. Cliff began to rapidly take in the scene. Warden Flint was standing with his left leg on the front tire of his Explorer, talking to a group of men standing in a semi-circle around him. Each man was holding a rifle or had one slung over his shoulder. Most of the men had sidearms, too. They all looked in Cliff's direction as he wheeled into the lot. Cliff immediately recognized two of the men. He had hunted with both of them, and he knew them to be the kind of guys who didn't cause trouble. Cliff alerted Dispatch that he had arrived at the scene. He crawled out of his cruiser and fixed his deputy's hat as he approached the group.

Flint stepped away from the group and approached Cliff. "Deputy," Flint dropped his chin in a quick nod. "I got a call about a rogue animal that attacked a group of campers here last night. About the same time that I got here these men arrived. A couple of them had children in the camp and said that they came home pretty shaken up. They came up here with intentions of going after whatever it is."

"What do you want to do?" Cliff asked, keeping an eye on the group.

"I've ordered a live bear trap from District. It should be here pretty soon. I want to set it up where the animal was last seen and try taking it alive."

"What about these guys?" Cliff asked.

"I'd rather they go back to their homes. I'm not sure I know what we have up here. Before we declare open season on whatever it is, I think we should at least try to get it identified."

Cliff nodded in agreement and stepped past Flint to the eager group of men who had been straining to hear what was being said. At the same time, another police cruiser rolled into the parking lot. It was Deputy Logan. As he crawled out of his car, Cliff felt a wave of relief. Logan's size was intimidating, even to an armed group of men.

"Fellows," Cliff began, as Logan reached his side. "I know that you are concerned with what happened here last night. But I think we need to give the Warden a chance to do his job."

"How are you supposed to catch something when you don't even know what you're after?" one of the men asked defiantly, "We need to hunt it down before it kills someone. It came awfully close to my daughter last night. And she's still freaked out about it!"

"I understand," Cliff replied calmly. "But we can't go shooting something that we don't have identified. If it isn't in season in Lycona, then you can't go hunting it."

Cliff watched the men look at each other and to Logan and him. If they had thought about a confrontation, Logan's added presence was a good deterrent. However, after a few shrugs, they turned back to their trucks. As the gravel began to grind beneath their oversized tires, Cliff turned to Warden Flint.

"What's going on up in these mountains?" Cliff asked.

"Have no idea," Flint replied, mopping the sweat off his forehead with a red handkerchief. "As I told you the other week, this ain't the first time I've been up here. I know Bragg has been up here, too. But I don't believe he found anything."

"Any idea what it is?" Cliff asked.

"Based on the reports that I've heard, I think we may have some kind of primate."

"Like a gorilla?"

"Something along that line, I guess. Some people illegally buy primates for pets. Then the pets either get too big to handle, or they escape and folks won't report them missing. It doesn't happen often; but it isn't out of the realm of possibilities."

Cliff thought the Warden should know about his own encounter and the sheer size of the thing he had seen. However, Flint would want to know why he hadn't reported it. Bragg's threat still loomed heavily. He couldn't afford what the truth might cost him.

The two men chatted idly for a few more minutes. Then, the rumble of the District's diesel truck could be heard grinding up the lane. Moments later, the truck eased to a halt with a bear trap in tow. Warden Flint turned to Cliff and Logan and asked, "You fellows interested in taking a ride up to Sanctuary Rock?"

Chapter Twenty-One

Cliff carefully jostled his police car along Cabin Road. He was careful to avoid the rocks and unattended potholes that still littered the newly-fashioned, forested road. In front of him crept a Ford that towed the bear cage. Cliff kept glimpsing at its iron-caged doors; wondering if they would be large or strong enough.

Cliff shook his head to clear his memory. Anxiously, he scanned the trees on both sides of his car. He glanced into his rearview mirror. Harris Long, owner of Camp Atawanda, was following closely in his white Suburban. Cliff had met Harris on a few previous occasions and had appreciated all his work to reclaim the mountainside. With Harris was the Native American who had been present the morning Cliff had been rescued. Behind them came Deputy Logan. Cliff shifted his eyes to the truck in front of him. Being sandwiched in between the vehicles gave him a slight feeling of security.

When they reached the opening at Sanctuary Rock, the four drivers corralled their vehicles in the grassy area near the forest's edge. The driver of the Ford began unhitching the bear trap at the direction of Warden Flint. Cliff fixed his deputy's hat as he exited his car and adjusted his mirrored sunglasses in the bright, afternoon sunshine.

"How are you feeling, Deputy?" Harris asked as he approached Cliff. "I understand you took a pretty good fall at this very spot."

"Much better, thanks," Cliff replied as he looked around the clearing. It had been just last week that Cliff had hiked here. He glanced over to the location where he had rolled out his sleeping bag and set up the trip wire. With great effort, he contained a shudder. The details of his night on this knoll were still not altogether clear. However, the things he was able to recall were enough to rattle him.

"You may remember Benjamin Walker. He's one of the guys who picked you up that morning," Harris said.

"Yes, I remember," Cliff said while shaking Benjamin's hand. "I owe you a big thanks for helping me out that morning."

Craig Logan joined their small huddle. He and Benjamin then walked off to watch the bear trap being set up.

"He's on staff here and has been a big help to me in dealing with what has been taking place," Harris said, nodding toward Benjamin. "We're all indebted to him."

"What kind of help has he been able to offer?"

Harris explained how Benjamin had wandered into camp not long after the sightings had begun. He shared how Benjamin had kept the work crews calm and had enabled them to get so much accomplished.

As Harris spoke, Cliff eyed Benjamin through the privacy of his sunglasses. His nourished physique and perfect teeth indicated to Cliff that he wasn't an average drifter. There was money in his background. His posture reflected a confidence that his dark eyes seem to command. This meant he was educated. Cliff wondered why a good-looking, educated, rich guy would come wandering into camp like a refugee. Something wasn't right. There was something else. It wasn't that he didn't like Benjamin; he would reserve that judgment for later. However, he had the feeling that he was the type of man who required caution. Cliff wasn't sure if he could be trusted.

////

Sandy packed his things at the Church office and loaded them into his Honda. He then drove to Ardelle's old home. Caroline's Hyundai and Ellie's blue Jeep were both in the driveway. Sandy knew she would probably be sleeping, but he really needed to talk with her.

Sandy knocked at the back door. Caroline soon swung it open.

"Hello, Pastor Sandy!" she said. Then she seemed confused. "What are you doing here?"

"Hi, Caroline," he replied. "We had a problem at camp and came home a little early. I was hoping to talk with Ellie. Is she home?"

"No," Carline said, shaking her head. "I haven't heard from her. Is everything okay?"

Sandy was surprised. The past twenty-four hours had pushed the staff beyond their breaking points. Everyone had just wanted to get home.

Sandy explained what had happened at camp and assured Caroline that Ellie was fine. He asked her to have Ellie call him.

Sandy crawled back into his Honda. He retrieved his cell phone and dialed Jocelyn. It rang twice before he heard her familiar voice. She sounded tired, but good.

"Jocelyn, this is Sandy," He paused and realized that he hadn't called himself 'pastor.' "How are you doing?" he asked.

"I'm okay. But I just heard the news; how are *you* doing?" she asked sympathetically.

It didn't surprise Sandy that she had heard so quickly. Pastors don't get fired everyday around Lycona, so the news had to have spread quickly. Sandy was glad for that. The fewer times he had to explain the mess the better.

"I'm doing okay, thanks," he replied. Sandy wasn't interested in dwelling on the subject, so he continued with the purpose of his call. "I was calling about Ellie. Do you know where she might be? I tried calling her, but I got her voicemail. I also stopped by her house, but Caroline said she never came home."

"I don't know, Pastor," Jocelyn apparently wasn't giving up on his title yet. "She didn't come back with us."

"What?" Sandy was surprised. "Wasn't she in your van?"

"She *was*. We were all loaded when Benjamin came out to talk with her. She got back out of the van with him and a few moments later came back for her stuff. She said that she would get a ride home with him."

Emotions that Sandy had only ever read about flooded his mind. They snaked their way through him, biting at every cell. They filled him with their poison until he felt bloated and repulsive. He tried to swallow, but his mouth had gone dry.

"Okay, thanks." It was all that he could say.

As he backed out of the driveway, Sandy realized that the worst day of his life had in fact gotten worse.

////

The live bear trap was a tubular, culvert-style cage made of steel and iron. The Wildlife Commission used it when bears became a nuisance. The bait was displayed on a large metal plate that was attached to a bar and spring. When the unsuspecting bear stepped on the plate, the cage door slid down the tracks and sealed in its quarry.

"What kind of bait will you be using?" Cliff asked the Warden after he had raised the sliding door.

"I had my driver bring in some leftover donuts from the office," Flint said as his driver appeared from the front of the truck with a brown paper bag. Flint looked in the bag and then let out a sigh of satisfaction. "I also had him stop at the market for some fresh fat." Flint withdrew a bundle of white newsprint. He unfolded it to reveal a pound and a half of pig fat. "Bears find this irresistible."

"But this is no bear," Cliff said confidently.

"I understand that. But I've got to start somewhere."

Flint wiped some of the fat along the opening of the bear cage and set a few donuts conspicuously nearby. The remainder of the meal was placed on the plate, and the trap door was set on its trigger.

Off in the distance, Cliff heard machinery running. He glanced to the adjacent hilltop.

"That's the new resort," Harris said, following Cliff's gaze. "You can't see it from Atawanda, but you can hear the work taking place."

"I didn't realize it was so close," Cliff said.

"It's *too* close," Harris replied.

Harris didn't need much prompting to start talking about the resort. He despised it. He admitted that the establishment was going to bring economic relief to the area. However, he didn't like sharing his primitive, environment-friendly mountain space with a commercialized machine that consumed vast natural resources with every ravenous gulp. He told how the workers were razing acres of forested area, moving tons of earth, and cutting new roads all over the mountain. The landscape of his beloved hillside was being radically redefined. The delicate balance of plant and animal life would soon be interrupted by the resort and its careless tourists.

"And don't even get me started on the casino," Harris complained. "It's one thing to have the vacationers and winter skiers here. They might have a small amount of respect for this place. But the casino will draw a completely different crowd. This mountain will never be the same."

"I thought the casino had to get approval first," Cliff said.

"Yeah, that's true. But there's no one to stop it now. It had to go to the zoning board for approval first. I heard it passed there with a vote of six to one. That means that at the next City Council meeting they will vote on the Board's recommendation. Weeks ago, I spoke with Ardelle Bingham about it. She and I didn't see eye to eye on the resort, but she was dead set against the casino. She told me there may have been a loophole or some way around it. But, when I heard she had died in that accident, the first thing I thought was 'there goes the mountain!'"

When Cliff heard Ardelle's name, he remembered his encounter with Hubcap Harcom and how he had first connected the Beast to

244

Ardelle's accident. Perhaps the mystery of the Creature was about to be solved. Perhaps it would even shed light into the death of Ardelle Bingham.

"What kind of loophole did the councilwoman think could stop the casino?" Cliff asked, returning to the conversation.

"She never said," Harris recalled. "And I doubt there's anyone out there who would know or care."

"Well, there's at least one. Didn't you tell me that there was a dissenting vote from the zoning board?"

"Yeah, but that's gone, too."

"What do you mean?"

"The dissenting vote was Clay Decker."

Chapter Twenty-Two

While Sandy's life was slowly falling apart, Ellie remained at camp. She grabbed her backpack and duffel bag from the van and slid its door closed. The van carrying Sandy had already left the parking lot. She gave a smile and wave to Jocelyn, who looked back. She watched the van pull away.

The past twenty-four hours had been trying for Ellie; she just wanted to go home. She wanted to talk with Sandy. She wanted to feel his hand in hers again. She wanted; no, she *needed* his embrace. Yet, she wasn't able to do those things. Not now. *This is so unfair for Sandy. I shouldn't have dropped my guard. I should have never let him get so close. He is the nicest, kindest man I've ever met. He deserves better than me.*

Ellie turned from the van to see Benjamin standing alone in the lot. "Okay, what's so important?" she glared.

"I just want to talk with you," Benjamin replied, smiling with hands raised. He glanced at the departing van to make sure they were alone. "It's been a long time."

"Listen, if you think threatening me into meeting with you is going to somehow make things better..."

"I didn't threaten you!" Benjamin objected. He then changed the subject. "You like the preacher, don't you?"

"That's none of your business," Ellie snapped as she threw her backpack over a shoulder and crossed her arms.

"He seems like a really nice man. The two of you will make a nice couple."

"Sandy is a *very* nice man. What sets him apart is that he's more concerned with others than himself." She hoped he could feel the barbs in her words.

"Nice guys can have a hard time understanding *certain* things."

"What do you want from me?" Ellie demanded, trying to get to the point of the conversation

"I need to make certain we are on the same page," Benjamin said, taking a step closer.

The departing van had kicked up a cloud of dust that suddenly blew their way. It filled Ellie's nostrils and dried her throat. She coughed and wiped her eyes. As Benjamin reappeared in the settling dust, she looked hard at him. He was no longer the tall, good-looking man she'd once thought he once was. They had met in college. They both had been seniors. Initially, she'd been taken by his charm, good looks, and money. Benjamin had been a philosophy major and seemed different from other guys. At first, he'd seemed to be a religious man. However, she'd soon learned that it wasn't in the charitable, self-sacrificing way that she would have expected. Rather, he'd loved to argue endlessly over religious topics and had been continually focused on his own unique views. She also had come to learn how self-centered he could be.

He had invited her to a party. It had been their first—and last date. Not many guys had had cars on campus. Benjamin had owned a sleek, red Mustang. He'd had no job, so she had assumed his money had come from his family.

He had picked her up and driven her to a small, rural house. It had been a hot autumn night, and a storm had been brewing on the horizon. She had ridden with the window open to let the wind whip her hair. At first, it had felt so exhilarating.

As soon as they had arrived, Benjamin had started acting differently. It had been a typical frat party with loud music and drinking. But Ellie had quickly become uncomfortable with Benjamin's behavior. He had frequently disappeared from her sight. When he had returned, he'd seemed more excited; more agitated. He also had started getting a little too touchy.

Two hours after they had arrived, someone suddenly had burst in, saying that the police were on their way. With the smell of pot hanging thick in the air, everyone had made a dash for their cars. Benjamin had grabbed Ellie by the arm and hustled her to his Mustang.

It had already become dark, and the storm had arrived as they'd made their getaway. They had barely made it past the first turn when they'd passed two police cars speeding in the opposite direction. They'd taken the next turn. Benjamin laughed triumphantly while Ellie gripped the door. The car had begun to weave.

Though she had pleaded, Benjamin hadn't decreased his speed. Soon he had begun weaving across both lanes. Rain had pelted their windshield. The more Ellie had begged, the louder Benjamin had laughed. Finally, the right tires had dropped off the road. Benjamin had countered by jerking the wheel hard to the left. The car responded smartly, and they'd been jettisoned across the center line into the other lane.

At that moment time had nearly stopped for Ellie. Everything had begun to happen as if in slow motion.

Illuminated by the headlights of the speeding car, Ellie had seen a figure suddenly appear. With amazing detail, she had begun to absorb everything. She had seen a blue raincoat and denim shorts. She'd seen white socks and white tennis shoes. She had heard a dull and lifeless thud, sounding as though the car had simply struck a pothole. She'd seen a figure lift high above the hood of the vehicle.

Helplessly, she had watched the body of a man contort unnaturally. It had seemed so surreal. He'd been lifted high above the hood of the car. She had seen a hand, a left hand with a gold-colored wedding band, strike the center of the windshield. She'd watched cracks in the glass snake their way across the windshield. She'd heard herself gasp.

Benjamin had begun counter steering. The speeding car reacted and began to propel across the road. He had slammed on the brakes and cut the wheel violently. The back end of the car had swung around and struck an embankment, kicking it straight. The wheels, already turned to the left, had caused the car to begin a sideways skid. The tires had searched for traction, but the wet pavement had provided no grip. They had spun completely around.

Eventually, they had come to rest across the middle of the highway. Benjamin had eased off of the brakes, and cut the wheel sharply to get back into his lane. He had stopped the car; both arms still locked on the steering wheel.

Ellie had been in shock. She hadn't even been able to scream. Finally, when she had found her voice, she'd cried, "We need to go back and see if that man is alright!"

Benjamin's arms had still been locked tightly. He hadn't moved. The only sound Ellie had heard was the rapid beating of the wiper blades.

"Benjamin?" She'd asked. "Are you okay?"

Benjamin still had not moved; he'd only stared ahead.

"Benjamin!" Ellie had screamed out his name.

Ellie's scream had jolted Benjamin back to reality. He'd glanced almost casually at Ellie and asked, "What?"

Frantic, Ellie had screamed again, "We need to go back and help that man!"

Benjamin had stared blankly at Ellie for a few more seconds. Then the blank look in his eyes had suddenly become replaced by something else. Something she had never seen before.

"No," he had replied calmly. "We can't. We probably can't help him anyway. We need to get out of here."

Ellie had been startled by his reply. She'd begun to cry and shake her head. "No, Benjamin," she had pleaded. "We can't leave that man! We have to go back and help him!"

"No!" Benjamin's demeanor had suddenly changed. His voice had become fierce and angry. "We are not getting out of this car!"

The snarl in his voice had frightened Ellie. In spite of her fear, she'd begun to fumble for the door handle.

"I've got to help him!" she had said.

Ellie had opened the door, but had left the seatbelt fastened. She'd been struggling to unbuckle it when she had felt Benjamin firmly grasp her left forearm. He had yanked it hard toward him.

"You are *not* getting out of this car!" Benjamin had growled. "Do you understand?"

His fingers had felt like claws digging into the soft flesh of her arm. She had tried to pull away, but she could not break free from his overpowering grasp.

"What are you doing?" She had asked through sobs that were beginning to pour from her lips. "Let go! You're hurting me!"

"I'm telling you," he had said, jerking her arm with each word, "that we are not getting out of this car!"

Ellie had stared at Benjamin in disbelief. His eyes had reflected something beyond wild.

"I am not going to spend the rest of my life in prison," he had continued. "Now, reach over and shut that door."

Ellie had become deeply frightened by the look on Benjamin's face and the commanding tone of his voice. She had never seen him like this before. Defeated, she had leaned toward the door and pulled it closed. Without letting go of her, he had throttled the car forward. Once they had gotten away, Ellie had jerked her arm free from his grasp. She had been amazed at the deep bruises left by his grip.

They had driven in silence for several miles. Benjamin had turned off on a side road and followed it until he'd come across an old dirt lane leading into the woods. He had followed that lane until they could no longer see the roadway. He'd then killed his lights and turned off the car. Ellie had become too frightened to talk.

"Stay put," he had warned. "I have to make a phone call."

With that, Benjamin had gotten out of the car. She had seen him place a call on his cell phone. She'd not been able to hear what he had been saying, but he had seemed furious. He had paced back and forth in the rain, gesturing wildly. He had stopped once and had appeared to be describing the damage to his car before continuing in some type of disagreement.

Ellie had thought about trying to escape. But she hadn't any idea where she was. Even worse, Benjamin had been standing so close that he could have quickly overtaken her. She had decided that the best way out of the situation was to remain calm and compliant.

Eventually, Benjamin had ended the call and crawled back into the car. He had started the car and turned its heater on to dry out.

"What is going on?" Ellie had asked after several moments. She hadn't possessed the courage to look at him.

"Everything is going to be alright. I called my father and he's on his way right now," Benjamin had replied. His voice and demeanor had seemed less agitated.

Ellie had felt a measure of relief. She'd believed she would be safe once his father arrived. *He will see the marks on my arm and take control of his son.*

They'd sat in the car for over an hour and a half. Neither of them had spoken. Twice, Benjamin had gotten out of the car when his cell phone had rung. Each conversation had been relatively short. There had been less arguing. Slowly, he had appeared to be relaxing.

The rain had stopped by the time a set of headlights had appeared behind them on the old road. Benjamin had told Ellie to remain seated as he'd walked to the other car. When he had returned, there'd been two men with him. The older man had resembled Benjamin. It spite of the late hour, he had been dressed in tan slacks, a white shirt, a tie, and a blue sports coat. The man with him had also been sharply dressed. He'd had a thick neck and his biceps had been bulging from beneath his jacket. He had looked like a thug from a gangster movie. Ellie had immediately gotten the impression that he was a bodyguard. The thug had opened her door and Benjamin's father had asked her to get out.

Ellie had crawled from the car. She had been cramped, and it had felt good to finally stretch. Still, she had been on edge.

"Miss Lawson; I'm Mr. Walker," Benjamin's father had begun. "I apologize for what has happened tonight, but I'm sure you can appreciate the importance of keeping this to ourselves."

Ellie hadn't said anything, but her hope of rescue had slipped away. She had glanced at Benjamin, who was looking at her.

"Benjamin is going to take you home now in this car," Mr. Walker had said, gesturing with a nod toward the car in which he had arrived. "There is nothing that anyone can do about what happened here tonight. However, we can prevent this from getting any worse. I am asking that you simply go home and forget that this night ever happened."

"Do you understand that your son may have just killed someone?" she had asked, pointing back toward the highway.

"Miss Lawson," Mr. Walker had said, taking a step closer to her. "An ambulance was already there, and it is gone. What has been done can't be undone. I am just asking that you don't make an unfortunate situation any worse."

She had been surprised that he'd known her name. "Do you expect me to walk away from seeing some guy getting killed by your son and pretend it never happened?"

"Miss Lawson," Benjamin's father's voice had become threatening, "you *will* forget about tonight."

Ellie had looked at Benjamin's father. It had been obvious by his demeanor that he had been a man who regularly exercised authority. It had also been apparent by the tone of his voice that he regularly received obedience.

"And just to make sure you forget about tonight," he had continued. 'I've taken out a little insurance policy."

Ellie had shot him a confused look.

"I understand that you have a sister and an aunt living back in Lycona?" he had asked rhetorically. "Your sister is Caroline, and your Aunt is Ardelle. Is that correct?"

Ellie had felt a wave of panic followed by an overwhelming sense of nausea.

"Good. I can tell that my information is correct," he had said with a satisfied grin. His eyes had then narrowed. "It would be awful if your baby sister and Aunt would be somehow dragged into this little mess."

The threat had been veiled, but Ellie had understood. "You keep them out of this!" She had shouted angrily. The thug had moved slightly closer to Mr. Walker in response to the level of emotion in her voice.

"That's what I'm trying to do," Mr. Walker had replied sarcastically. "Keep them out of this. Now just go your way. Don't say a word of this to anyone, and all of this will simply go away. But if you so much as breathe a word of tonight, your aunt and sister will most certainly *get involved.*"

Ellie had stared hard at Benjamin's father, hoping that he would flinch, or show some sign of weakness. But his face had remained solid as stone. She'd had a sense this was not the first time he had made these kinds of threats.

At that moment, a subtle ringtone had sounded. Mr. Walker had withdrawn a Blackberry from his breast pocket and had clicked a few buttons. "Ah," he'd said. "Just in time."

He had turned his phone so that Ellie could see the screen. Curiosity had gotten the best of her. She had bent slightly forward and peered into the screen. As her eyes had adjusted, she suddenly had recognized the familiar shape of her Aunt's house and her Buick parked in the driveway!

Ellie had leaned back in horror. She hadn't found her words. Benjamin Walker's father, satisfied with the reaction, had smiled and put the phone back into his jacket.

"You see Miss Lawson, I have friends everywhere. I even have a few friends in your hometown. And right now one of them is parked outside of your house. Should I learn that you've shared our little secret with anyone, this friend will pay another visit to your aunt and sister's place. But it won't be to take a picture. So, do we have an agreement?"

Ellie had been filled with both rage and fear. She had wanted to scream and fight, but the thought of someone parked outside of her Aunt's home at this very moment had crippled her. She had thought of innocent Caroline; how she had already been through so much. She'd known she had to protect her. Her mind had scrambled for possible solutions, but she'd been at a loss. Finally, she'd nodded a weak reply.

Ellie and Benjamin had made their way back to the waiting car. To her surprise, it had been the same make, model, and color as Benjamin's. She had crawled into the vehicle, amazed at the turn of events. The thug had then exchanged the license plates. Benjamin had spoken briefly with his father and then gotten into the driver's side. Within minutes, they had returned to the highway. He had driven her back to campus without saying a word. When he had eased up in front of her place, Ellie had grabbed her purse and flung the door open.

As she had quickly exited the car, she'd heard Benjamin's voice. "Remember: your sister!"

Reports of the accident had been plastered in all of the papers. It had also run on the evening news for over a week. Tommy Michaels, just twenty-five, had run out of gas and had been walking to get help when they'd hit him. He had left a wife and small boy at home. When Ellie had first seen his face on the news, she'd raced to the bathroom to throw up. Everywhere she had turned, someone was commenting on the accident. Her friends had wished the driver would get caught and go to jail. Some had wanted the death penalty.

Ellie had ached to tell someone what had happened. The burden had seemed too great to carry by herself. She hadn't even cared if she went to jail; at least she would have had a clear conscience. However, the fear over what might happen to her sister and aunt had kept her silent.

Two weeks after the accident, an envelope had appeared under her door. It had contained a photograph of her sister. Weeks later, another one had appeared; and then another. Most had been taken at the house while Caroline was waiting for the school bus. Occasionally, close up pictures of her sister going shopping or attending a school football game would appear. These had sent cold chills up Ellie's spine. It had meant that someone was getting close, very close, to Caroline. Eventually, they had started appearing less frequently. But just when Ellie had started to feel normal again, an envelope with another photograph would arrive. Then the terror would begin again.

A day after the accident, the police had showed up on campus. They had been following up on some leads, and had interviewed a number of students. They also had examined every red car parked at the college. Ellie had been terrified that they might question her. They never did. She had heard that they had talked with Benjamin and had looked at his car. Eventually, the police had stopped asking questions and coming by the campus. It had been hard knowing that Benjamin had been getting away with murder, but she'd had too much at stake to say anything.

That fateful night had changed Ellie forever. After her mother had died, she'd reacted by becoming reckless and rebellious. She had partied and done whatever she'd pleased. She had resented being told what to do and had felt she could find her own way to happiness. She had gone wherever her wild heart had led her; until it led her to a lonely stretch of highway in the pouring rain. From that moment on, she had become a different woman. It had become hard to smile; and she'd trusted no one. Overnight, she had become serious and somber. She had promised herself she would never be so reckless. She also had vowed never to trust anyone.

Ellie had barely been able to finish her senior year of college. Afterward, she had returned to Lycona, but had felt she was just a shell of her former self. She now felt responsible for her sister's well-being and took local, menial jobs so she could stay at home.

////

As Ellie stood looking at Benjamin in the parking lot at Camp Atawanda, she felt the anger, terror, rage, and fear all over again. She hated this man. He had taken so much from her, and each time a secret photograph appeared, she felt robbed. She had prayed she would never see him again. When he had walked through the cafeteria doors last night, she had been shocked beyond words. Seeing him had made her forget the terrifying encounter with the Creature. The monster in front of her was far more horrifying.

"What do you want?" she finally asked him as they stood alone in the parking lot.

"I think we need to come to some kind of understanding," Benjamin repeated himself, taking a step closer. Ellie didn't respond, so he continued. "I like this place; this town. I think it's a place where I could settle down. In fact, there's a job offer in the works right now. If I accept it, then I'll be staying in Lycona."

"I don't want you living here!" Ellie shot back. "Not here. Not my town!"

Benjamin smiled. "I appreciate your input," he said sarcastically. "But you don't have a say in where I'll be living. If I decide to stay here, you can either accept it and stay, or accept it and leave."

This was too much to bear. It was only with herculean effort that Ellie was able to keep her temper in check. She wanted to lunge at the man. She wanted to fight. She wanted to scream. But, she also knew that that kind of reaction could endanger Caroline. She maintained her composure.

"And if I decide to stay," Benjamin continued. "I need to remind you of a promise you made to keep quiet about our little secret."

"I haven't told anyone that you killed a man," Ellie spat.

Benjamin glanced quickly around the parking lot. His face then contorted into something that Ellie had seen once before.

"Don't you *ever* say anything like that again!" he whispered forcefully. "Your aunt may be gone, but you still have a sister!"

Their conversation was interrupted by Harris Long, who walked out of the camp office. Ellie strode quickly to him and asked for a ride back to town.

Chapter Twenty-Three

"Dad? What are you doing here?"

Sandy stared in disbelief at his father, who was in the doorway. It was Sunday afternoon, and Sandy had just missed his first church service ever. He had hoped some church members might stop to see how he was doing. He hadn't expected to see his father.

"I decided to visit you in church today," Owen began. "I had really hoped we could talk. However, when I got there I heard the announcement that you were no longer the pastor. I came to find out what had happened."

The last time Sandy had seen his dad, he'd been filled with so much hurt and anger. He'd had no will to speak with him. So much had changed since then. The bottom had fallen out of his world, and he desperately needed someone's support. Seeing a familiar face brought a strong surge of relief. He really needed a friend; even if it was his father.

"Sandy? Are you okay?" Owen asked when Sandy didn't reply.

"… Dad" It was all Sandy could say before he threw his arms around his father.

If Owen was stunned by his son's reaction, he didn't let it show. Instead, he wrapped his arms around his son and held him in the doorway.

"Please, come in," Sandy said as he pulled away. "I would really like to talk with you, too."

Sandy led his father into the living room, and they both sat down. The hug that his father had given him had ripped him open like a breached dam. Sandy soon began pouring out his troubles. It was as if there had never been a rift between them.

Starting with the phone call from Harris, he described everything that had transpired. He shared about the tragic deaths of two of his closest friends in Lycona. He told his father about the Creature and how he had been accused of endangering the lives of the children by not reporting the phone call. He then described how Ardyth Van Horten had likely convinced the church council to wash their hands of him. He also spoke about Ellie and how much she had meant to him. Slowly, Sandy felt the weight of the past few weeks being lifted from his shoulders. It felt good to finally talk with someone.

"What are your plans?" Owen asked as Sandy finished.

"I don't know. Everything seemed to happen at once. I haven't had time to think about it."

A pause in the conversation allowed Sandy to reflect on how good it felt to be able to unload. However, he had been so anxious to talk that he had forgotten that his father had come to talk to him. He knew it was time to deal with his father's troubled past.

"Well, now it's your turn," Sandy said as he finished his story. "I know you have some things to say."

Sandy felt ready to listen; ready to handle what had happened. He couldn't ignore what he had learned about forgiveness. He had also experienced what it was like to need the help of others.

Owen nodded and leaned back in the couch. He inhaled a long breath and began.

"Two years ago," Owen said gently, "my church hired a new secretary. We worked together every day and started to get close."

Owen paused for another breath. His eyes fell to the floor. With his eyes still fixed downward, he explained how he had allowed his calling to the church to take precedent over his calling to his family. He had become focused on what he believed were his gifts, rather than what he had been given. His pride had set him up. He'd thought he was invincible. He'd thought he was fireproof. Instead, he had become spiritually weak. The emotional attachment to his secretary had become stronger. Eventually, he'd fallen into deeper sin with her. Though no one else had known, he'd felt exposed. He'd been trapped. He'd felt that he couldn't go back, nor could he go on. His only recourse had been to step down from the pulpit and leave town in shame.

"I had no where to go," Owen admitted, looking up. "She took me in for a few weeks. I stayed there because I didn't know what else to do. Finally, I realized that I'd rather be homeless than live as an adulterer, so I moved out."

It was draining for Sandy to listen to his father. He'd expected this moment to be hard. It was. Ever since he had heard the news, he had pitied his mother. Now, for the first time, he pitied his father. He pitied him because he was a broken, hurting sinner who needed forgiveness. Sandy was beginning to see his father through new eyes.

"When you visited me a few weeks ago, she wasn't with you?" Sandy asked, recalling the soft, foreign voice he'd encountered when he had called the hotel.

"No. I've been alone for months."

"What about going home?" Sandy asked.

"A few weeks ago, your mom and I started talking. I hurt her very, very deeply in a way that I can never repair. However, she has an amazing faith in God. There may be some hope for us again. But that will take time."

Owen looked at Sandy through eyes welled with tears. "I don't deserve it, but I've come to ask for forgiveness, Sandy."

Sandy had been leaning forward with hands clasped. He had been listening intently.

"Thanks, Dad," he replied slowly. "I know what it means to make mistakes; and I know what it means to need forgiveness. I know God has forgiven you. I forgive you, too."

The look on Owen's face changed. There was relief.

Then Sandy added, "Where are you staying?"

"I've got my old car back. I've been sleeping in it. I've noticed a few job openings in the sawmills around here. I'm hoping I can get a job."

For the first time, Sandy realized how rough his father looked. He hadn't shaved in days. His hair seemed dirty, and his clothes were wrinkled. He looked the part of a homeless man.

"I am allowed to stay here for a few more weeks. You are welcome to move in with me," Sandy replied.

A soft knock at the door interrupted them. Sandy excused himself, hoping to quickly dismiss the visitor.

"Ellie?" he asked in surprise as he opened the front door.

"Hi, Sandy," she replied quietly. "Can we talk?"

Sandy heard his father make his way out of the living room. He knew Owen was leaving to give Sandy time with Ellie. Sandy introduced them as his father shook her hand.

As Owen opened the screen door to leave, Sandy asked him, "By the way, who preached in my place at church today?"

Owen paused at the door and looked over his shoulder. He said, "A young man by the name of Benjamin Walker."

////

Cliff was halfway through his Sunday shift when he put a call in to Warden Flint about the bear trap. Flint said he was visiting it daily. The trap had not been sprung, and the bait hadn't been taken.

Cliff ended the call and continued his patrol through sleepy Lycona. On most days, police work in Lycona was slow. On Sundays, it nearly halted. He was thankful for days like these. They gave him time to think.

Cliff was still perplexed over why Bragg had halted him from investigating the Creature's involvement in the councilwoman's death. *Does Bragg have some kind of interest in the animal? Why does he want me to stay away?*

Then there was the threat. Bragg hadn't just ordered Cliff to drop it—he had *threatened* him.

Absentmindedly, Cliff had made his way out of town on his patrol. He soon realized that he was on the same mountainous road where the councilwoman had crashed. An idea struck. He had to do this.

As he ascended the steep hill, the forest closed in tightly against the highway to his left. The other side was hemmed in by a steep precipice.

Eventually, Cliff eased to a stop in a truck pull-off near where the Buick had been found. The highway wound around a sharp bend at this point. A new section of guardrails marked the spot where the car had left the roadway. Cliff got out of his cruiser and walked to the edge of the road. He sniffed, but could smell only the sun-baked tar of the pavement beneath his feet. There was no scent of the pungent smell with which he had become familiar.

He peered down the steep embankment. About seventy-five feet of clear-cut area spanned the gap from the roadway to the edge beneath him. A treeline began there, and the descent became steeper. Overturned dirt and small saplings crushed by the weight of the rolling car clearly marked the ugly path it had taken. A huge oak tree bore scars from where the Buick had come to rest. It must have been a horrifying plummet.

Cliff climbed over the guardrail and carefully descended the hillside. He dug his boots into the soft dirt and held on to smaller vegetation to keep from falling. Small pieces of the Buick were still

266

scattered about. He didn't know what he was looking for. He just felt the need to explore.

The debris field increased as he neared the oak tree. Shards of glass littered the area. The scene still testified to the violence of the wreck.

Cliff finally reached the oak. He leaned against the tree and looked around. He spied something lying behind the tree. Finding a stick, he reached down until he was able to snag a small, colorful purse. It looked like a woman's makeup bag. He unzipped it and examined its contents. Among the mascara and lipstick tubes, he discovered a cell phone. He tried booting it up, but the battery was either dead or damaged. He could see condensation bubbles beneath its screen.

Cliff climbed back up the bank and returned to his car. He put the makeup bag in a plastic evidence container. He slipped the cell phone into his pocket.

Chapter Twenty-Four

"What?" Sandy and Ellie both shouted.

"Benjamin Walker was their preacher today. Do you know him?" Owen asked, eyeing them both.

"I know a little about him," Sandy said, shifting uncomfortably. "How did things go?"

"It was the strangest service I've ever seen," Owen replied, stepping back inside. "Something is definitely going on in that church, and it's not good."

"What do you mean?" Sandy asked.

"He first talked about the Creature that you saw at camp. Frankly, what he had to say was the most ridiculous thing I've ever heard. He read from Genesis and tried making a connection between the Nephilim mentioned there to this animal."

"The Neph-i-what?" Ellie asked, struggling to repeat the word.

"The Nephilim is a word of uncertain origin mentioned only twice in the Bible," Sandy cut in. "No one really knows what it means, but there's a very old tradition which suggests that it describes a race of beings who were the product of fallen angels and humans."

"Is that true?" Ellie asked. She seemed a little troubled at the thought.

"It's a little far-fetched if you ask me," Owen grumbled, wagging his head.

Sandy redirected to Owen. "Besides not handling the Scriptures very well, what else went wrong?"

"I knew something was happening when I saw the church packed: wall to wall people," Owen continued. "It turns out that at least two other congregations came out to hear him. He talked about the Nephilim for a while, and then he began talking about the New Testament. Worst stuff I've ever heard. It was like straight out of Zeitgeist."

"Zeit-what?" Ellie asked, trying to understand these new terms.

"Zeitgeist is a movie available on the internet," Sandy replied. "It has the feel of a professionally done documentary and has been seen millions of times. The movie makes amazing claims about the origins of Christianity. However, most of the claims have no historical truth to them. It parades stuff that was debunked a long time ago."

"Mr. Walker doesn't know what he was talking about," Owen continued. "To make matters worse, there were clergymen in the congregation. No one objected! They just ate everything up!"

Sandy blinked hard. Ever since coming to Lycona, he had labored to bring solid Bible teaching. It had been a hard task since many in the congregation didn't have a solid foundation in the Scriptures. The thought of a stranger coming in and tearing apart the congregation with lies was too much to bear.

"You need to do something," Owen said, looking directly at his son.

"Like what?" he cried in desperation. "They won't even let me back in the church!"

"I'm not sure," Owen replied. "Pray about it. I don't know anything about the monster running around in the woods, but I can guarantee you that there is a *monster* loose in your church!"

////

After Owen left, Sandy turned to Ellie and invited her to sit down with him. To his surprise, she declined.

Lately, Sandy's sense that something was wrong had been inconveniently accurate. He was feeling it now.

"I've been worried about you," he said. "I've left a couple of messages, but you never called back."

"Listen, Sandy," she began. "I need to talk with you about what happened between us at camp. You are a wonderful man; the most wonderful man I've *ever* met. But I just don't think things will work between us."

Sandy was flabbergasted. For several weeks, he had been fostering the hope of a relationship with Ellie. After their kiss, he had thought she felt the same way.

"I don't understand," he stammered. "I thought that…"

"I'm sorry," Ellie interrupted. "I shouldn't have strung you along. I need to end things right now!"

"Does this have anything to do with Benjamin?" Sandy asked.

"Yeah," she paused and dropped her gaze to the floor. "It does."

////

Sandy sat alone at his kitchen table. His head was in his hands. His adulterous father had ripped his family apart. Sandy had been fired from his job. He had been ordered to leave his life's calling. His replacement was not only tearing his church apart, but had stolen the woman who had captured his heart. *My faith has never been so viciously attacked.*

Attacked. It struck a chord within him. *Attacked.* He was under attack. He wondered why he had not recognized this before!

Something grave must be hanging in the balance. Why else would my faith be so tested? Why would I be the target of so many blows? The Kingdom needs to be my focus. This is not a time for self-pity. This is the time for prayer and growing strong in spirit!

Sandy fell to his knees in his kitchen. He thought of Clay and the quiet strength that was in his heartfelt prayers. Clay's body had been disabled from the trials he had suffered. Yet, Clay had been the strongest man Sandy had ever met. Sandy knew that Clay had been made strong in spite of his weaknesses. On his knees, Sandy now sought that same strength in spite of his own.

Chapter Twenty-Five

On Monday morning, the *Lycona Dispatch* ran a full, front-page article on what was being dubbed, "The Lycona Monster." Eddie Law had finally been permitted to run the story. It described the close encounter at Camp Atawanda and featured interviews with a number of Eddie's other sources. A photograph of Benjamin Walker appeared on the front page. In it, he was leaning against the church office desk with his arms crossed. He flashed a confident smile and was wearing his fringed, buckskin shirt. The photograph was taken from a low angle, looking up. It gave Benjamin a "bigger than life" look. The article identified him as Lycona Community's Interim Pastor.

Sandy read the article to Owen over breakfast. Benjamin was extensively cited, giving his explanation for the Creature. Eddie described the "cutting edge" Bible study classes that Benjamin had been leading. He called them "insightful and provocative." The article stated that the study classes had been moved to the church and were being offered several nights each week. The newspaper encouraged anyone with questions to bring them to the meetings for Benjamin to answer.

The television news media descended on the town on Tuesday. They remained throughout the week. The Lycona Community Church became a backdrop for most of the features. Several telecasts were filmed from the church lawn. Sandy guessed that the congregation enjoyed seeing their church on the evening news.

Sandy's phone soon began to ring with requests for interviews. He had seen the Creature close up, and the media was hungry for a story. Even Eddie called. Sandy politely refused.

With each news article and broadcast, Sandy and Owen felt more troubled. The recent events had propelled Benjamin into the spotlight. He suddenly had become an authority on the Creature. However, it wasn't only his interpretation of the Lycona Monster that disturbed them. Benjamin had taken advantage of his position and had begun to interject his unorthodox religious views. His authority on the Lycona Monster was subtly transferred to his authority on the Bible.

Initially, he'd been identified as Community's Interim Pastor. Soon, the word 'interim' slipped from the print.

On Wednesday, Beatrice appeared at Sandy's door with the last of his things from the office.

"You've gotta do something about what's happening," she said, handing Sandy a box crammed full of his items.

Her eyes squinted from the smoke rising out of the cigarette dangling from her lips. A long line of ashes precariously hung from the cigarette, threatening to fall on Sandy's floor.

"What am I supposed to do?" he asked, his eyes fixed on the column of ashes.

"I have no idea," the cigarette bounced with each word. "Van Horten has everyone thinking all this publicity is gonna make the church grow. She also has people convinced that Benny is the reason for the turnaround. That woman is plain evil, and he don't know the first thing about being a pastor. I swear, he's gonna wreck that church if you don't do something!"

As she turned to leave, a gust of wind caught the cigarette. It created a tiny storm of ashes, which blew into Sandy's face.

That night, Owen attended one of Benjamin's studies. No one recognized him as Sandy's father, nor would anyone have cared. They were intently focused on Benjamin's teaching. Owen listened as Benjamin taught for over two hours. Benjamin then fielded questions from the very large crowd. Everyone was desperate for answers. Members of the media, who were also present, jotted down notes that were to be included in the following day's news.

"This has got to stop!" Owen said as he walked into the parsonage that night. "Nothing angered the Apostle Paul more than false teaching. And this is as false as it gets. Benjamin is standing in front of that church openly undermining the Scriptures. By doing so, he is poisoning the faith of that congregation. Once he convinces everyone that the Bible cannot be trusted, then *he* becomes their authority; their object of faith!"

"I know, but what am I supposed to do?" Sandy pleaded. "They won't even let me back in the church. Even if they did, Benjamin isn't going to stand back and just allow me to tell everyone that he's wrong!"

"You need to challenge him in the open," Owen replied. "The people need to hear the truth! They need to hear valid responses to his teaching. His ideology has *got* to be held up to the light so that everyone can see it for what it is!"

"But how?" Sandy begged.

"I've been thinking about that, and I believe that I may have an idea. However, you need to remember something important. This is not about revenge. This is a spiritual battle. This is about shining a light into what has become a very dark place."

////

Sandy left a message for Eddie Law. It took a while for Eddie to return the call. The very plain man had suddenly become very extraordinary; and busy. Calls were pouring in from news agencies with requests for interviews and remote broadcasts. The news media was even willing to work around his non-descript personality to put him on camera for a few minutes. Eddie had also become Benjamin's liaison for the media. Benjamin gave Eddie the interviews, while Eddie maintained contact with the news outlets. He was becoming a very popular man.

"I'd like to give you my version of what happened at Camp Atawanda," Sandy said when Eddie returned the call. "However, before I do, I want you to agree that I can control what gets printed."

"And why would I do that?" Eddie chuckled.

"Because if you do, I will give you the only known photograph of the Lycona Monster."

Eddie set a new land-speed record getting across town.

////

Thursday's *Dispatch* carried a large black and white photo on its front page. Sandy had snapped it while sitting next to Ellie at Sanctuary Rock. The photo wasn't completely clear. However, there had been just enough moonlight for the picture. It showed two campers and a counselor running across the open field. Their images were too blurred to be identified. However, at the bottom of the photograph was a large, grainy figure. The editor had circled the image and magnified it over the same photo. It resembled a large stump. Upon closer examination, however, it was obvious that the image was not a stump. It was a crouching figure.

Eddie kept his promise and printed details of how Sandy had lost his job. Lycona Community's former pastor decried Benjamin's explanation of the Monster and suggested that the community was being falsely led by his teachings.

Almost the moment the paper hit the newsstands, the television crews were at Sandy's doorstep; just as Owen had predicted. Although they wanted more Monster stories, they were also interested in the controversy. Sandy was interviewed by three news stations in a few hours. During each interview, he admitted that he didn't know the origin of the Creature. However, he denounced Benjamin's interpretation, pointing out his inept handling of the Bible. Sandy was calm, but did not mince words. At each interview, he looked directly into the camera and warned that Community's current pastor was incapable of teaching the Scriptures.

Sandy clearly laid the gauntlet down as each interview concluded, declaring, "I will meet Mr. Walker anytime–any place–to discuss these topics, *if* he has the courage to meet with me."

As soon as the TV crews finished Sandy's interviews, they raced to interview Benjamin. They played Sandy's challenge and asked for a response. Benjamin kept a calm appearance, but he was caught off guard. Eddie had blindsided him by allowing Sandy's story to go to print. Though he didn't appreciate being publicly rebuked by Sandy, he relished a good argument. He accepted the challenge on camera. His interview was broadcast right after Sandy's on each station.

////

"We will not give that loser the time of day!" Ardyth Van Horten snorted. She set the remote control down and looked at Benjamin. He was sitting in Sandy's old chair behind his old desk.

"I had that man fired because he was incompetent," she continued. "He's only doing this to get back at me. The church's budget is finally growing. The offering from last Sunday alone was more than he ever collected in a whole month! I will not let this happen to my church!"

"Ardyth," Benjamin said, "I've been studying these topics for years and can assure you that Sandy Kelly doesn't know what he's talking about. Don't worry. I can handle him."

"No!" Ardyth commanded.

"Listen, Ardyth, you and I are a lot alike," Benjamin continued with a disarming smile. "We don't run from our problems. We face them. I have a feeling that people probably underestimate you. However, when they try standing up to people like you and me, they find out just what we're really made of."

It had been a long time since anyone had tried to flatter Ardyth Van Horten.

Chapter Twenty-Six

Saturday began with clear skies. However, the summer humidity was bringing trouble. Hemmed in by the mountains, purple rain clouds began to assemble like vagrant hoodlums. They were looking for a fight.

"I would rather *you* handle this," Sandy said to Owen. They sat at the kitchen table and were looking over notes that Owen had assembled from Benjamin's sessions. In addition to his own, Owen had collected other people's notes from previous meetings.

"Sandy, you'll do fine," Owen encouraged. "You've studied this topic, and you know it as well as I do. Besides, my reputation is finished. No one will accept what I have to say about the Bible or God. It's a fact that I have already accepted."

"Yes, and I've been meaning to talk with you about that, Dad," Sandy said. It was a name he was beginning to call his father again.

"I know this is hard," Sandy continued somberly, "but I don't think that you can go back to preaching again; not after what you did."

"I know," Owen said, nodding. "I've already come to terms with it. As a fallen leader, I believe that I must surrender my claim to leadership. Leaders face a stricter judgment, to paraphrase a passage from James. I know that God has forgiven me, but that doesn't mean that I am automatically restored to my former position in the church."

Sandy's cell phone interrupted them. It was Eddie Law. After Benjamin had accepted Sandy's challenge, Eddie had moved quickly to arrange things. He had never been near the center of anything this exciting. Quite unexpectedly, he'd found himself enjoying the attention.

Television crews were still in town covering the Lycona Monster story. Eddie had known that a public debate might entice them to stay a few days longer. His new-found popularity had caused him to think of wider possibilities. He'd begun to think beyond Lycona. If he moderated a televised event, he might catch a producer's eye. After running Sandy's interview, Benjamin had ended the exclusives with Eddie. They were barely on speaking terms now. However, the debate could redirect his career.

Eddie had already arranged the debate for Saturday night. Sandy had asked for more time. However, Eddie had pushed it; hard. He wanted the publicity to continue. The only matter that hadn't been agreed upon was the topic. Sandy had offered "The Reliability of the Gospels." Eddie was now calling to share that Benjamin had agreed. Eddie insisted, however, that the topic of the Lycona Monster also be discussed. Though he had little interest in that, Sandy reluctantly agreed.

The newspaper had already run a front page article on the debate. The local TV stations were running features on it. Eddie told Sandy that a lot of interest was being generated. It was to be held at Lycona Community Church.

"I need your help in organizing my thoughts, Dad," Sandy said as he ended the call.

"Of course, Sandy," Owen replied. "But let's pray first."

////

Cliff stepped into Mason Carter's electronic repair shop. The door jingled a little bell perched above. Mason sat hunched over a workbench. A movable arm reached above him, extending a powerful magnifying glass and bright light. Smoke from a soldering gun swirled around him. When he finished his task, he lifted his safety glasses and switched the light off.

"Hey, Cliff!" he said as he turned to see his visitor. "Sorry that it took so long to get it done."

"Hey, Mase," Cliff answered. "Don't worry about it. I've been working the night shift for the past few days. Whenever I work that shift, I'm out of touch with everyone. There was no way I could have stopped in before today."

Cliff and Mason each moved toward the sales counter that stretched between them in the middle of the shop.

"Did you have any luck?" Cliff asked.

"A little," Mason replied as he wiped his hands on a rag that he had pulled from his pocket. He bent beneath the sales desk and began rummaging for something.

"I'm curious," Mason said looking up, "you guys have a tech department at your crime lab. Why would you come to me with this?"

"It's a little complicated," Cliff replied. "For now, let's just say that I'm working on a hunch."

Mason found what he was looking for. He stood up, holding an envelope in his hand. He slid its contents onto the countertop.

"It's the councilwoman's cell phone, alright," Mason announced. "I was able to get the cell phone's number and match it with hers."

"Were you able to get it turned on?" Cliff asked.

"Unfortunately not. The body had a bad crack. Too much water had gotten into it. The battery was ruined, and some of the circuitry was bad, too."

"What about its content?"

"Well, you're *partially* in luck. I've never worked with these things before, so I had to do a little research. After downloading some third-party software, I was able to get into it. Eventually, I was able to extract some of its data."

"What did you get?" Cliff asked with rising interest.

"I couldn't get any GPS info, web browsing history, or emails. However, I was able to extract her call log and text messages."

Mason reached into the envelope and withdrew several folded papers. He set them on the countertop beside the phone.

"This is the printout of that data."

////

Cliff drove beyond Lycona and pulled off along a deserted stretch of highway. He withdrew the printout from the envelope. The data was not easy to decipher. He studied it until it began to make some sense. Text messages were categorized by date and cell phone number.

He skimmed over the messages until one caught his eye. It read, "Be careful." The message came from Ardelle's cell phone. The timestamp showed that it was hours before her accident. Cliff jotted down the recipient's phone number and began to look for more messages to or from that cell. There were others.

Cliff began to write down the messages in their order. The theme of the texts wasn't clear. However, Cliff could tell that Ardelle Bingham and someone had been having a tense conversation. She had warned the recipient that there were "powers," who would not be happy with their work.

Cliff didn't recognize the recipient's cell. However, based on the area code and exchange, he knew it was a Lycona number. He decided to take a chance. He punched the number into his own cell phone and called it.

"Hello?" a female voice answered.

"Hello, ma'am," Cliff replied. "This is Deputy Cliff Janowski of the Sheriff's department. With whom am I speaking, please?"

"Hi, Cliff. This is Anne Decker. What can I do for you?"

////

Sandy prepared all day for the debate. However, his thoughts kept turning to Ellie. He repeatedly opened his phone to look at the picture he had taken of them. She had smiled so sweetly with her head on his shoulder. She'd genuinely looked happy.

Sandy had a hard time understanding what had happened. She had really started opening up to him at camp. He felt that their time together had been genuine. Her laugh. Her smile. Their kiss. All of it had appeared real. It didn't make sense that she would suddenly have an interest in Benjamin; a man she had just met.

Sandy wondered if Ellie would come to the debate. Would she sit beside Benjamin? Would she support the man Sandy needed to expose? How could she be drawn to a man who opposed Sandy, and God, on so many things?

Sandy shook his head to free himself of these hurtful thoughts. He needed to focus on tonight. He had a very difficult task to accomplish. Still, he missed her terribly.

////

It was Saturday afternoon. Caroline had finished her shift at the Timber Creek Cafe. Thunder warned of the coming storm. The rain hadn't started, but it was coming.

Caroline walked to her car, which was parked in the alley beside the restaurant. She planned to go home, take a shower, and make it to the church for the debate. She was one of the few parishioners at Lycona Community who didn't like Benjamin. She missed Sandy and was looking forward to seeing him again.

As Caroline neared her car, she reached into her purse to retrieve her keys. Suddenly, something caught her attention in the car's window. It was a reflection. Someone was behind her. Before she could react— before she could even turn around, a strong arm grabbed her! Her scream became lodged in her throat as a gloved hand wrapped itself around her mouth. She struggled to free herself, but she couldn't move.

284

Caroline was shoved into her own car. A black hood was quickly thrown over her head. She never saw her captor.

////

Cliff left Anne Decker's house with renewed purpose. He knew what he had to do. Although he still had many questions about the events of the past few weeks, he finally had a few answers. However, one thing was decided; he had to deal with his own personal demons. It was time to face the music.

Driving into Lycona, Cliff made his way straight to Lycona Community's parsonage. Carly had told him that Sandy was still living there. Cliff felt badly for Sandy. He knew he was a good man. He was also one of the few people Cliff knew he could trust.

When Cliff reached the parsonage, he decided to park his patrol car around the corner. He had some suspicions, and he didn't want to involve more people than was necessary. Secrecy was the best plan for now.

"Do you have a few minutes?" Cliff asked, standing at the doorway.

Cliff was relieved to find Sandy at home. The last time they had talked, Cliff had intended to share his burden. Now, he desperately needed to finish that task. He had to clear the air.

"Well, I have an event at the church tonight," Sandy replied. "But I think that I have a few minutes."

Sandy ushered Cliff into his living room. They both sat down.

"How can I help you?" Sandy asked.

"Do you remember when I stopped by your office to talk?" Cliff asked.

"Of course," Sandy replied. "Something was on your mind, but we didn't get a chance to talk about it."

"Well, I really need to finish that conversation. Are you alone?"

"Yes. Dad has been staying with me, but he just stepped out. What's going on, Cliff?"

Cliff lowered his head in thought, wondering where to begin. He lifted his gaze to Sandy's. He saw only tenderness.

Cliff began with his first encounter with the Creature and described the events that led him to Sanctuary Rock. He told Sandy about the terrifying attack that had put him in the hospital. He described how he had reason to connect the Creature to Adrelle Bingham's accident. He also described how Sherriff Bragg refused to allow him to investigate the Creature's association with her death.

"I don't understand," Sandy interjected. "How could he keep you from doing the investigation?"

Cliff blinked. "He threatened me with something I had done in the past; something that I need to tell you."

Sandy looked questioningly at Cliff.

"It was seven years ago," Cliff began. "Carly and I lived in Clinton, and I worked for the Clinton Police Department. She was diagnosed with leukemia. She got very, very sick and couldn't work. Our bills started piling up. My insurance wasn't good, and the medical bills were astronomical. Carly said we should just 'trust God,' but I was the one facing the bills. I didn't know what to do. I stopped paying the mortgage just so we could eat. The bank tried working with us, but they soon threatened to foreclose."

"I didn't know that you two had gone through that," Sandy said. "I'm sorry."

"Please," Cliff said, holding up his hand. "I'm not saying this to excuse myself or get sympathy. Just hear me out."

"Go ahead," Sandy nodded.

"I got an offer one night," he continued. "An offer to make some easy, fast money. I never thought that I would stoop that low, but I was desperate. I hated dirty cops. Then I became one."

Cliff looked at his former pastor. He felt encouraged by the compassionate look he received.

"I got paid to look the other way," Cliff continued. "There was a neighborhood known as Brookvale. It was in an area known for drug trafficking and everything else that comes with that. I had to inform my contact of my shift schedule. I then received instructions on what hours I needed to be somewhere else. I also redirected other officers from there. I knew the kinds of things that were going on, but I couldn't see any other way out. Within a few months, I had caught up on our mortgage and paid off most of the bills."

"What happened next?" Sandy asked.

"Things started to escalate with the people who were paying me. They wanted more favors. They wanted cop protection. I needed to get out."

"What did you do?"

"Carly started getting better right around that time, and this job in Lycona opened up. It was a way out of the mess that I had created. We moved here, and I tried putting it behind me. Yet, I have always hated myself for what I did. I betrayed my badge. I betrayed my community. I betrayed Carly, and I betrayed myself."

Sandy nodded. "Does Carly know?"

"No, I couldn't tell her. She hates dirty cops as much as I do; and I was afraid that she would leave me. No one can love a hypocrite."

"And that's how Bragg stopped you?" Sandy asked.

"Yes. I don't know how he found out."

"How can I help you?" Sandy asked.

"Recently, I've been made aware of some things that need to come to light. Before that happens, I have to remove this threat. I am going to tell Carly, and then I am going to the DA's office to turn myself in. I'd like it very much if you would go with me."

"Absolutely," Sandy replied. "I believe that..."

There was a sudden, hard pounding at Sandy's front door. Sandy shot Cliff a confused look and excused himself. He walked to the front door and opened it.

Ellie stood outside. The wind preceding the coming storm was whipping her hair. The blackened sky seemed to illuminate the pale look on her face. Her eyes were red with tears.

"You cannot go through with the debate tonight!" she demanded. You have to tell everyone that Benjamin is right, you are wrong, and that you are leaving town!"

"Ellie? What's wrong?" Sandy asked.

"Please, please!" she cried. "Please, tell me you will do what I ask!"

"Why? What's happening?" Sandy exclaimed.

Ellie buried her face into her hands, muffling her own voice. Then she cried out, "My sister has been kidnapped! Someone has Caroline!"

Chapter Twenty-Seven

"What happened to Caroline?" Sandy asked.

"She's been kidnapped!" Ellie cried. "We can't call the Sheriff! You have to do whatever they say! Please, Sandy! Please, tell me that you'll listen to them!"

Cliff had made his way to the door. When Ellie saw him, she shrieked and turned to leave. Sandy reached out and took her by the hand.

"It's okay, Ellie," Sandy said. "Don't be afraid. Cliff can help us."

"Ellie, tell me what happened," Cliff said calmly. "You can trust me. I will do everything I can to find your sister. I promise."

Ellie's eyes darted from Cliff to Sandy. She seemed to be weighing her options; trying to decide whether to trust Cliff.

She finally relented. "Okay, please help me!"

Ellie stepped inside, allowing the screen door to close behind her. She frantically described receiving a phone call from a man who had stated that he had Caroline. He had demanded that Ellie force Sandy to go to the debate and renounce his opinions. Sandy was to admit defeat and leave town. If this happened, her sister would not be harmed. The phone had then been handed to Caroline, who had screamed Ellie's name as the call was ended. Ellie had tried calling her sister's cell, but she had gotten no answer. She also had checked the diner. They'd said that

Caroline had left work, and no one had seen anything unusual. Her car was still nowhere to be found.

"Do you have any idea who could have done this?" Cliff asked.

"No," Ellie said as she looked down and shrugged her shoulders.

"Ellie," Cliff said more forcefully. "You're not telling me everything. If you want me to find your sister, you have to tell me what you know!"

Ellie closed her eyes. Sandy heard a sick groan escape her lips. She looked up, and for the first time in her life, began to talk about what had happened at college. She didn't hold anything back. Intermingled with her tears, all of the anguish of the past few years came pouring out.

Ellie told Cliff and Sandy what Benjamin's father had done. She also talked about the photographs that she had received over the years. Steadily, her voice grew stronger as she recounted her story. Sandy was finally gaining insight into Ellie's life. Her complexity and the emotional walls she'd erected were now making sense. He also realized why Ellie had broken up with him. It hadn't been because of love for Benjamin; it had been to protect Sandy from him!

"This doesn't make sense," Sandy said to Cliff. "Why would Benjamin do this? Can you go arrest him?"

"No. There isn't enough evidence to charge him with anything." Turning to Ellie, Cliff said, "did you recognize the voice of the person who called? Was it Benjamin or his father?"

"It wasn't Benjamin," she said. "But I can't say whether it was his father. I just don't know who it was!"

"That's okay," Cliff said. "What do you know about Benjamin's father?"

"A lot," she replied coldly. "His name is Reginald Walker. He's the CEO of a huge software company that has military contracts. He has money, and he's very powerful."

Sandy had been holding onto Ellie's hand. She quickly pulled away and readjusted so that she could hold his hand, too.

"Do you remember what the caller said about the Sheriff's Department?" Cliff asked.

"He said," Ellie squeezed her eyes shut in concentration, "that he would *instantly* know if I had called the Sheriff."

"Bragg," Cliff muttered.

"What?" Sandy asked.

Cliff turned to Sandy and explained how he had been suspicious of Bragg ever since he had threatened him. His recent conversation with Anne Decker had further strengthened his skepticism.

Suddenly, their conversation was interrupted by a car pulling into the driveway. Sandy groaned as he saw Beatrice slam its door shut. She charged onto the porch holding an envelope over her head to shield herself from the sprinkling rain.

Sandy pushed the screen door open. "Beatrice," he began, "this is not a good time."

Beatrice cocked an eyebrow as she saw Sandy, Cliff, and Ellie standing just in the doorway.

"What's happening?" she pried.

"I don't have time to explain," Sandy said curtly. "What can I do for you?"

Keeping her eye on Cliff and Ellie, Beatrice extended the wet envelope she had been using as an umbrella.

"Here are the points Benjamin is going to make tonight," she said. "These are copies of emails with some professor he's been writing to."

"How did you get these?" Sandy demanded.

"He leaves his computer turned on at the office. I just read his emails, like I used to read yours," she replied without a hint of shame.

"Well, thank you, but no thank you," Sandy replied. "Throw those away!"

"Wait a moment," Cliff jumped in. "Have you been around Benjamin lately? Has he done or said anything strange?"

"Everything that boy does is strange," she said, turning to Cliff. "What do you mean?"

"Just anything out of the ordinary?" Cliff coaxed.

"Well, he got a phone call on his cell yesterday," she mused. "I walked to his door to listen. I heard him asking why they wanted 'the combination.' He gave a number and hung up."

"Do you remember the number he gave?" Cliff asked hopefully.

"Well, what do you think?" She seemed a little hurt.

////

The sky had finally burst. Driven by the wind, the rain was blowing horizontally. While he raced out of Lycona, Cliff struggled to see out of

293

his windshield. He kept his siren and lights turned off. Yet, he pushed his car as fast as he could safely go.

When he reached the heavy steel gate on Cabin Road, Cliff breathed a prayer that his theory was correct. He also breathed a prayer for Caroline and for himself. He could not risk calling for help, God would be his only backup.

Standing in the pouring rain, he spun the dials to the numbers Beatrice had remembered. The lock fell open.

Soon, he was bouncing along the rough road in his patrol car. The rain was beginning to flood some of the lower sections of the road. The howling wind was bouncing sticks and small branches off of the hood of his vehicle. Flashes of lightning burst like warning flares. Nature itself was at war with him.

Eventually, Cliff reached the bottom of Sanctuary Rock. He turned out his headlights and opened the car door. Although it was still daylight, the purple sky made it seem like night.

Cliff un-holstered his service weapon and looked around at the forest. A horrifying thing had happened to him in these woods. This time, however, he felt no fear. All the might of the Creature itself could not keep him from his duty. He was too determined to be afraid.

Cliff began to ascend the small hill. Rain pelted him. Mud and clay washed down the road, covering his boots and splashing his pants. Yet, his soiled uniform seemed cleaner to him than the stains on his soul. *This whole mess is my responsibility. My betrayal has put a lot of people at risk.*

Cliff reached the top of the hill and saw the cabin. Parked beside it was the car that Ellie had described as belonging to Caroline.

Crouching low, he saw a light from inside the cabin. He needed the element of surprise. This would not be easy. It was twenty-five yards across the open field to the cabin. He could easily be spotted.

Crouching as low as possible, Cliff made a dash for the cabin. When he reached its corner, he straightened. Gun in hand, he inched closer to the door.

Cliff never saw it coming. The blow was as hard as it had been silent. A terrific force slammed his body against the cabin wall. He caught a whiff of cedar as his face dug into the cabin. His neck snapped back. Cliff's sidearm fell from his hand. He toppled into the mud with something heavy on his back. A strong arm wrapped around his neck.

"You shouldn't be here, Janowski," Craig Logan breathed into his ear.

The muscled arm began to squeeze. Cliff struggled to breathe, but was being choked by Logan's strong grip. Strangely, he felt no panic or fear. Only remorse. The weight of blame rested heavily on his shoulders. His sins in Clinton had kept him from speaking the truth. His silence had placed many in harm's way. It had allowed bad things to happen to good people. Now, the life of an innocent girl was in the balance, all because Cliff had placed a price tag on his integrity.

He then remembered Carly. The remorse he felt turned to sorrow. He knew that his sins would shame her. She would be the widow of a dirty cop. Perhaps he deserved this end, but she didn't.

These final thoughts of Carly stirred Cliff. He couldn't allow her to bury him in the shadow of those sins. For Carly's sake, he had to fight. He had to find redemption.

Cliff was lodged in the mud with the full weight of Logan on his back. Logan's large arm was wrapped around his neck, squeezing tighter. Digging deep inside for everything he had, Cliff began to hoist himself. Muscles that had been fed on steroids and groomed in the weight room were now pitted against those that had earned their keep setting miles of fence post and bailing hay in the hot sun.

Slowly—incredibly—Cliff pushed himself out of the mud with Logan on his back. Logan's face was still buried in his left ear, cursing with every foul breath.

As the light in his eyes began to dim, Cliff took his open right palm and swung it over his own neck. His palm connected perfectly with Logan's nose. Cliff heard the snap of broken cartilage.

Blood spattered from Logan's nose, and his eyes instantly watered. Involuntarily, Logan let Cliff go. Sucking air, Cliff wheeled around and threw a crushing hook to Logan's left temple. Logan went limp and crumpled like a discarded garment.

Gasping, Cliff fell to his knees. Adrenaline kept him from blacking out. Still breathing hard, he cuffed the unconscious Logan. Cliff found his weapon and made his way to the cabin door. He paused for only a moment to get a breath. He had to keep moving.

The door was unlocked. Cliff crept inside. The room was vacant. Cautiously, he began clearing each room. In the last bedroom, he found Caroline: alive. She was tied to a chair in the middle of the room. He cut the zip ties that held her hands. She lept from the chair into his muddied, wet arms. Cliff finally breathed again.

With Caroline safe, Cliff returned outside to Logan. He was stirring in the mud, trying to right himself. Cliff turned him over. He was spitting the blood that was streaming from his shattered nose.

"Who's behind this?" Cliff demanded.

Logan cursed. Cliff bent down and took Logan by the neck.

"If you want a chance in court, you'd better start talking!" Cliff shouted. "Did Bragg put you up to this?"

"What?" Logan asked with a confused look. "No, Bragg didn't have anything to do with this."

"Then who are you working for?" Cliff barked.

"Van Horten." The name came out covered in blood.

Chapter Twenty-Eight

Sandy, Ellie, Owen, and Beatrice sat in the front pew of Lycona Community Church. In addition to church members, it seemed the whole community was in attendance. The vicious summer storm hadn't stopped anyone. It was standing room only. A television crew had set up to cover the event. A live feed was being broadcast on their website.

A few of the parishioners with whom Sandy had been close stopped to wish him well. Most others, however, ignored him.

Owen had his eyes closed in prayer. Sandy held Ellie's hand. Beatrice shoved another piece of nicotine chewing gum in her mouth.

Across the aisle sat Benjamin. He was with Mitch, the young man that Sandy had met at camp. Mitch jerked his blond head about and looked excited. He seemed to enjoy being part of something so big. He also kept trying to talk to Benjamin. Sandy noticed that Benjamin appeared annoyed with him.

Missing from the church was Ardyth. Her absence surprised Sandy. He had expected her to be there to taunt the has-been pastor. He was relieved not to see her.

Having to publically admit Benjamin was correct and withdraw from the debate upset Sandy's stomach. However, it sickened him even more to think about Caroline. Clearly, there was no question about what had to be done.

At seven o'clock sharp, Eddie Law walked to the front of the church. Eddie was wearing a new pinstriped suit. He looked like a very unremarkable man in a very nice suit.

Eddie raised his hands to get everyone's attention.

"I'd like to welcome everyone to tonight's debate," he began. My name is Eddie Law, and I will be moderating the event."

As Eddie continued his introductory remarks, Sandy's cell phone vibrated. He almost shouted as he read the message from Cliff: "FOUND CAROLINE. SHE IS OKAY. TAKING HER TO THE HOSPITAL." He was startled to read the next message: "BENJAMIN MAY NOT HAVE HAD ANYTHING TO DO WITH THIS."

Owen rushed Ellie out of the church and to the hospital. Sandy was buoyant with relief. After he breathed a prayer of thanksgiving, he looked at Beatrice sitting beside him. She winked and offered him some gum. Sandy laughed to himself. *If I were the pastor of this church, I'd give that secretary a raise. And then I'd fire her on the spot!*

At Eddie's invitation, Sandy and Benjamin moved to two chairs that were behind the pulpit, both facing the audience.

After Eddie had introduced Benjamin and Sandy, he set the parameters for the debate. They would each make opening remarks and then offer rebuttals to one another. After rebuttals, they would be permitted to ask each other questions. Each presentation would be timed by Eddie.

Benjamin took the podium first. He seemed confident and continually flashed a broad, toothy grin. Sandy had expected the buckskin shirt, but he was dressed professionally in slacks and a nice shirt.

The first matter to be discussed was the Lycona Monster. As Sandy had expected, Benjamin began his discussion with the Nephilim mentioned in Genesis. He insisted that the Creature came from a line that had begun when angelic beings had taken women as wives. He described the Nephilim as a "hybrid" being: part human, part spirit. It was his belief that they meant no harm, but had come to bring a message. As an example, he cited the Nephilim's visit to Hank Deal's farm. He recalled the subsequent methane explosion that had been in the newspaper. The conclusion he drew for the audience was that the Nephilim had come to warn Hank of the danger.

Sandy saw some nodding in agreement. Benjamin seemed to be playing on their imaginative superstitions and poor Biblical foundation. It was clear that he had already won their confidence. Sandy's task would not be an easy one.

A round of applause eventually served as the segue between Benjamin and Sandy. As Sandy took to the podium, he caught Benjamin's eye. If Benjamin had expected him to capitulate, he didn't show it.

"I don't know what the Lycona Monster is," Sandy began with a steady voice. "However, I find Mr. Walker's arguments void of both sound logic and good Biblical reasoning. Tonight, I hope to expose the weaknesses of his points. I pray that you will each keep an open mind as you listen to both sides of the issues we will be discussing."

Sandy encouraged the audience to find the Bibles in their pews. He had them turn to the sixth chapter of Genesis. Slowly, he read the first four verses of the chapter.

"I'd like to call your attention to verse two," Sandy began. "We find there that the 'sons of God' married the 'daughters of men.' Mr. Walker just stated that the phrase 'sons of God' means angels. Perhaps that's what it means." Sandy paused for effect. "However, that's not the *only* possible way to understand the verse."

Sandy then directed the people to Hosea 1:10, which contained the phrase, "sons of the living God." He pointed out that this phrase was clearly a reference to human believers, not angels. He then cited passages from the New Testament that mentioned "sons of God." He noted that in each reference the phrase meant "godly people," never angels, and certainly never a "fallen angel."

"Since the Bible often uses the phrase 'sons of God' to refer to human believers," he started, "what would prevent us from assuming that the phrase in Genesis might *also* be a reference to godly men?"

Sandy paused as he looked to the audience. He wasn't sure if they were following him.

"Go back with me," he continued, "to the fourth verse of Genesis chapter six."

Sandy then reread the verses very carefully: "*There were giants in the earth in those days; and also after that, when the sons of God came in unto the daughters of men, and they bare children to them, the same became mighty men which were of old, men of renown.*" Sandy glanced at the audience.

"In this particular translation," Sandy continued, "the word Nephilim has been rendered 'giant.' For the sake of argument, let's say that the Bible *does* teach that angels married mortal women. The Nephilim, however, could still *not* have been the product of those marriages. Why? Because verse four tells us that the Nephilim were *already* present before these strange marriages were said to have occurred! Whoever the Nephilim were, the Bible tells us that they were already on the earth both before and after the sons of God took these women as wives!"

Sandy quickly glanced back at Benjamin, who was looking intently at a Bible. Benjamin looked up at Sandy. He smiled, but it didn't seem as broad or confident as before.

"If Mr. Walker," Sandy said, turning again to the audience, "would like us to believe that the Nephilim are the offspring of angels and women, then he should demonstrate that the phrase 'sons of God' must *necessarily* mean angels. Furthermore, he must explain why Genesis teaches that the Nephilim were present before these odd unions ever occurred!"

Sandy then addressed Benjamin's idea that the Lycona Monster had come to bring a message. He referenced the many newspaper articles involving encounters, and he pointed out that they all lacked the report of any message being delivered.

"If the Lycona Monster," Sandy said, "came to bring Hank Deal a message about the explosion that nearly killed him, then we must admit that it failed miserably. Why? Because Hank never got the message! One would expect a supernatural hybrid to have better communication skills!"

There were a few chuckles. Sandy felt that he was beginning to connect with the people.

Sandy then read Matthew 22:30. This would be his final point.

"In this passage, Jesus suggests that angels do not marry. Don't you find it a little strange that while God forbids angels from marrying, He apparently gave them the ability to procreate, as suggested by my opponent? Why would God give them the ability to sire offspring, as well as the urge to do so, yet without any permissible outlet? Does that sound like something God would do?"

When Sandy had finished, Benjamin took the podium again. He reread the Genesis passage, emphasizing the phrases while pumping his hand. However, he didn't add any new understanding to the passage. He made no new arguments.

Benjamin then turned to Job, chapters one, two, and 38, which contained references to "sons of God." He suggested that the phrase meant "angels" in all three passages.

"And I fail to see the relevance of the Hosea passage that the former pastor brought up," Benjamin said with a smirk. "It's clearly not the same phrase, and consequently, it is not relevant to this discussion."

Benjamin shrugged his shoulders as he began his conclusion. "So you see, it *is* reasonable to infer that the phrase means angels in Genesis. The Bible could not be clearer: 'sons of God' is a reference to angels. My opponent is simply trying to avoid the obvious fact."

He had completely avoided the difficulties Sandy had raised with Genesis 6:4.

When Sandy returned to the microphone, he quickly admitted that angels were likely in view in Job 38:7.

"However," he added, "in Job chapters one and two, which say, that the sons of God presented themselves to the Lord, we do not have to *necessarily* hold that this means angels. There is nothing in the text itself which requires that understanding. Certainly, godly men may have assembled before the Lord, just as we do today. Mr. Walker is reading into the passage the interpretation that suits him best. Those of us who are good critical thinkers will keep our minds open to *all* the possibilities. Doing good Biblical study means that we don't make up our minds before we read the passage."

Sandy sensed he had everyone's attention. "Mr. Walker suggested that the phrase in Hosea is not the same, and is therefore irrelevant. This is because the verse says 'sons of the *living* God.' The only difference is that the word 'God' is modified by the adjective 'living.' I believe that that adjective could be imported to all the other phrases without changing their meanings. Therefore, I disagree. The phrase is in fact *very* relevant."

Sandy paused and sifted through his notes. He glanced at Benjamin quickly, who shot him a glance. For a flash of a second, Sandy detected a frustrated look of anger.

"You will also note," Sandy concluded, "that Mr. Walker avoided Genesis 6:4. Therefore, I believe this verse still stands as a solid obstacle to his conclusion."

Eddie then invited Benjamin to ask Sandy a question. Without moving from his chair, he asked Sandy to identify the Lycona Monster, if in fact it was not the Nephilim.

The weakness of the question surprised Sandy. He noticed that Benjamin seemed to catch the mistake a little too late. Sandy turned to the microphone and pointed out that not knowing the identity of the Creature did not automatically make it the Nephilim.

"I'm not an expert in the animal kingdom," Sandy continued, "however, I've had a lengthy conversation with Warden Flint. He explained to me that to this day there are new animal species still being discovered. Before we begin conjuring up strange spiritual entities, shouldn't we at least investigate the possibility that a previously unknown animal exits? God has woven into this world many mysteries that we are only beginning to unravel. To paraphrase Proverbs 25:2, God takes great delight in concealing secrets, and gives *us* the delight in discovering them.

The idea of fallen angels and mortal women having children together is an intriguing, scandalous thought. Although I have serious reservations regarding the theory, let's suggest for the moment that it's true. That being the case, I could not imagine how knowledge of those interactions could possibly benefit our walk with God. As Christians, we are called to love others and imitate Jesus. Knowing who or what the Nephilim are should have no bearing on that calling."

Sandy paused before making his final and most important remark on the topic. "We need to remember that the Apostle Paul warned Timothy not to 'give heed to fables,' which only stir up questions and fail to edify the church. Just as in Paul's time, it seems that today there are many who are more anxious to pursue sensational mysteries rather than to seek the deep secret of living a changed life for Christ. If there's a 'fallen angel' at work right now, I suspect that it's trying to distract us from keeping our eyes on Jesus, not roaming our woods."

Eddie then encouraged Sandy to ask Benjamin a question. Sandy challenged Benjamin to read from Genesis 6:4 and explain how his theory worked with the passage, which suggested the Nephilim were already present before the celestial marriages occurred.

Benjamin approached the microphone, but seemed to stumble through the passage. He seemed perturbed. It was blatantly obvious that Benjamin had never considered the wording of verse four. His effort to downplay Sandy's point was weak and ineffective. Sandy glanced at the audience. Some seemed to be studying Benjamin in a new light. They had never heard him challenged before.

Eddie then took to the podium. He made a few remarks and moved to the topic for which Sandy was most prepared: whether the Gospels were reliable. Ever since coming to the area, Benjamin had been making this his focus. To Sandy, this false teaching was the real threat. It was the real danger. It was the real *monster among us*, he had thought.

This time Sandy went first. From the notes Owen had gathered at Benjamin's lectures, Sandy had a sense of what his arguments would be. Therefore, he decided to attack these thoughts first, putting Benjamin on the defensive. However, it was a risky move. If Benjamin had prepared other points, Sandy would be in trouble. He would have wasted his introduction by not building a case. Benjamin would then have the clear advantage.

"It is my understanding," Sandy began, slowly and deliberately. "That Mr. Walker has been suggesting to this church that the ancient manuscripts used for the Gospels were written long after the originals were penned. Therefore, he suggests, this gap in time allowed the Gospel message to be exaggerated or altered as it was being copied. He also insists that the message found in our New Testament reflects a *later* teaching of the church and not one that was part of the original.

I believe that a bold claim like that demands substantial proof. We cannot simply accept his word on the matter. He must demonstrate how the central teaching of the Gospel has been changed, and he must show us where those changes are found."

Sandy could sense that he had the audience's attention. However, he knew that this could easily become a very tedious discussion; one that might be difficult to understand. In his lectures, Benjamin had over-simplified the process by which the Gospels had been preserved. It had then become easy for him to discredit the procedure. As he and Owen had discussed, Sandy had to keep his speech plain and his points easily understandable.

"We don't know exactly when the Gospels were first written down," Sandy began, "although it probably wasn't for at least several decades after Jesus' life. However, it is doubtful that the Apostles would have forgotten what had happened. For example, I can vividly recall things that happened to me a decade or two ago, and those things weren't as memorable as someone walking on water. Also, the Apostles were telling and retelling these stories often. Especially in Jerusalem, they were probably telling them to an audience who had actually witnessed some of the events. Therefore, it is highly unlikely that the public would have allowed the Apostles to exaggerate the stories of Jesus, which they themselves had witnessed."

Sandy then began discussing the process by which manuscripts had been copied to produce new generations of manuscripts. He talked about how they were widely dispersed to early churches and recopied. Sandy explained how many of these later manuscripts, in various languages, are with us today.

"It is a well-known fact," Sandy carefully noted, "that there are many, many differences among the manuscripts that we have available. However, the vast majority of these differences are considered very minor. These include such differences as spelling errors, word order, or erroneous word insertions. They are easily noted, but have no bearing on the doctrine of the church."

Knowing Benjamin might try to introduce his illustration of "the telephone game," Sandy wanted to be the first to address it.

"Manuscripts are written documents, not oral tales," Sandy pointed out. "Preserving manuscripts is not like the children's game played at parties. In the game, something is whispered from one to another, without the benefit of the message being repeated. When manuscripts are copied, the originals continue to maintain a vital role. They were likely used multiple times and remained available while the new ones were being used. New generations of documents could be checked against old ones.

Preserving scripture was no *telephone game*," Sandy said firmly. "It was a careful process with a focus on preserving what was sacred. No one considered it an amusing pastime, sport, or something to be entertained by."

Sandy then addressed whether there was proof of the Gospel message being altered. One by one, he began citing passages that he knew Benjamin had used in recent teachings. He first exposed the discrepancies these passages seemed to pose. With each passage, he either showed how the problem could be harmonized, or explained how the issue had no bearing on church doctrine.

"The last example that I'd like to give," Sandy said in conclusion, "is Matthew 24:36." From his lecture notes, Sandy knew this was Benjamin's passage of choice.

"Some people like to point out that in the earliest manuscripts containing this verse, Jesus denied having knowledge of when He would return. They claim that later church leaders became uncomfortable with Jesus' ignorance, and so they edited the verse to reflect a revised theology of Him.

Indeed, later manuscripts do not contain the phrase 'nor the Son,' which would make it appear that the verse was altered. However, Mark 13:32, creates a problem for those who like to teach this theory."

Sandy heard the rustling of pages behind him as Benjamin was quickly turning to the passage he had just mentioned.

"In that passage, Mark records the very same conversation that Matthew recorded," Sandy continued. "Yet, all manuscripts of Mark *clearly* record Jesus claiming no knowledge of His return. If the later church had decided to alter Jesus' message to reflect their changing idea of Him, they obviously didn't do a very good job! Why would they fix one verse, but leave its parallel verse completely untouched?"

Eddie had been waving at Sandy to tell him he was out of time. Sandy sat down while Benjamin took the podium. Sandy breathed a prayer that his speech had been clear enough to follow.

As Benjamin launched into his opening remarks, he was obviously nervous. By the way he shuffled through his notes, he also seemed very unprepared. It soon became apparent that Sandy had hit all of Benjamin's points. The tactic had worked. Benjamin was now rowing upstream. All of the Scriptural issues that he had planned on raising had already been addressed and dismissed by Sandy. Benjamin had not anticipated having to deal with Sandy's replies during his opening remarks. He was flustered. Additionally, Sandy found that Benjamin seemed unfamiliar with the objections he had just raised. Sandy prayed the audience would recognize Benjamin's weakened arguments.

They continued taking their turns addressing the issue. Sandy watched as Benjamin grew more frustrated with each round. Obviously, he was not used to being challenged. He was not used to having someone else in control. His tone became sharper. His face became molded into an angry, red scowl. Instead of trying to make his points more easily understandable, he raised the volume of his voice. He became more animated as his irritation intensified. Sandy noted that more than just a few onlookers seemed surprised with Benjamin's increasingly agitated demeanor and growing volume. By the time Eddie closed the debate, Sandy felt that Benjamin was losing his confidence and his grip over the people.

As Eddie began his closing remarks, Sandy saw Sheriff Bragg slip into the back of the church. He was eyeing Benjamin. When the evening's events concluded and the audience was dismissed, Bragg made his way through the crowd and leaned over to quietly speak to Benjamin.

Beatrice had edged closer. She later told Sandy that the Sheriff had asked Benjamin to come to the department to answer a few questions. Sandy hadn't heard the conversation. He was already making his way out of the church and to the hospital.

Chapter Twenty-Nine

As soon as Craig Logan lawyered up, he began to talk. He had overheard Clay Decker and Ardelle Bingham talking at City Hall one night. They had discovered a way to stop the casino's construction. Knowing that Ardyth had been a big investor, he'd shared the information with her. Ardyth had hired Logan to "convince" Clay to let the matter drop.

In order to avoid the death penalty, Logan confessed to the murder of Clay Decker. He claimed that he had found Clay working beneath his car and had acted impulsively. He said that Ardyth had been furious at first. However, when no one had discovered the truth, her attitude had begun to change.

Logan knew that Ardyth had met Benjamin at camp when he shuttled her to check the resort's progress. She'd been able to fire Sandy, whom she had replaced with Benjamin. She'd told Logan that she feared the debate might interfere with her control over Benjamin and the church. Therefore, she had ordered Logan to figure out a way to stop it.

Logan claimed that he had refused. However, she'd had too much over him. He'd had to try. Logan said that by that time, Ardyth had become drunk with power and control. After getting away with Clay's murder, she'd thought that she was invincible. For this reason, he had decided to abduct someone close to Sandy to force his hand.

Logan had chosen to grab Caroline. He'd known all about her; he had been taking pictures of her for years. Formerly, he had worked security for Benjamin's father. Taking the photos had been fast, easy money.

In the interrogation room next to Logan, Ardyth Van Horten sat in handcuffs. She had been picked up while watching the debate on her computer. When Sandy did not capitulate, she had frantically started calling Logan. By then, the Sheriff had arrived and was pounding at her door. Belligerent and vulgar, she had been brought in. She claimed she didn't need an attorney, and soon began a boastful confession. Afterward, she was strip-searched and changed into an orange jumpsuit. Her complaints of phlebitis were largely ignored.

Sheriff Frank Bragg confessed that his failing health had been affecting his ability to lead the department. When Cliff had challenged him about Ardelle's accident, his pride had gotten in the way. He'd been afraid he had missed something vital, so he had made Cliff back off. Two years earlier, he had arrested a man with ties to a Brookvale gang. The gang member had leaked the information about Cliff to Bragg. Bragg had decided to keep the information a secret in case he had ever needed it. Bragg retired immediately.

Ardelle's accident was reinvestigated. No indication of foul play was ever found. It appeared that she had fallen asleep at the wheel. No evidence connecting the Lycona Monster to her death was ever discovered.

Cliff sat down with Carly on Saturday night. With immeasurable grief, he confessed to what he had done. Carly wept as he poured out his story. Her tears, however, were not born out of his betrayal. Rather, they came from an intense love for a man who had demonstrated that he would go to any lengths to care for her. He asked for forgiveness. It flowed as freely as her tears. She promised that whatever happened, she would stand by him, just as he had stood by her.

Monday morning, Cliff, Carly, and Sandy went to the Lycona County DA's office. The DA was swamped with charges and investigations that had poured in over the weekend. When the DA looked into the matter, he could find no record of a crime committed in Brookvale during the time frame Cliff had described. Therefore, there was no crime to which he could be linked. In exchange for the names of Cliff's contacts in Clinton, and in light of his meritorious service, the DA did not process any charges against him. Logan's corruption had brought enough bad publicity.

Although Owen continued talking with Sandy's mother, she wasn't ready to reconcile. The wound was still too raw. Perhaps in time. Until then, Owen got a job at Camp Atawanda in exchange for room, board, and a little pay. Occasionally, he was seen coming into town for materials in the Suburban. Mitch rode with him, chattering constantly. It never seemed to bother Owen.

Caroline sustained no serious injuries in the abduction. However, the emotional trauma was difficult. Fortunately for her, she had a sister who knew what it was like to walk through difficult times. Caroline would not walk alone.

In an email that Clay had sent to Ardelle Bingham, Anne Decker discovered the casino loophole. The casino's water demands would create a conflict in water contracts Lycona held with surrounding communities. Anne quickly petitioned the local courts, and an injunction to stop the casino was granted. The matter became a legal battle. The state was only granting two casino licenses that year, and there were three companies filing for them. Just as Clay had predicted, the two licenses were granted while the Lycona case remained tied up in court. The casino never came to Lycona.

Several of the big news outlets interviewed Eddie Law, but made no offers. One day, he decided to grow a mustache. It made him look—well, different. Three weeks later, one of the smaller TV stations called him. He was interviewed and hired on the spot. He never shaved again.

Two months after the debate, Beatrice suffered a stroke. With Sandy holding her hand in the hospital, she offered an unorthodox prayer that bordered on the profane. Yet, it was one of the most honest, heartfelt prayers Sandy had ever heard. She made a full recovery and began reading her Bible during cigarette breaks.

Immediately after the Sheriff began questioning Benjamin, he stopped cooperating. He got an attorney; so did his father.

Ellie had provided enough details regarding the death of Tommy Michaels to prove she had been present when he was killed. However, without his admission, investigators had a difficult time connecting Benjamin. The tedious task of building a circumstantial case against him would take time.

Lycona Community Church quickly removed Benjamin from its payroll. Sandy was offered an apology and his old job. There were many good reasons not to accept it. However, the experience with Benjamin had proved that the congregation was in desperate need of solid leadership. They were like sheep without a shepherd.

Sandy never felt that he had "won" the debate. However, he found that it had sparked the congregation's interest. They had never heard anyone objectively discuss their faith. They had never heard reasons given for why the Gospel records should be accepted. As a result, many became hungry to learn more about the historical roots of Christianity. These were all good reasons to stay.

He also had another very good reason to stay: Ellie.

Epilogue

For eons, the heavily wooded mountains have stood as tall, muted sentries over the Lycona basin. At any given moment, on every forested acre, some secret is being sheltered by the woodland giants. These silent watchmen jealously guard each story; they keep every secret.

As in all mountains, undisclosed pathways swirl and duck where no foot will ever tread. Like wooded corridors, they lead to sacred quarters, which for the present are sealed by the Hand that fashioned them. In the fullness of time, their secrets will come to light–not a moment before.

The Lycona Monster was never seen or heard from again. The deeply-wooded hills swallowed it without a trace. The code of silence, which governs the forested brotherhood, is an honored system. It would be useless to challenge it.

As Harris Long predicted, the new resort changed the mountain forever. It became a capital for tourists who came to have their pictures taken beside a life-sized statue of the Creature. If the Mountain objected, no one knew. It remained as still and silent as it had always been.

/ / / /

Then the LORD *answered … out of the whirlwind, and said … Where wast thou when I laid the foundations of the earth? declare, if thou hast understanding. Who hath laid the measures thereof, if thou knowest? (Job 38:1-5) (selected)*

AUTHOR'S NOTE

A very small portion of the inspiration for this book came while I was solo-backpacking a section of the Appalachian Trail a few years ago. A very peaceful night was suddenly shattered by three very terrifying screams coming from the ridge above me. I had never heard anything like it before, and was never able to identify its source. Indeed, the woods can be a mysterious place.

ACKNOWLEDGMENTS

Whenever an author's name appears on a book binding, it is tempting to think he or she may have completed the project alone. Although that may be the case for some, I haven't the skills or creativity to make that kind of claim. There are numerous people who have contributed to this story, each of whom I would like to gratefully acknowledge.

There are three gentlemen who provided considerable technical direction for a number of the scenes. They are Brian Retzler, Randy Datsko, and Mark Fulk. These guys took time out of their days to meet with me, return my calls, or send emails (Brian went the distance and included detailed photographs!). Their insight really helped shape this story and keep me on track.

I would also like to recognize two excellent thinkers whose work helped influence this book. Daniel B. Wallace, Ph.D., is a professor at Dallas Theological Seminary. He is also the executive director of the Center for the Study of New Testament Manuscripts. Dr. Wallace doesn't know that I exist. However, he has taught me through his books,

RSS feeds, and blog postings. He has done some amazing work in his field.

The second man is Mr. Steve Gregg of TheNarrowPath.com. Steve has been the single most influential Bible teacher in my life. His online lectures and daily live radio program have shaped my theological understanding in a very profound way. His critical approach to the Scriptures fits very naturally into my own way of thinking. My life was changed the day that I "accidentally" found his ministry.

I am also eternally grateful for the work that Sarah Rouch put into this book. I asked Sarah to edit the manuscript. She did more than just edit. She became my writing coach. Her insights and feedback were crucial. I could never have done it without her.

Lastly, I want to thank my wife, Cynthia. She always encouraged me to keep writing. She was also gracious while I did nothing but eat, sleep, and talk Nephilim for the past few months. Thanks, babe.

www.ingramcontent.com/pod-product-compliance
Lightning Source LLC
Chambersburg PA
CBHW021202250626
47155CB00008B/2637